THE LIAR'S CHILD

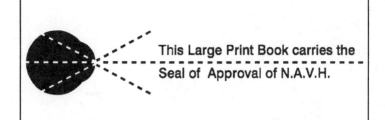

THE LIAR'S CHILD

CARLA BUCKLEY

THORNDIKE PRESS
A part of Gale, a Cengage Company

Farmington Hills, Mich • San Francisco • New York • Waterville, Maine
Meriden, Conn • Mason, Ohio • Chicago

Copyright © 2019 by Carla Schwarz Buckley.
Thorndike Press, a part of Gale, a Cengage Company.

ALL RIGHTS RESERVED
The Liar's Child is a work of fiction. Names, characters, places, and incidents are the products of the author's imagination or are used fictitiously. Any resemblance to actual events, locales, or persons, living or dead, is entirely coincidental.
Thorndike Press® Large Print Thriller.
The text of this Large Print edition is unabridged.
Other aspects of the book may vary from the original edition.
Set in 16 pt. Plantin.

LIBRARY OF CONGRESS CIP DATA ON FILE.
CATALOGUING IN PUBLICATION FOR THIS BOOK
IS AVAILABLE FROM THE LIBRARY OF CONGRESS

ISBN-13: 978-1-4328-6563-4 (hardcover alk. paper)

Published in 2019 by arrangement with Ballantine Books, an imprint of Random House, a division of Penguin Random House LLC

Printed in the United States of America
1 2 3 4 5 6 7 23 22 21 20 19

For Kate Miciak — who believed,
and Ruth Elaine Buckley — who will
be missed.

PROLOGUE:
HANK

It wasn't as though anyone came right out and said it in so many words. That wasn't how small towns worked. No, it was mostly raised eyebrows, grunted half sentences. People knocked on Hank's door, shuffled on his porch. They waylaid him at the post office. They tried to be reassuring. *Not your fault, Hank,* they'd say. *Could have happened to anyone.* They cleared their throats, squinted into the distance. *It was right under our noses,* they murmured. What they really meant was, Right under *your* nose.

Half a million kids go missing every year. Most of them run away or are thrown out of their homes by their families; the rest are kidnapped. These are just the cases reported to the police. So it's a rough estimate.

Look around your neighborhood, at the kids playing in the streets or walking to school. Hold up your hand and blot one of them out. Imagine him wavering, the lines of his body and clothes and backpack gently blurring into a sharp bolt of sunlight, or slipping into a shadow at the end of the playing field. There, between the trees. Gone.

Most abductions are what's known as *custodial interference,* kidnapping by a family member defying a court order. The FBI doesn't look into these cases. They leave it to the local cops to handle the interviews and hunt down leads. You might think that these kids are safe, given that it's a loving parent who's taken them, but you'd be wrong. Although most of these kids are recovered and returned to the custodial parent, some end up dead, pawns in ugly games that had been going on since long before they were born. You've seen the headlines, clicked through to the images: the car floating in the lake, the dizzying span of a bridge, the house reduced to ash.

A smaller number — just over a hundred kids a year — are abductions by non–family members. Still usually someone the child knows. That kidnapper has spent time learning the kid's habits, marking his vulnerable moments in each day, maybe even casually befriending him, getting things to the point where he willingly agrees to walk away from his friends or his own front lawn and climb

8

into a stranger's car.

The remaining kidnappings are true stranger danger, crimes of opportunity seized during a sliver of time when no one is watching. A day is made of those slivers, isn't it? Sure, your kid can walk three houses down to her best friend's house. Why not let your son play ball with six or seven other kids in a park you can see from your back window? It's helpful when your daughter offers to run over to the bread aisle and grab the hamburger buns while you load a plastic bag with heads of broccoli and wonder whether you can convince your kids to eat them.

Of these true stranger abductions, half the kids make it back to their families and the other half are murdered, usually within the first three hours of being taken. A very few — three percent of all abductions — remain lost, their whereabouts never discovered. Ask any parent what terrifies them the most, and this is what they'd say.

In a town so small you could drive all the way through in seven minutes, a missing child was big news. It had been before, and it was once again. This time, though, two kids were involved. For a while, no one talked about anything else. It got so if Hank saw someone walking toward him with that purposeful gait, he'd yank down the brim of his cap and hurry past. Let them think he'd gone back to drinking. Let them think too many memories had driven him to it.

But it wasn't what folks did say that he didn't want to talk about. It was what they didn't: How, if Hank had devoted his life to finding lost children, had he missed spotting the two staying right next door?

A brown cicada shell, front legs bent and praying. The bug that had lived inside it had crawled out and left behind its skin, perfectly whole. The crooked antenna, the fat eyes and curved back. The only difference from the bug and its shell is the split down the middle, easily pressed back together and made whole.

CHAPTER 1
CASSIE

Cassie could never tell, when she pushed off the railing behind her, whether she'd make it to the other side. There was always that sickening instant as she hung suspended between the two balconies when she imagined misjuding the hard lurch forward. Would someone be looking out their window at the exact moment she plummeted past to lock eyes with her and register the horror? She'd be screaming. She always screamed when startled. It annoyed her mom endlessly. *Would you cut that out,* she'd snap, as if Cassie could control it. Cassie would be screaming until the pavement met her body and that would be that.

She hadn't planned on sneaking into the vacant apartment tonight. Everyone had been sitting around the bonfire, complaining there was nowhere to go, when Cassie had found herself saying, *I know a place.* No one paid her any attention. Why should they? They were in high school and she was the seventh grader they let hang around sometimes. Cassie summoned her courage and said it again, blushing when Danny turned to her with sudden interest. His red hair curling out from beneath the brim of his black beanie, Death Cab T-shirt hanging from his shoulders, and jeans dragging to the ground, hems torn and shredded. He got up, and so they all did — Mikey P, Bruno, and Lexi — following her over the dunes, where the huge beach houses sat facing the ocean, and down the sandy road that led around the Paradise and into the courtyard. As they made their way through the parked cars to the staircase, Cassie began to have second thoughts. Did she really want to give up her secret hiding place, the one space she had to herself, away from her little brother and her mom? Once the four of them claimed it, would it ever be Cassie's again? Worse, what if Danny saw it and laughed at her? She might be shut out of his group, never allowed to return.

They waited outside on the walkway as she let herself into the dark apartment where her parents and little brother slept. She tiptoed to the sliding glass door, unlatched it, and stepped out onto the balcony. She climbed onto a chair and then the railing, pressing her palm against the wall for balance. Stretching out a foot, she hooked her leg over the railing of the balcony next door.

There was always the chance a renter in one of the beach houses on the other side of the alley might look over and spot her. It was almost Memorial Day. Every week, a new wave of vacationers arrived, unloading luggage and beer cases and dogs that ran around wagging their tails and making her brother stand on the balcony and stare. Cassie wasn't worried about the vacationers, though. Even if someone did glance up, who would think to call the police? They lived in their happy world. They never saw Cassie in hers.

The first time, Cassie had landed hard on the balcony. Boon had been the one to notice her bloodied knees and palms the next day, reaching out a finger that she'd smacked away. But it had been enough for their mom to frown at Cassie. *Gym class,* Cassie had lied. Landing wasn't the hard part, though — fixed by lining the balcony floor with cushions hauled out from the sagging sofa inside — it was the jumping.

She counted. *One. Two. Three.*

She sailed weightless. She thought her heart would explode with joy.

■ ■ ■ ■

She didn't see any of them again for almost a week. After school, she dumped her backpack at home and headed out before Boon could whine about wanting to play, wanting a snack, wanting help with his spelling words. She checked all their favorite places. The fishing pier. The arcade. The Baptist church playground, where they liked to sit on the swings and smoke. The thrift store, the dollar store. But the Cassie-shaped space she'd carved out among them had lasted just the one night before closing up again, leaving her standing alone on the outside again.

She was coming back from the beach when she entered the courtyard and spotted Bruno and Mikey P over by the swimming pool. They didn't live at the Paradise. None of them did. Danny lived with his mom and two little sisters in the trailer park. Lexi lived with her stepdad the next town over. Bruno lived a couple blocks away with some old lady Cassie figured must be his grandma. Cassie had seen them together once at the grocery store, the old lady pushing the cart and Bruno walking along beside her and looking bored.

Were they waiting for her? Did that mean Danny was coming, too? She felt a flicker of hope. Why else would they be here, hanging around a crappy pool that was still too cold to swim in?

She took a step toward them and another, and then she was committed. She opened the gate. Neither of them looked over. She stopped to stand in a nearby pocket of shade trying not to look obvious about it. She was wearing her black jeans and black shirt, too, and she was hot.

"That was fucking hilarious." Mikey P was talking to Bruno. Mikey P had one side of his head shaved. The other side was wavy and slick with grease. The long silver chain threaded through his belt loops banged against his thigh. He sat down in one of the pool chairs and pulled out his phone.

"Yeah." Bruno stood there striking match after match and tossing each one hissing into the pool. A small nest of them bobbed on the sparkling water.

Cassie should say something. The only thing to talk about was the apartment. How should she say it? *That apartment's still empty.* Did that sound slutty? Did it sound like she wanted to have sex with all of them? She'd never even kissed a boy. What about *Ready?* No. That was even worse. All she knew was that she had to get Danny to spend more time with her.

Bruno straightened. She followed his gaze and saw Danny walking toward them. She felt her cheeks grow warm. She'd been sitting way at the back of the auditorium at the talent show, when he walked across the stage with his guitar. He sat down and everyone went quiet. The music floated to the ceiling and rained down onto her head and shoulders like soft pieces of gold. He'd been singing for her, and her only. She'd been waiting all year for him to realize it.

Mikey P shoved his phone into his pocket and stood. He looked over at her. "Hey, so can we go to that apartment again?"

"She's cool. You're cool, right?" Danny grinned at her, and she smiled back. He saw her, really saw her. She wasn't some lame seventh grader. She was the girl willing to leap from balcony to balcony four stories up.

"Sure," she said. She guessed they weren't waiting for Lexi. That was fine with Cassie. They'd all almost gotten caught the other night. That had been scary, freezing behind the door as footsteps hurried past. Lexi had giggled. Cassie had wanted to stab her.

Usually, Danny led the way, with Bruno at his side. Then Mikey P and Lexi, bumping elbows or holding hands, then Cassie, following behind like an afterthought. But this time, Danny stood at the gate until Cassie came through it, and then to her amazement and shocked delight, he began walking alongside her. Could Mikey P and Bruno register this development? What if he grabbed her hand? Her palms were sweaty. She didn't dare rub them on her jeans.

A black car rolled through the gates ahead of them. Danny turned his head to watch it coast by. Three people inside, Minnesota plates. They had to be lost. People from other states didn't move to the Paradise.

Danny had slowed his step, and their arms brushed. Her skin buzzed electric. She glanced at him, but he was staring at the car. Bruno and Mikey P had come up alongside them. Now all three guys were watching the car as it pulled in front of the management office. The back door opened and a woman climbed out.

"Now we're talking," Danny said.

"Got a few miles on her," Mikey P said. "But I'd take her for a spin."

"I'll give her to you when I'm done," Bruno said.

Cassie felt a hole open up deep inside. What was so special about that woman? Cassie would have passed her a million times and never given her a second look, but Danny sure was looking. Was it the color of her hair, not red but not blond? The way her ponytail swung and clipped her shoulder as she glanced around the lot? The length of her legs? How she filled out the top of her white T-shirt? Cassie shrank inside her pretend bra, made of a tank top she'd taken scissors to.

The woman went into the office. Danny leaned against the fountain with his arms folded, staring. There was nothing to see. They'd been on their way to the apartment, and now they weren't. Cassie had no idea why. Something about the woman had stopped them all in their tracks.

The door opened. The woman came out. Behind her was Ted, holding his huge ring of keys. Ted, whom everyone called the Lazy Moron and who never did anything unless a fire was lit under him. The pony-tailed woman must have lit a fire. She had flame-thrown the Lazy Moron out of the air-conditioning and into the heat.

"Hey," Cassie said, but no one was listening.

The woman walked up the stairs with Ted. They reached the landing, passed the railing overlooking the courtyard, then turned to take the next flight of stairs. They went higher and higher, past the second floor, past the third. Cassie knew where they were going, she just *knew,* and she was helpless to do anything but watch. They were all watching. When Bruno stepped in front of her, his head craned, she shoved him back. He stumbled, rubbed his arm. "Bitch," he snarled, but she ignored him. Ted and the woman turned onto the fourth-floor walkway. They walked past Cassie's apartment and stopped in front of the apartment beside hers. They went inside and the door closed behind them.

That apartment had been empty for months. Cassie had watched the family move out. They'd complained loudly to Ted about the fighting coming from Cassie's apartment, said it kept waking up their baby.

As soon as they'd gone, Cassie had walked over to the railing and looked across to the balcony next door. A foot, she'd estimated. Maybe a little more.

All she had to do was be brave enough to make that leap.

CHAPTER 2
SARA

They'd assigned her a man and a woman — the woman was there to accompany Sara into the restrooms and motel rooms along the trip from St. Paul to the Outer Banks, places where the man couldn't go. Nicole, her name was. His was Luis. Or so they said. Sara didn't care. She'd been playing this game longer than they had.

They rode in a dark sedan with tinted windows. They followed a circuitous route, driving west, then south, and finally east, stopping along the way in small towns to change vehicles — pulling into an empty parking lot, Luis getting out first to walk around and check the new car, shining a light beneath the undercarriage and passing a handheld device along the dashboard before Nicole would let Sara climb out of one backseat and into the next. The vehicles were exactly alike, the differences among them being the way each smelled. The first had reeked of popcorn, and the second, a sharp pine scent. This one, stale coffee.

When they stopped for the night, Nicole would check out the motel room while Luis waited in the car with Sara. Then Nicole would wave Sara out of the car and inside the room, closing the door quickly behind them and sliding the chain. Then it was lights-out — no TV, no reading, no chitchat. Sara was skilled at getting people to talk about themselves, but she didn't even try with these two. What was the point?

Where have you always wanted to live? the Director had asked, back at the beginning, when they first started talking about using her instead of prosecuting her. California, Sara said, instantly, maybe Seattle. They picked North Carolina. The Outer Banks was filled with vacationers who came and went, they explained, and permanent residents who wanted to keep to themselves. No one would pay Sara the least bit of attention. As long as she kept her head down, she'd be okay.

It had been a long journey conducted mostly in silence, leaving behind sleety avenues and overcast skies before winding through serrated mountains and emerging into a land transformed by greenery and flowers. When at last they drove onto the long, narrow bridge soaring over the ocean, Nicole rolled down the windows. "Smell that air."

Sara said nothing. It wasn't California or Seattle.

The Outer Banks was a strip of land hanging out in the Atlantic, accessible only by bridges at the northern and southern tips, studded with magnolia trees and palms. Signs bristled. Peaches, barbecue, fresh boiled peanuts. Churches and Brazilian waxes.

Luis slowed the sedan and flicked on the turn signal. Sara glanced at the strip mall opposite, the faded placards taped to shop windows. This was an area in transition, though whether it was trending up or down, she couldn't tell. She'd usually spent her time in neighborhoods that had already decided.

They bumped into a courtyard. THE PARADISE, the sign said. It didn't look like paradise. The grubby building in front of her rose four bleak stories connected by stark concrete walkways. The roof was patched. Beach towels sagged over railings; miniblinds dangled over every window. The parked cars were older models with sagging bumpers and decaying panels. The only thing running in the stone fountain were rivulets of rust beneath the spigots. Three teenage boys and a girl stopped to let them drive past, all four dressed in black. Making a statement. Clueless, Sara thought.

Luis braked to a stop.

"This is it?" Sara couldn't keep the horror out of her voice.

Luis glanced back at her. Of the two, he'd turned out to be the friendly one. He and Nicole had probably flipped a coin, deciding who would play good cop. "It's on the ocean."

Maybe he was afraid she'd refuse to get out of the car. The Paradise was a full block from the ocean, a line of private residences standing between it and the water. She could hear the ocean and smell it, but she couldn't see it.

Sara got out to talk to the building manager. Luis and Nicole waited in the car. Inside, a circulating fan beat the humid air. The guy behind the counter glanced up. Bald, fat, sweat prickling his upper lip. "Help you?"

"I'm here about an apartment."

"Name?"

She didn't even stumble. "Sara Lennox." It was her first time using it.

What name do you want? the Director had asked. Sara had just been escorted from jail

25

back to her house. She didn't have time to think. She cast her gaze around her living room, let her eyes settle on the faded spines of her two favorite books from a childhood that now seemed to belong to someone else. She took Sara from one and Lennox from the other. She'd hoped they'd feel familiar, but they turned out to be just four syllables, easy to spell.

The manager tapped his keyboard and frowned at the computer. "Lennox, Lennox." His brass name tag dragged down the pocket of his short-sleeved shirt. Ted. "Got it. Fourth-floor single. That right?"

"I guess."

He studied her. Was she supposed to sound more certain, as if she'd been the one to decide on this dump? Well, she hadn't. He reached into the drawer for a ring of keys and, groaning, pushed himself up.

There was no elevator. They took winding metal steps slick with salt spray, the soles of her black pumps sticking and unsticking, the manager wheezing in front of her. Cars baked and winked below. Those kids were still by the fountain, their faces lifted to watch Sara's progress. The boys wore the smirk teenage boys did, but the girl looked furious. One of the boys turned to say something, and the girl gave him an angry shove that sent him reeling. Temper, temper, Sara thought.

Ted was panting by the time they reached the fourth floor. He clomped onto the walkway, stopped. He unlocked a door and swung it open, stepping back.

Sara stepped into a wall of heat. It was gloomy in the apartment, all the shades closed. Ted reached for a light switch, and the space sprang into view: one room divided into living, dining, and kitchen. Scuffed blue walls, mushroom-colored carpeting. Beige cabinets, chipped Formica counters. The furniture was yellow pine. The previous residents had left chaos behind. Pizza cartons, beer cans, cigarette butts, crumpled paper napkins. The space reeked of weed.

"Huh," Ted said, and she glanced over to see he was frowning at the cushionless couch. "I'll get that taken care of. Bedroom's this way."

He led her down a hallway to a dim, square space. Double bed, cheap dresser, nightstand and lamp. A single window. A plastic-framed, full-length mirror had been nailed inside the closet door, reflecting back a wavering image of her. The bathroom was sour with mildew.

In the living room, Ted yanked the vertical

blinds aside with a clatter, then slid open the glass door. The apartment filled with the crash of the surf.

A narrow balcony hovered in midair, a sheer drop of forty or fifty feet to the alley below. Ted grunted and stooped to pick up the missing cushions. "Former tenants," he said, as if that explained everything.

The railing was sun-warmed. Black paint crumbled against her palms. Below, the pitched gray roof of a beautiful house shoulder to shoulder among other large homes. Every day she would have to look out over their rooftops to glimpse the ocean glinting in the distance. She was fine with that. It would only fuel her rage, make it easier to con them.

Ted stood waiting for her decision. As if it was her decision to make. But she played the game. "I'll take it."

He didn't ask for ID. He named a monthly rent, tacked on a security deposit — twice as much as she used to pay for a condo in a trendy neighborhood filled with cafés and quirky boutiques. She opened her wallet and counted out the bills Luis had given her. Ted folded them in half, tapped them into the shirt pocket beneath his name tag. "Need help moving in?"

"I've got it." She had two suitcases, all

she'd been allowed to take.

He nodded, no doubt relieved at being spared the climb. She'd be making it, though, two, four, maybe six times a day. Was this really going to be her life?

Down in the courtyard, Luis had pulled the car around and parked it in the speckled shade of a mimosa tree, engine running, air-conditioning blasting. Nicole had moved to the front seat. Sara opened the rear passenger door and got in. Nicole had a habit of clutching her cellphone even when she wasn't using it. She was doing that now.

"How'd everything go?" Luis asked.

What was there to talk about? They'd picked a place. She'd seen it. "Fine."

He nodded, pleased. "You hungry?"

They drove her to a seafood restaurant up the coast for dinner, found a table sheltered beneath an umbrella, and ordered steamed crabs. It was the first time they'd eaten in public, the signal that their mission was over and she was now where they were supposed to leave her. Luis and Nicole took chairs against the wall and did more looking around at the other diners than enjoying the view. The server tossed a sheet of brown paper across the table, then heaved over a bucket of crabs that slithered to an aromatic stop, brilliant red shells with white bellies and black eyes.

Luis showed Sara how to smash the shell with the wooden mallet, pry off the armored chest, and pull apart the legs, teasing out the tender bits of crab with the sharp metal tool. It felt animal to eat this way, indulgent. Her fingers were stained orange. Candles flickered. The moon rose, a mottled silver-gold disk. Luis and Nicole drank iced tea. She downed two margaritas, licking the salt from her lips and wondering if she could get away with ordering a third.

Nicole went over everything again. A car was waiting for Sara at the dealership; she'd be able to open a bank account using her new driver's license and social security card. She'd have to be smart, Nicole warned. Make sure she kept her doors locked. "Don't draw attention to yourself. Don't go anywhere. You need to get drunk, get drunk in your house. No dancing on tables, no guns." No picking up strangers. "Absolutely out of the question," Nicole said, although Sara hadn't argued.

They'd deleted Sara's Facebook page, taken her cellphone with its contacts list. The new phone had only one number in it: Luis's, for emergency purposes only. Down the road, if Sara started dating, she could never tell him who she was. Who she had been. That part of her life was over.

The sun had set, and the tables were filled with people laughing and eating dinner. The marshals were leaving the next day. But they'd be back. There had never been a breach in the program's history, and these two didn't plan to be the first. They'd considered every exigency. They'd peered around the sharp edges and shone a bright light into every dark corner, and laid it out — a life in which nothing would ever again happen.

They didn't know what Sara had hidden in the lining of her suitcase.

CHAPTER 3
WHIT

It wasn't much as far as gift shops went — a few flower arrangements in a refrigerated case, a carousel of picked-over get well and welcome baby cards, a cluster of bright Mylar balloons, candy bars, gum. The woman behind the cash register shifted her weight from side to side and glanced at the clock on the wall. Whit had been on his way to the cafeteria when he'd spied the sign off the hospital lobby. Here, he thought, was at last something he could do. He knew which toy immediately: a German shepherd with a pink felt tongue, buried beneath the other stuffed animals. His son wanted a dog more than anything, but they didn't allow pets at the Paradise. When they got Boon out of here, they'd move someplace where his kid could have as many dogs as he wanted. Hell, Whit would get him an entire petting zoo.

Diane didn't look up as Whit slid open the glass door and stepped into his son's darkened room. She was huddled in the chair beside the bed, her legs curled beneath her and her forehead resting on her cupped palm. "Thanks," he told the tech standing by the monitor. She nodded, slipped out. The deal was Diane wasn't allowed to be alone with Boon, not for one second. It didn't matter that she was his mother.

Whit pried off the lid, blew on the surface of the hot liquid. "Here," he told Diane, and after a moment she reached for the cup. Her hair was a mess, her skin blotchy, her eyes swollen from crying. From the way she held herself, he could tell the ibuprofen was doing nothing for the migraine.

The pediatric unit meant cartoon decals on the walls, cheerful sheets, and nurses in rainbow scrubs. The doctor had a little stuffed koala hanging from her stethoscope. Boon would love that, if he'd only open his eyes.

Boon lay flat on his back, his hair stiff from sweat, in exactly the same position he'd been in when Whit left the room. Boon was a restless sleeper, but he wasn't sleeping now, was he?

The doctor didn't think there'd be brain damage, but it was too soon to tell. They'd brought him in just in time, she told them. Whit hadn't corrected her. It hadn't been

Diane or him, but a stranger who'd saved their son. An IV ran from Boon's arm tucked beneath the sheet to the pole beside his bed; a heart monitor dragged a blood-red line across the screen. The nurses were watching the numbers from their station outside the room. If anything looked the least bit alarming, someone would rush in. The numbers meant nothing to Whit. All he knew was that if his son was okay, he'd be asking question after question. *But why?* was his favorite.

Whit pulled the toy dog out of the plastic bag and set it beside Boon where it would be the first thing his son saw when he opened his eyes.

"Where's Cassie?" Diane's voice rasped, as if she hadn't used it in years.

"With the guidance counselor." They'd had to pull Cassie out of class. After talking to the police, then the social worker from CPS, Whit had paced in the hospital corridor, listening to a heavy silence until Cassie's young, breathless voice piped in his ear — *Dad?* — and he suddenly stopped, his legs unable to move. "She's okay. I got to her before Child Services did." Robin, the woman's name was. She'd insisted on talking to him privately, and all he could say, over and over, was that his wife had made a mistake. A terrible, terrible mistake. But the expression on Robin's face told him that there was no excuse for making a mistake that landed your five-year-old in the hospital.

"How much did you tell her?"

"The truth, Dee. I told her the truth." He yanked his tie free and shoved it into his pocket, sat beside his wife. She held her hand opened on her thigh, a plea for forgiveness.

"She must think I'm a monster."

"Of course she doesn't. No one thinks that." But Diane's hand lay there untouched, inches from his. "My mom's going to pick her up from school. She'll take her to the apartment and stay with her."

Diane squeezed her eyes shut. The last thing she needed was to have his mom stop by the hospital to see Boon. *Now's not a good time, Mom,* Whit had told her. Like Diane, she couldn't stop crying.

"What do you think they'll ask her?"

"I don't know, Dee. Probably a lot of the same things she asked us." *Where do your children sleep? Does anyone else live with you? Do you eat together as a family? Who helps your daughter with her homework?* Then the questions Robin wouldn't ask a twelve-year-old: *Has your wife ever been diagnosed with a mental illness? Have you ever been concerned for Diane's safety, or that of your children?*

"She's going to take our kids away, Whit. I know she is."

He glanced to the bed, to their son's slack face. "She won't do that."

"You don't know that." Diane started to cry again.

"I do." Robin had been clear. Diane had been the one to forget their son was asleep in the backseat of her car. She'd driven to work and gone inside to start her shift, while the temperature outside hovered in the low eighties. A pleasant day, he remembered the TV weatherman saying. But inside the car, the heat had climbed higher and higher. Diane had given Boon cold medication that morning. He lay there, head lolling against his shoulder, sweat trickling down his temples, soaking into his shirt as his pulse raced and his round cheeks turned bright red. A woman pushing her baby in a stroller had spotted him.

The nurse lingered outside the glass window, watching, frowning. Whit reached over and took his wife's hand, at last, in his.

CHAPTER 4
SARA

The office sat in a strip mall between a dry cleaner and a used bookstore. Sara drove around, looking for a parking space. She was still getting used to the car, an older, boxy, blue Kia that belched exhaust and trembled at high speeds. *Can you drive manual?* they'd asked her, and she'd assured them she could, not thinking about it because there were so many other things to think about. But now, as she gripped the knob and ground into reverse, she decided this was just one more hurdle the Feds had stuck in front of her. They'd made a list, no doubt. Taking bets on how many Sara could climb over before falling flat on her face.

A handwritten sign taped to the inside of the door told Sara she was in the right place. The bell overhead jangled as she let herself into a narrow space divided by a counter. Armchairs in faded fabric sat around a scarred coffee table. On the other side of the counter, shelves stretched floor to ceiling, a jumble of cleaning solvents, boxes of rags and wipes, buckets, brooms. A woman emerged from a back room, glossy black hair swinging behind her. Her upper arm was blurred with ink, her lower lip pierced with a gleaming silver hoop. "I'm Terri. You Sara?" Without waiting for an answer, she said, "Glad to have you aboard. We're heading into our busy season. I can use all the help I can get."

The two of them had talked on the phone, a quick screening process. *Do you use?* Terri had asked, and Sara had had to think for a moment before understanding.

Now, she looked Sara up and down. "You're what, a small? I'll get you a uniform. You can change in the back."

The closest Sara had ever come to wearing a uniform had been those nine months in juvenile detention. When she came out of the small room in a green polyester polo shirt and tan shorts, Terri stood by the door, holding her car keys. "Normally, I stay here to handle the calls and issues that come up, but I always train the new girls. It's not brain surgery, but there's a way I like things done."

Sara understood. She was the same way. She liked Terri — a woman who sized up a situation and acted. In another life, Sara could have used her. Well, there would be other Terris along the way. There always were.

Terri accelerated her white minivan through intersections and roared around corners, pinning Sara against the seat and setting the strand of purple beads clacking from the rearview mirror. The usual routine, she explained, reaching for a cigarette, was one or two houses in the morning. Ditto for the afternoon. Depending on how bad they were, Sara might or might not get a lunch break. The only thing Sara had to keep in mind was to make sure she was out before the renters showed up. If she did a good job, she could move up from rentals to the occupied houses, which paid more. Sara kept her gaze trained on the undulating sand dunes. She didn't want to appear eager. Better to have people want to talk you into something than to be in the weak position of asking.

They pulled up to a three-story house standing on stilts. Pampas grass, a thick wall of bamboo. A fence curved around a shimmering pool. Terri unlocked the trunk and lifted out a vacuum cleaner. "Grab those buckets, will you?" Mops, she said, would be inside the house somewhere.

They hauled everything up the wooden stairs to the front door. A floral wreath hung there. Plaster cherubs held up a wooden sign: WELCOME HOME. Terri pulled a key from her pocket. "Sometimes the renters are still clearing out. You'll see them running around, throwing things into their cars. Try not to get in their way. Park on the street, wait for them to pull out. If it looks like they're going to be a while, let me know. I might need you to move on to the next house."

The house was a sprawling expanse of aqua walls and gleaming marble floors. Everything was glass and white wicker and stainless steel. Outside the picture windows, the ocean glared. Sara had never been in such a beautiful home. She ran her hand along the smooth leather couch facing the view. There were lavish bouquets of silk flowers everywhere. One of Sara's foster moms had shaken paper flowers in plastic bags filled with rice to clean them, spending hours jabbing them into vases.

"We start at the top, work our way down. You do bathrooms. I'll do bedrooms. Shower, tub, sinks, mirrors, toilets, in that order. Wash the floors last. People are supposed to take everything with them when they leave, but they don't always. Make sure to check for used soap, shampoo, stuff like that. It all has to go."

They headed up the carpeted stairs, and Terri disappeared into a bedroom. Sara sprinkled cleanser into the shower, worked the sponge around the steel drain. The rough tiles cut into her fingertips. She turned on the water and watched the powdered grit swirl away. She held up the bottle of glass cleaner, tried to remember which two cleaning ingredients emitted fatal fumes when used together. Ammonia and something. Bleach? God. She didn't want to die scraping off someone else's toothpaste dribbles.

"You know you're supposed to wear gloves, right?" Terri stood behind her. She handed Sara a pair of purple latex gloves, shook out a plastic trash bag. Sara wiped her palms on her jeans and tugged on the gloves. Terri opened the medicine cabinet, the cabinets, held up a black hair elastic webbed with hair. "See? This is the kind of stuff you need to make sure you catch. Renters don't want to know other people have been here before them." She dropped the elastic into the plastic bag.

Sure. Marks were like that, too. They all wanted to think they were special. It was what made them vulnerable.

In the kitchen, Terri checked inside the refrigerator. "It's empty, but it's not always. I don't know what people are thinking. Do they really believe the next family wants their opened cartons of cream and frost-bitten chicken patties?" She rattled out a plastic drawer and carried it over to the sink. "I have a strict policy about throwing out whatever leftover food you find, even if it's unopened. I can't run the risk it'll make you sick, or that the renters will come back and claim it. You'd be surprised. Other companies might let you keep it, but that's not how I operate."

There was no shame in taking food other people didn't want. No shame in eating it, either.

They stopped for lunch at a food truck parked in an empty lot. The cook greeted Terri, asked her how it was going. Sara studied the list of items scrawled on the black chalkboard in different colored paints. Terri poked a straw through the lid of her plastic cup. "Try the fish tacos."

They sat at a picnic table beneath the spreading arms of a pink crepe myrtle, its creamy trunk stripped clean of bark. Sara tried not to study the tattoos writhing around Terri's arm. She never could figure out if people liked strangers staring or if

42

they took affront. She herself would never adorn her body with something memorable or permanent. She lifted her taco and took a bite, drank some sweetened tea. Terri lit a cigarette. "So, what brought you to the Outer Banks?"

Sara was prepared. Keep it simple. Keep it vague. "I just needed a change."

"Yeah? Where you from?"

"Small town out west. You wouldn't have heard of it."

"I know all about small towns." Terri flicked ash. "Where you staying?"

"The Paradise."

"Huh. Sounds familiar. Didn't something just happen there?"

Sara shrugged.

"Yeah. Something. It's been all over the news. Oh, well. I'll think of it."

They drove to a complex of stucco townhouses surrounded by grass so emerald green it looked fake. Terri carried the vacuum cleaner and Sara grabbed the buckets of cleaning products. "You have to be careful letting yourself into the condo units," Terri warned. "You can't always tell if the renters have left by checking to see if there are cars outside. I once walked in on a couple still in bed." She ripped open a box of dust-cloths.

Sara forced a smile. She snapped on a pair of latex gloves and lifted the lid to the commode. There in the water floated a wrinkled condom.

What kind of animal tossed condoms into the toilet? Sara pictured the guy, naked and smug, peeling off the latex and dropping it into the water, not giving a damn whether or not it plugged the pipes. Lucky Sara, getting to clean up after him. Well, it was either this, or prison.

She picked up the toilet brush.

She stopped at the liquor store on the way back to the Paradise. Second time she'd been to the place, and the same taciturn man rang her up. He didn't seem to recognize her, but she'd have to think about rotating her purchases. She was keeping an eye on herself, too. Just half a bottle a night, two thirds, tops. The minute she reached a full bottle, she'd cut back.

She collected her groceries from the trunk and locked the car behind her. A seagull spun in greedy loops in the clear blue sky. She crossed the courtyard and started climbing stairs. Music with an urgent, angry beat was playing nearby. Someone was grilling. A man slowed as he came down the stairs, muscular arms and chest. Sara ignored the smile he gave her. She was thinking about dinner. Mint chip or Cherry Garcia? Fresh and crunchy, or sweet and rich? Both, maybe. Definitely.

On the landing, however, she stopped. A woman stood outside Sara's door, fist raised to knock. Twenty-something, jeans, yellow blouse, wavy brown hair. She clutched a clipboard. A lumpy canvas bag sagged by her feet. Her posture — relaxed but with a hint of authority — set off warning bells.

Not a Fed. Way too casually dressed. Maybe she was selling something, taking a poll. "Can I help you?" Sara asked.

The woman gasped, then turned. Her eyes were bright behind colorful striped glasses. "Oh, you surprised me! I hope so. Is this your apartment?"

A lanyard swung from around her neck. The moment Sara saw that, she got it. She knew this woman. Not by name, of course. The woman was a stranger, but Sara knew her just the same. "That's right."

"Oh, good. I'm glad I caught you. I'm Robin McIntyre. I'm a social worker with Child Protective Services." Robin smiled, held out the business card she'd been gripping. "I'm working with the family next door. Would you have a few minutes to chat?"

Working with. What a joke. Sara took the card, didn't look at it. "I wish I could help you." A flat-out lie. "But I don't know them. I just moved in a few days ago."

"I see." Robin's smile didn't falter. "Well, maybe you've noticed them, coming and going?"

"No, not really."

Robin hesitated. She was waiting for Sara to express a natural curiosity about what was going on. Sara would ask if everything was okay, and Robin would explain how it wasn't. Sara would show concern. Rapport would be established. When Robin returned — and she would, because once social workers had hold of you, they never let go — Sara would be glad to see her. She would have started paying attention to the family next door. She might have something new to tell Robin.

Sara shifted the bag to her other arm. She was tempted to mess with Robin, ask a bunch of long, twisty questions that led nowhere and took up Robin's entire evening. Robin wouldn't be so quick to knock on Sara's door again, would she? She'd learn she wasn't calling the shots. But Sara's feet ached and her ice cream was melting. "I have to put away my groceries . . ."

"Yes, of course. But you'll call if you think

46

of anything?"

"Sure."

Sara went into her apartment, kicking the door shut behind her, and set her groceries on the counter. She'd been truthful when she told Robin she didn't know her neighbors. But people couldn't help but be aware of their neighbors when they lived side by side with tissue paper for walls. She had heard the shouts and slammed doors, the raised voices. *Goddammit, why do you always . . .* She'd glimpsed the wife on the balcony painting her long nails while the husband stood over her. *I thought you were coming straight home,* she said, holding up a hand and critically examining it.

Something came up.

*You always say that. Everything's always more important than me. Or should I say, every*one? She scraped back her chair and stood abruptly. A pretty blonde with smooth, tanned skin. She grabbed the bottle of nail polish and pushed past her husband. He watched her go, face rigid with anger.

A marriage made in heaven, Sara had thought.

She walked over to the trash can, pressed the lever with her foot, and dropped Robin's business card on top of that morning's damp coffee grounds, the empty bag of chips, the pale slices of cantaloupe rind. And then she remembered: Robin with her head cocked as she studied Sara — she'd recognized Sara for what she was, too.

CHAPTER 5
WHIT

His mother called twice before he and Diane left the apartment. Should she clean inside the oven or just wipe it out; should she ask his father to shave even though it was his day off; should she make a casserole or were sandwiches okay? She worried that they, too, were being judged. It didn't matter how much he reassured her. When she swung open the front door, he saw she'd taken effort with her own appearance. Her pale eyelashes were spiky with mascara. "Well, hey, you two! Come on in."

Diane gripped coloring books against her chest, a rainbow assortment of markers. *My mom has all that stuff,* Whit had reminded her, but Diane had ignored him, agonizing over what to bring. "Boon? Cassie?"

The social worker sat alone on the couch, sweaty glasses of iced tea on the coffee table in front of her.

Diane whirled to face his mother. "Where

are they?" Her voice was shrill with panic.

"Bert took them down to the creek."

"What? But you knew we were on our way!"

"I know, but it's such a nice day . . ."

"Three hours. That's all I get. *Three* lousy hours, and they're at the *creek*? I can't *believe* you!"

The social worker was sitting right there, watching everything. "Honey." Whit put a hand on Diane's arm. "It's not a big deal."

"It is a big deal! You know it is. You can see them whenever you want, but I have to wait until it's *convenient.*"

This last word was aimed at the social worker. Robin. Diane had to wait for Robin's schedule to accommodate a visit. Whit was allowed to visit anytime. He'd go every day after work, which made for long days. Diane would pepper him with questions: Had the kids asked after her? Had they talked about what happened? Had Whit explained it had been a mistake? Nothing he said calmed her, no amount of detail was enough. It had almost gotten to the point where he didn't even want to tell Diane he'd been to see the kids.

Robin rose from the couch, serene and smiling. In her job, she probably was used to hostility. He hoped she would see it for what it was and not hold it against them. She was younger than he'd expected some- one in her position to be, late twenties, and she always seemed weighed down with fold- ers and satchels that she shifted from shoulder to shoulder, from arm to arm. A barrier, he thought, defining her space and keeping them on the other side of it. "Hi, Diane. Whit."

"Hey. Thanks for meeting us here." He came forward, hand extended.

"Of course."

Robin had told him she spent a lot of time on the road, that she had thirty or so families under her care. He had listened politely, but the whole time he'd been think- ing about how he needed her to take his family off her list.

"They don't even know, do they?" Diane fired this at his mother, still fixated on Boon and Cassie. "You didn't even tell them. They'd never have gone to the creek if they had any idea I was on my way."

Whit hated the helpless expression on his mother's face. She was bone-tired. They all were, but Diane couldn't see that. "You and I can go find them if you want. Right, Robin?"

"Sure," she agreed, but she followed closely behind as Diane went through the kitchen and smacked open the screen door. He caught the door just as it came flying back, held it open for the social worker.

The wooded lot was studded with new things: a turtle-shaped sandbox, a tire swing dangling from a tree branch, what looked like the framing of a playhouse. His father was in construction. Maybe he was letting the kids help out, the way he'd taught Whit when he was a kid. His parents had been thrilled to find such a large piece of land when they moved here soon after Cassie was born. No doubt, they'd pictured Hallmark summers with their grandchildren, hiking through the forest, crabbing. Sitting around the campfire and telling ghost stories. They were getting their dream, just not in the way any of them had figured.

Someone was crashing through the brush, twigs snapping, his father's sarcastic voice saying, "Next time, huh?" They pushed through the trees, Boon and Cassie, his father right behind them.

Diane went running.

By the time Whit and Robin got to her, she'd scooped Boon into her arms and was reaching frantically for Cassie. "My babies! Did you miss me?"

Cassie went limp.

"I don't even get a little hug, not even a

teeny smile for your mother? After I came all this way to see you?"

Whit tried to see his wife through their eyes, to see what they saw. Look at the way Boon was pressing against her. Surely that made up for the fact that he refused to get into the car now unless the windows were open. Did Robin know Boon insisted on sleeping on his closet floor? Or that Cassie had broken into her grandparents' liquor cabinet and lied about it? Nothing had been taken, Whit's mother assured him, but she was upset — and for good reason. Cassie had always seen a lock as a challenge. *We're raising a burglar,* he'd joked with Dee after Cassie got into the medicine cabinet and spilled Dee's pills everywhere. But that had been when she was younger. It wasn't so funny now.

I want to go home, Cassie had screeched when he tried to explain that it was this or staying in a stranger's house. What kind of thing was that to have to tell your kid? Had he made the wrong choice, farming out his children to his folks? What child didn't want to spend a few days with Grandma and Grandpa being spoiled out of her mind? Cassie was lucky to have two willing and able grandparents. It wasn't like Diane's mother was any sort of an option. Helen could barely remember what day it was, let alone that she had two grandkids.

But Cassie was miserable about missing the last days of seventh grade. She hated how Grandma made okra. She claimed Grandpa was a pervert because he smacked her on the behind. Whit studied Cassie, standing stiff and unhappy, her arms folded, scowling at her mother. His daughter was so angry these days. She and Dee fought constantly. Dee didn't like how Cassie chewed her fingernails. She didn't like Cassie's tone. Dee snooped, Cassie insisted, tried to control her every move. Small skirmishes quickly escalated into full-out shrieking matches. *You're the adult,* Whit would tell his wife after Cassie had run to her room and slammed the door. *Exactly,* his wife would snap.

He tried to see Diane through the social worker's eyes. She'd gotten too thin. Too agitated. That first night, she'd gone on a wild cleaning frenzy, washing the windows and scrubbing the floor with a toothbrush; just as abruptly, she'd stormed out of the room to lie curled in their darkened bedroom. She hadn't eaten for days, then last night he'd heard her well past midnight, rustling packages and clattering dishes. That morning, wrappers and empty containers were jammed into the trash bin, crumbs scattered across the counter. All week, he'd come home from work to find her sitting in the same place she'd been when he'd left ten hours before, still in her bathrobe, her hair a rat's nest. *You can't let the social worker see you like this,* he'd warned her, and she'd raised red-rimmed eyes to his, but wouldn't answer.

"So you went to the creek, huh, baby?" she was asking Boon now. She licked her thumb to rub at a dirt smudge on his chin. "Did you catch anything?"

"We saw you on TV," Cassie said, baiting her mother.

Diane threw Whit a look of despair. *Rescue me,* her eyes pleaded.

His parents had promised not to turn on the TV until the news coverage had died down, but it was impossible to keep Cassie away from the remote. Short of unplugging the set, what could they have done? At least they didn't own a computer. The stuff online was far worse. "Well, everyone was worried about Boon. But he's okay now, right?" Whit tousled his son's hair. "Aren't you, buddy?"

"I got you a present, Mommy." Boon dug in his pocket and held out a river rock. His palm was lined with dirt, his fingernails black. He had Wolf tucked under one arm, blue button eyes glinting, pink felt tongue damp and dragging.

"Wow." Diane rubbed her thumb across the stone's smooth surface. "That's beautiful, sweetheart. Thank you."

"It's for making wishes."

"A wishing stone! Exactly what I needed." Diane hugged him, a little too hard. "You guys have gotten so big! I can't believe it. Don't you think so, too, Whit?"

It had been only a week, but she was right. They did look older, somehow — like they finally understood the world wasn't the shiny place they'd been promised it was.

Cassie sat on the rim of the sandbox and wouldn't say goodbye. Whit sat beside her as she dribbled sand from the small plastic shovel. He told her they loved her and would see her soon. Were words enough? He was still leaving her behind, and they both knew it. He kissed her on the top of her head, and she swatted at him, then flung the shovel down.

He went to pry Boon away from Diane.

Boon had his arms wrapped around her neck. Diane clung to him, dragged the flat of her hand against the cotton of his shirt. "How much longer?" she begged Robin, who merely shook her head, lips pressed.

"Hey, buddy. Time to say goodbye." He put his hands around Boon's narrow rib cage.

"No! I don't want to!" Boon tightened his grip around Diane's neck.

"I think Grandma has cookies for you."

"Snickerdoodles," Whit's mom said, too anxiously. "Your favorite."

"I don't want cookies."

"How about coloring? You want to draw your mommy a nice picture?"

"No!"

Diane put her lips to his ear and whispered. Boon whimpered, then loosened his grasp. Whit lifted him away. He handed his son to his mother, who put Boon on her hip and kissed his forehead. "There's my big boy. You two go on now. We'll be fine. We're going to eat cookies and do some more coloring in those books Mommy brought, aren't we, darling?"

"I guess . . ." Boon was a heartbeat away from crying.

Whit's mother lingered in the doorway as they walked to the Explorer. The social worker wouldn't leave until she'd made sure Diane was gone. Like his wife was some sort of pervert or criminal. He tried not to be angry. He told himself it was up to him to keep things together.

On the ride home, Diane sat silent and hunched, rubbing the stone Boon had given her.

He glanced at her, tried to dredge up a neutral topic. "Maybe we can walk down to the beach when we get back to the Paradise. I'll have a few hours before I have to get to work." She loved hunting for shells. She never tired of it.

She stared out the window. "I hate that they're there. That backyard is a wilderness."

"You have to snap out of it, Dee."

Her thumb worked over the gray stone. She'd painted her nails pale green, a color she said Cassie would get a kick out of. But their daughter just snorted when Diane showed her the bottle and offered to paint her nails to match. "I can't believe the way Cassie acted. How could you let her get away with that? And the clothes she was wearing. She looked like a hoodlum. What was your mom thinking?"

"What did you want me to do, Dee? Send her to her room?" Diane didn't know about the liquor cabinet. He and his mother agreed it would only make her more upset. Diane might say something stupid to Robin. She was so caught up in her own emotions

58

that she couldn't see beyond them.

"She told her teachers I was too sick to take care of her. Sick? What kind of thing was that for her to say? What if they believed her?"

"She's just embarrassed. No big deal. It doesn't mean anything."

"Easy for you to say!"

"Dee, she just needs time. They both do. They're going to bounce right back from this. You'll see." Was he telling her this to reassure her, or himself?

"What about *me,* Whit? Did you see the way that woman looked at me? How am I supposed to get through this?"

"We have to be strong for the kids, Dee. Why don't you go see a movie or something tonight?"

"I'm not in the mood."

"What about your mom? I bet she'd like a visit."

Diane didn't answer.

"Come to the Seaside tonight. I'll get you a nice table, see if I can join you for dinner. Robineaux won't be there." The hotel owner never worked Sundays.

"Everyone else will be."

Whit knew the rest of the Seaside staff talked.

Thinks the world revolves around her, his

father said the first time he met Diane. *Like the rules apply to everyone but her.* He'd never volunteered an opinion on the girls Whit had dated before, and Whit had defended her. Diane was beautiful, vivacious, full of life. She challenged him. Maybe she got lost a little in her own thinking, but who didn't? His father had turned the page of his newspaper. *That's not the kind of woman you can make a life with.*

Whit could leave, take the kids. He'd thought about it. But everyone else had walked away from Diane — her dad, her friends, even her mother. He wanted to be the one who stayed.

The answering machine was playing when they stepped into the apartment, a woman's soft voice, urgent and twisted. The dark hiss of words — *fucking cunt has no business having kids* — spooled out before he could get to the machine and stab the button. *Kid could have died . . .* The ugly words hung in the air.

He pulled Dee into his arms, inhaled her vanilla scent. "We'll get through this, babe. Couple more days, the kids will be home and we can all get back to normal." He prayed it was true. Robin had given them no time line. Everything was in free fall.

"I'm a terrible mother."

"You're a great mom. You just made a mistake." He'd repeated it so often the words had grown flat. He could dress it up any way he wanted to, but the facts remained. Diane had almost killed their son. "Look how you got Boon to calm down today. What did you tell him, anyway?"

Silence. She turned her face away. "Nothing."

He dropped his arms. So the secrets were starting again.

CHAPTER 6
SARA

Sara paced, and thought about timing. Timing was everything. Her dad had taught her that. You could fudge on every other aspect of a scam — the approach, the profile you faked, the team you assembled, but if you blew the timing, you had nothing. Worse than nothing. You'd caused the wrong people to sit up and take notice.

The apartment had grown dark. She flipped on a light when she heard a soft thud. Strange new places had strange new noises, she reminded herself. Still, she turned in a slow circle, tense and listening.

There it was again, louder this time. It seemed to be coming from the balcony, which was impossible. Only Spider-Man could scale that outside wall. Sara stood in the middle of her living room and squinted at the glass. Someone was crouched there. A woman, her face turned away. No, a teenager, dressed in dark clothing. While

Sara waited for her heart to stop hammering, the girl straightened and saw her. They looked at each other.

Sara strode forward and yanked open the door. The roar of the ocean swept in and with it, the girl. Not even a teenager. Younger than that. The girl from the courtyard, the one Sara had spotted the day she'd moved in two weeks before. The one with a hair-trigger temper. She clutched a camouflage sleeping bag in her arms.

"What the hell were you doing out there?"

The girl pushed past to Sara's front door, flipped the dead bolt. She'd obviously done it before.

"Wait a second —"

But the door was already closing, footsteps clattering away.

It was almost as if Sara had imagined the encounter, but no, the sliding door was still open, the ocean breeze lifting the blinds and rattling them. The balcony was barely big enough to hold two plastic lawn chairs and the overturned crate wedged between them, left behind by the previous tenant. Wind swirled her clothes against her as she turned her phone's flashlight on and shone the beam around. There were sneaker prints on the dirty cement where the girl had stepped, but where had the girl herself come from?

No ladder hung from the railing. No trees nearby, nothing between the building and the rooftops across the alley. Sara leaned over the balcony railing. Nothing there except the sharp corners of other balconies, from the apartments on either side. The one on the right was twelve feet away. Too far. But the other balcony, the one on the left, was closer. Less than half a yard away. The girl had to have come from there. So this girl belonged to the feuding husband and wife, the one whose family was being investigated by Child Protective Services.

Sara was no judge of children's ages, but the girl couldn't have been more than twelve. Would a twelve-year-old really have had the courage to leap over fifteen inches of empty air hanging forty feet above hard pavement? Remembering her own childhood, Sara thought, Well, maybe. Depended on what she was running from. Or to.

Sara had almost forgotten the girl until the next evening, as she parked her car after a long, crappy day and got out to make a long, crappy climb up four flights of stairs to her crappy apartment — crappy new *home*, she reminded herself. She plucked at the collar of her shirt as she crossed the humid courtyard. A tern strutting across the cracked pavement squawked and flew off as she limped past. She'd sprained her back wrestling that damn vacuum cleaner out of her trunk. Every muscle in her body throbbed.

Inside her apartment, she toed off her shoes and poured a glass of wine. Same Chablis she always bought. They didn't tell her she had to change *everything*. She took a sip and closed her eyes. For a moment, almost like home.

At the sound of a thump, her eyes flew open.

She put down the wine more roughly than she meant to, slopping some out of the glass, and strode to the sliding door. Furious, she yanked it open.

"What the hell?"

Pale heart-shaped face, brown eyes, blond hair straggling past her shoulders. She was dressed in jeans and an oversize black shirt that hung on her small frame, just as she had been the night before, a skinny little vampire wearing black lipstick and smudged eye shadow, figuring it made her look older. "I thought you weren't home." Small chin lifted, voice challenging.

"Clearly, I am."

"What's the big deal?"

Were all kids this clueless? Did Sara have

to spell it out for her? "What if I'd been naked?"

"Ew."

"How old are you anyway?"

"How old are *you*?"

Wow. They glared at each other. Then the girl's eyes strayed past Sara's shoulder to the kitchen.

Sara folded her arms. "You have any idea how dangerous it is climbing over that railing? And how stupid?"

Another shrug. The girl held the same lumpy sleeping bag bunched in her arms. To soften her landing, Sara now understood. Which explained the sofa cushions lining the balcony, the pizza cartons and beer cans scattered across the counters. The girl had turned the place into her own private hangout.

"This is *my* apartment," Sara said.

"You just moved in. You'll be moving out. I've lived here for *years.*"

"Well, I live here *now.* You can do whatever you want when I'm gone. While I'm here, you respect my boundaries, and I'll respect yours. Meaning: I won't tell your parents you're sneaking out and you stop climbing onto my balcony."

The girl shrugged. "You gonna make me climb back over?"

Sara thought about it. That was exactly what she should do. But what if the kid slipped? All hell would break loose. Cops, reporters. She stepped back to let the girl into the apartment. Then she moved into the kitchen and flicked on the overhead switch. She watched the girl as she did so, and sure enough, the girl stopped halfway to the front door, and turned. Sara moved to the refrigerator. The girl relaxed. Sara moved to the sink. The girl stiffened.

Aha.

Sara crouched and opened the cabinet beneath the sink. She'd done the usual upon moving into the apartment: a cursory cleaning, tossing out bed linens and a mildewed shower curtain, before organizing things the way she liked them — the floor lamp moved to a more interior corner, the pillows plumped and set up on their edges. Now, she moved aside the bottle of glass cleaner, the dishwashing detergent. There, at the very back, wedged behind the pipes, a silvery rectangle. Sara reached in and tapped it free. She rose with her find: a bulging fabric makeup bag, zipped shut.

The girl's cheeks reddened. "That's *mine!*" She came around the counter and lunged.

Sara dangled it high out of reach. "We

have an agreement?"

"Fuck you!"

"I'll take that as a yes."

They glared at each other a long, hard moment, then Sara lowered the bag.

"Bitch!" The girl snatched it away, spun on a heel, then stomped out, slamming the door.

Sara had been called worse. She locked the door after the girl and retrieved her Chablis from the table. This had been some unexpected excitement, in this boring beach town. She couldn't believe people chose to live out their lives here. What did they do with themselves? Play minigolf, sing karaoke?

She'd been here two weeks. It felt like two decades.

The marshals would be contacting her soon. They'd told her they wanted to know if anything odd happened, even something minor. Should she mention the kid to them? No, she decided. She'd told the girl she wouldn't tell anyone. Where Sara came from, people kept promises.

CHAPTER 7
WHIT

It wasn't until the end of the day, as he was on his way home and stopped at a red light, that Whit pulled his cell from his pocket and scanned the texts. Sure enough, Diane. She'd just learned about a school fundraiser. The last one of the year, and they couldn't miss it. People would talk if they did. In Diane's world, that was all that mattered. Not Whit, who'd had a hellish day. Not the expense, which they couldn't afford. But what people thought of her.

He could lie, claim he'd had to work late. He could find a bar instead, sit in welcome solitude for a few hours, go home after the charade was over. He thought of his kids, watching the door and waiting for him to walk through it. They'd been home a week. The light turned green. Whit hesitated, then turned left.

The Jade Palace was crowded. He spotted Diane and the kids at a four-top in front of the plate-glass window. Hostesses liked to place Diane where passersby could see her from the sidewalk. She made a nice advertisement, with her bright hair and animated face. Diane knew it, too. An actor on the small stage of her own making.

She was wearing the green tie-dyed dress he liked, the one that gathered at her waist and showed off her bare arms. She smiled brightly as Whit made his way toward them, her face glowing, then leaned forward and hissed as he pulled out a chair. "Jesus Christ. Is it too much to ask you to answer me when I text you?"

"Busy day," he said, shortly. Of course she'd forgotten what day it was. "Let's see. What's everyone in the mood for?" Boon was sitting low in his chair. The place must have run out of booster seats. His son could barely see over the tabletop. He had Wolf propped on his lap. The stuffed dog had been a hit, but it was a painful reminder to Whit of how he'd nearly lost his boy. He waved over the waiter, asked his son, "Hey, buddy. Know what you want?"

"Um." Boon gnawed his lower lip. "Fried rice?"

"Can I have fried rice, *please*," Diane corrected.

Boon nodded. "Please?"

"One order of fried rice," Whit told the waiter.

"Chicken," Boon whispered.

"Right," Whit said. "Chicken fried rice. Cassie?"

Cassie sat there with her arms folded. She wore heavy black clothes, despite the heat. Her bangs were slicked back with gel. A tiny skull hung from the black satin cord around her throat. Whit dealt with teenagers all day long, as they descended on the hotel with their parents. Those girls blended together in one shiny-haired, giggling, cheerfully dressed bunch in ripped jeans or pastel dresses hanging from skinny straps. Nothing like his kid. What was Cassie supposed to be, a junior punk rocker, some sort of band groupie? "I don't care."

"Stop it," Diane snapped. "Pick something."

"I'm not hungry."

"How about lo mein?" Whit suggested.

"I hate lo mein."

Last time, she'd insisted it was her favorite. "Egg rolls?"

"I don't care, Dad. I don't even want to be here."

Yes, she was making that clear. "Egg rolls," he told the server. "How about you, Dee?"

She studied the menu. She was torn, Whit

71

knew. She was still upset, but they were out in public. She'd never let it show. "I don't know, darling. What do you think?"

"How about sesame chicken? That's one of your favorites."

She pursed her lips, then sighed. "All right." She handed the waiter the menu. "No MSG, please. No dark meat."

The man nodded, looked to Whit.

"I'll have Mongolian beef."

The waiter swept together the menus, went through the swinging doors to the kitchen.

Whit loosened his tie. "So how was everyone's day?" No one answered. Diane was applying lip gloss, Cassie biting her thumbnail. "Boon?"

His son was looping a straw wrapper around Wolf's neck. "We had Field Day."

"That sounds like fun."

"Uh-huh. I got two medals."

"Good for you, buddy."

Cassie rolled her eyes. Her lips were rimmed black, the remnants of that awful lipstick she insisted on wearing. "*Everyone* gets medals in kindergarten. If you have a pulse, you get a medal."

"Still." Whit needed a beer. He looked around for the waiter. "Two medals are quite an accomplishment." He ruffled

Boon's hair. "How about you, Cass? How was school?"

"Fantastic. Josh Bierman gave me the finger in the hall, and Taylor barfed in the cafeteria."

"Poor Taylor. Hope she feels better soon."

"Yeah. In about nine months."

He threw a startled look at Cassie. Then he glanced at his wife. Did she have any idea this kind of thing was going on in middle school? But his wife was smiling around the restaurant, waggling her fingers at people she recognized.

She felt his gaze on her and glanced at Cassie, reached over and tucked a strand of hair behind their daughter's ear. "You're such a beautiful girl. I'm so glad you took after me."

Cassie jerked away from her mother's touch.

The food arrived, steaming bowls of white rice in perfect mounds. Whit ordered a beer. Boon stripped apart the wooden chopsticks and used one to jab a piece of chicken.

"That's not how you're supposed to do it," his sister said.

"Yes, it is." But Boon sounded doubtful.

"Really? Have you ever once seen anyone use a chopstick like that?"

"Why are you so *mean*?" Boon tossed

down his chopstick, swung at his sister with his stuffed dog. She blocked him with her elbow.

"Behave yourselves," Diane said. "Both of you."

"Here, Boon. Let me show you." Whit held up the chopsticks, forming a V. "See?" He fitted them between Boon's small fingers, cupping his son's warm hand in his own. Boon nodded, but when he went to pinch up a circle of carrot, the chopsticks slid apart. His face crumpled. "That's okay, buddy. It just takes practice. Come on, Cass, you, too. This is a life skill. Right, Dee?"

She glanced toward the front of the restaurant. Another family had arrived, husband, wife, three kids. They stood there, waiting for someone to seat them.

Diane's face lit up. "Oh look," she said. "She's PTA president," she told Whit, as she pushed herself up and waved. "Hi, Leigh Ann," she called.

Leigh Ann turned her head, still smiling. Her smile froze when she saw Diane. She looked back to her husband, said something. He nodded. Whit could see the effort the man made not to look in their direction. Diane lowered her arm and sank back down. Her cheeks were bright pink.

"It's all right," Whit said. The mantra of their marriage. *It'll be okay,* he'd assured her when his father refused to attend their wedding. *Things will get better,* he'd told her after Boon was born. *We'll figure it out,* he'd said after Social Services took away their kids.

"Everyone's staring."

"No, they're not." Anyone's feelings would be hurt. But when Diane got upset, she swept everyone along with her. She made everyone miserable.

"Like she's so special?"

"Just forget it, sweetheart. Don't let them get to you. You're bigger than that."

"After all the bake sales I ran for that bitch? Agreeing to be room mom when no one else would take the job?"

Boon was sitting very still. Cassie had her head lowered and was pouring soy sauce onto her plate, black rivers of the stuff. Her food would be inedible.

"You know what? I'm going to talk to the principal. I'm going to tell her exactly what kind of cow Leigh Ann Dowd really is."

"Diane, calm down. You're not going to do anything of the sort."

"She's the one who should be embarrassed. Treating a parent like that."

Diane was spiraling. It could go on for

hours. He forced a smile. "Have I told you how beautiful you look tonight? I like your hair like that."

She put her hand to her curls. "I could have been PTA president. Everyone wanted me to. All the teachers stopped me in the hall and *begged* me." Her voice was rising. Nearby diners were looking over.

He put his hand on hers. "Just give it time. People will forget."

"Forget what?" She shook off his hand. "My terrible transgression? I didn't do anything wrong. It was a *mistake*! It could have happened to anyone!"

But it hadn't. It had happened to them.

Diane marched ahead, winding around the pedestrians on the sidewalk, blond hair gleaming and growing faint in the distance. Whit went more slowly, letting Boon choose the pace. Maybe not surprisingly, Cassie hung back, too. They all knew, without exchanging a word, that it was sometimes better to give Dee some space.

But the moment they rounded the landing and heard the thumping bass coming from behind their closed apartment door, Whit knew it hadn't done any good. The door was unlocked. He swung it open to Amy Winehouse's smoky contralto. *I won't go, go, go.* At least Diane was home. Sometimes she'd stay out all night, coming home around dawn and climbing on top of him. *I was worried about you,* he'd tell her. *Mm,* she'd reply, lowering her mouth to his.

"You two better go to bed," he told his kids. Diane was standing out on the balcony, gripping the railing and staring into the night. The kitchen light slanted across her smooth back and shoulders, lit up the skirt of her dress.

Boon clapped his hands over his ears. Cassie took him by the shoulder and steered him down the hall. Their door closed.

Whit lowered the music, went to the fridge, and grabbed a couple beers. He carried them out to the balcony. "Beer?" He cracked one open and held it out.

"I hate this place, Whit." Diane took the can. "I've had it."

"It's just one woman —"

"It's not just one woman, Whit. It's the moms at the bus stop. The idiots in the grocery store. Those horrible phone calls." Cassie had intercepted the last one, snatching up the phone and eagerly saying, *Hello?* Then her face had drained of color. Now when the phone rang, she and Boon ignored it.

"Things will die down."

"I want to move."

"And go where?"

"I don't know. Out of this horrible town."

"We can't afford to move."

"Don't be like that. Don't be cheap. You're general manager. You can do whatever you want."

"Sure." He drained his beer, crumpled the can.

˜She glanced at him. "You didn't get the job."

So she hadn't forgotten what today was. She'd just written a script that suited her.

"That son of a bitch," she said. "Robineaux picked someone else?"

"Thompson." It stung to admit it.

"That fucking weasel? He doesn't know how to run a hotel. He ran a movie theater, for God's sake."

"Let it go, Dee. It's over."

"But you've been acting general manager for months. You told Robineaux that, didn't you? You reminded him?"

"He knows, Dee."

She narrowed her eyes. "What is it? What did you do, Whit?"

Here they went again. She was suspicious of Holly. She accused him of spending too much time with her. "I held on to my job, Dee. That's what I did."

She raised her chin. She was stunning, standing there, her chest rising and falling, the shadows slipping over her perfect skin. Her long cascading curls haloed by light. She had lost her job, right after the Problem, as she called it. Things were always other people's fault. Never hers. She wasn't even looking for a job. Whit had called in a favor, found her a few shifts at the dry cleaner.

"You don't respect the guy. Maybe he senses that."

"Sure," he said, sourly. "My fault. That's what happened."

"You promised me. You promised me the world. But all you wanted was to fuck me."

"As I recall it, babe, it was a two-way street."

"You need help, Whit. You really do." She tossed the can over the railing, a hissing spray of beer. It clattered to the alley below.

He followed her inside, closed the door. She was at the refrigerator, rooting around. He knew better than to challenge her — sometimes their arguments ended with her packing up the kids and sneaking away while he was at work — but he couldn't help himself. "I'm not the one who almost killed my kid."

She froze. Then she whirled to face him. "If you're so wonderful, Whit, how come we

79

still live in this dump? We can't even afford the first floor. No, we have to be stuck all the way up here. Save a few bucks on rent."

"As I recall, you're the reason we got kicked out of the last place." The fridge door was hanging open. He reached around her to close it.

"What the fuck does that mean?"

"You want to leave, Dee? Go ahead — leave. But you're not taking the kids."

She stepped close to him, her face tilted up to his. "Oh, you'd like that, wouldn't you?" Her breath was warm, beer-scented. "You'd love it. You'd tell them all sorts of things about me, turn them against me."

"Calm down."

"Don't tell me to calm down." She leaned closer. "You coward." She put her hands on his chest, pushed him. "When are you going to stand up? Be a man?" Another shove. "You just sat there and let Robineaux walk right over you. You didn't even fight for the position."

"Fight for it? I never had a chance. *You're* the reason I didn't get the promotion. You and your fucked-up life."

"Me? That's a real joke. It's you, Whit. You're pathetic." Her mouth twisted. "If our son turns out anything like you, he's never going to amount to shit, either."

Whit knew what he needed to do — what he always did. Say soothing things, hold her while she sobbed in his arms, then lift her and put her to bed.

But tonight, that wasn't what happened.

The skeleton of a baby crab, white as paper, with pointy claws and two tiny holes where shiny black eyes used to be.

CHAPTER 8
SARA

On her day off, Sara pulled on her bathing suit and an old cotton shirt that hung to her knees, and fitted her feet into the cheap yellow flip-flops she'd bought at the grocery store. She'd never swum in the ocean, had never so much as dipped a toe in anything but bath or ice-cold lake water.

The courtyard let directly into the alley that ran behind the building. She crossed it and followed the sandy pavement to where a path had been hollowed out through the dunes. Others were headed in the same direction, carrying coolers and sun umbrellas, the conversation between them loud and happy, their noses and shoulders burnished a hard red. Some nodded to her, and she nodded back.

When she reached the summit, a gorgeous gallop of sand and water and sky stretched as far as she could see. Colorful umbrellas dotted the curving shore. The surf thundered. Yesterday the water had been green, and other days, it was gray.

Home. It still felt nothing like it.

She'd been locking up her accounting office when they came for her. Three black sedans rolling to a stop in the small strip mall, crowding out the parked cars. She stood there with her car keys and workout bag as they showed her the piece of paper that said they were going to take apart her office, dig into her computer files, open her business safe. They drove her to the police station, where she was charged with tax fraud. They were going to make an example of her. She was going to prison. Five years, if she was lucky. Ten years if they were.

Unless.

Show us where your client got his money. Tell us how he instructed you to hide it.

Kids dashed in and out of the waves, squealing. No one paid Sara the least attention as she wandered along the beach. She was just one more anonymous face. She wrapped her towel around her shoulders, removed her flip-flops. It was cooler than she'd expected, and windy. The sand was hot beneath her bare feet. A crab skittered past and she gasped. She extricated a shell from a slick tangle of seaweed, whorled and ridged and sharpened to a point, then tossed it aside. Later, she would look it up and find it was an oyster drill — the snail that used to inhabit it would smear the hard shells of oysters with a substance to soften the shells so it could pluck out the poor defenseless creatures hiding inside. A ruthless bastard. A lesson that appearances could be deceiving. She should have held on to it.

She stepped over a jellyfish with long shimmering tentacles stretched out behind it as though it were desperate to drag itself back into the water. A seagull shrieked overhead, and she shaded her eyes to search for it in the sky. She'd once known a guy who could tell birds apart by their flying behavior. On the lakeshore, he'd lift an arm, trace the swooping patterns. *See?* he'd say. *That's a bald eagle. That's a hawk.* She'd nod and say she saw it, too. But all she saw was a bird.

She watched people venture into the ocean, studied the way they flung themselves in or turned sideways to give the waves less to grab on to before diving into the water. She dropped her towel and waded in.

The waves pushed and pulled at her, unexpectedly strong. Something grazed her thigh and swam away. She held up her arms as the water gathered itself into a towering wave. Then she was yanked below the water.

Bubbles surged around her. Swirling debris. Shards of sunlight. She somersaulted and, when her head broke the surface, sucked in a panicked mouthful of air before being dragged back under. Another tumbling suck of air, another glimpse of sky before the water slammed in over her. She was being swept out to open sea. She flailed and kicked, trying desperately to break the water's grip. But it held her tighter.

Fingers closed around her arm and hauled her up. She coughed, bobbed. A man paddled beside her, fat, sunburned shoulders, and white hair streaked across a balding head. "Best not to swim alone. Even if it looks calm."

Wheezing, she nodded her thanks.

He stroked away. Panting and humiliated, she turned and swam toward shore. Her hair hung stiff with salt water; her knees and legs throbbed, scraped raw by the ocean bottom. She limped back to the Paradise wrapped in a damp towel. Her rescuer would brag about how he'd saved some dimwit out in the middle of the ocean. Guess she didn't know about riptides, he'd boast. Maybe his wife would lean close and kiss him, feeling a deep emotion for him she hadn't felt in a long while. Their friends would raise their glasses to him, the way he'd seized the advantage of being in the right place at the right time. Sara spooned potato salad from a deli container and wondered what that would feel like.

She'd tried going straight — earning her GED, then working nights to put herself through college. She'd charged low rates, promised a quick turnaround. She'd slowly built clientele. She'd been shocked at the end of the year to realize her bank account was empty. It hadn't taken much. Her car breaking down. Student loans. She'd sat in the coffee shop that served as her office, going over the numbers and feeling an increasing swell of panic, when a guy slid into the chair opposite. A representative, he told her, of someone who wanted to hire her, a businessman based in Chicago looking to branch out into the Twin Cities. They'd heard of her. They knew who her father was. She'd closed her laptop and set it aside. *I'm listening,* she'd said.

Later, she figured out just what this businessman bought and sold: people. Mostly women, down on their luck. Women like her. Still, she stayed.

She was getting ready for work when she heard an enraged shout from the apartment next door. Seven in the morning. She held up her uniform shirt, wondering if she could get away with wearing it two days in a row. A door slammed.

When she stepped outside her apartment, she saw a dark-haired boy sitting on the concrete walkway, his back against the wall. He had his head bent and was clutching a stuffed German shepherd by its front legs. The thing's fur was worn in patches; one of its plastic eyes dangled from a thread. It grinned inanely. "You okay?" she asked the kid, without thinking.

The boy glanced up. His eyes were red and swollen, his hair matted against his damp forehead. "Wolves can't go to school."

"Of course not. That would be dangerous."

"Even nice wolves?"

"Even nice wolves." She had no idea what they were talking about.

His mouth turned down. For God's sake, was he about to start crying again? She pulled her purse over her shoulder. She had to get going. But she found herself saying, "It's not like wolves can learn to read or write."

He let out a shuddering breath. "I guess." He sniffled. "Have a nice day."

"You, too," she told him, glad to leave this

little drama.

Still, his words stuck with her as she mopped floors and misted glass surfaces with window cleaner. Was she having a nice day? She wasn't behind bars. Was that enough?

CHAPTER 9
WHIT

He'd showered and shaved, combed his hair, tied his tie, patted ointment on his knuckles. It was a long day spent sitting at his desk. Eight-thirty. Had Cassie made the school bus? Three-fifteen. Was Boon crossing the highway now, darting between speeding cars? Just get through the day. That was all he could do.

He wanted to call the kids on the drive home, but he had to do everything exactly the same as always. No detail to alert the police.

He let himself into the apartment. Boon sat washed in the glow from the TV, holding Wolf.

"Hey, buddy. Where's your sister?"

"Bedroom."

Today was like any other day for Boon, Whit reminded himself. He had no idea. "How about your mom?"

A shrug.

"You don't know where she is?"

A headshake.

Whit reached for the wall switch, flipped on the overhead light. The kid's hair branched out in every direction. Was he wearing the same striped shirt he'd worn yesterday? And why was he wearing only one sock? "How about I give your mom a call, see what's going on?"

" 'Kay." Boon rubbed one felt paw between his fingers, wouldn't look up.

Diane's cellphone went straight to voicemail. Eight-fifteen. "Where are you, honey? The kids and I are worried." He paused, wanting to say more, but broke the connection. He had to play it out. "Boon, did your mom say anything this morning about going somewhere this afternoon?"

A shrug. "She was sleeping."

Boon would have thought Diane was having one of her headaches. It happened frequently enough. The three of them would tiptoe around, talk in whispers. The door hung ajar now — no doubt one of the kids had cracked it open and peeked in. "You didn't see your mom before you went to school?" Their stories had to match exactly, even though the kids couldn't know that.

Boon shook his head, eyes still on the TV.

Whit looked around at the bare counter,

the empty hook where Diane's purse usually hung. Should he try her cell again? "I'll get dinner started." He tried to sound upbeat, like none of this was any big deal. The police would ask about his movements. Everything he did and said in these early hours mattered. He opened the refrigerator, moved things around, brought out a plastic container labeled in Diane's exuberant hand. "How about spaghetti?"

" 'Kay."

Whit rummaged around in the freezer compartment. No garlic toast, but there was a bag of frozen peas. The kids liked peas. "Why don't you go wash up for dinner, buddy?"

Boon nodded but didn't move.

"Boon," Whit said. "Turn off the TV. Right now."

Boon scrabbled down from the couch.

As soon as Whit heard the water running in the bathroom, he dialed the dry cleaner, waited a noisy minute before Diane's manager came on the line. "She was scheduled to come in at ten." Her voice was surly.

"You haven't seen her?"

"No. And she didn't even call in. Tell her to come pick up her final paycheck. I'm real sorry, Whit. You know I tried to help you out."

"Yeah. Thanks."

Whit stirred the spaghetti, turned down the flame. Boon shuffled out of the bathroom, dangling Wolf by the tail. "Dinner will be ready soon. Why don't you get out your homework?" Boon liked doing his spelling page. He considered it a game.

"I forgot my pencils at school."

"I bet we have one around here." Whit pulled open the junk drawer, shuffled through the rubber bands, batteries, take-out menus. "Here," he said, handing his son a red pen.

"My teacher won't like it."

"She'll understand. Go get your folder, buddy. You can work at the kitchen table."

Whit went to check on Cassie.

Light from the hallway fell into the darkened bedroom. "Cass?"

Silence.

"You okay?"

She rolled over onto her side, putting her back to him.

"How was school today?"

Nothing.

No one from school had called to let him know she'd skipped class again. "What's the homework situation?"

She didn't answer.

He doubted she'd cracked a book. She

could do the work. She just didn't want to. "Let me look at it and I'll sign off on it, okay?" This was what her teacher had instituted, in an effort to teach Cassie responsibility. Half the time, Cassie just forged Diane's signature. It was unsettling how good she was at it, too. Diane had been infuriated. She told Cassie that everything Cassie did was a reflection on her, and to stop being so selfish. Cassie needed to pull her grades up. She needed to make something of her life. It was a familiar complaint. Whit would try to intercede, tell Diane their daughter was old enough to learn from her own mistakes, but Diane never heard any of it. Their battles raged around and round, exhausting them both, neither of them emerging the victor. "We'll talk about it after dinner, Cass. I'm making spaghetti, the kind with meatballs."

Silence.

"Cassie —"

"Fine."

But she didn't move. He'd give her a minute.

Boon was bent over his spelling sheet, pen gripped between his fingers. He'd positioned Wolf so the toy could read the page, too.

"How's it going, buddy?"

" 'Kay."

Whit looked down. Instead of forming letters, Boon was drawing faces in the margins, empty eyes and slashes for mouths. Whit decided to let it go. "I'm going to make another phone call," he told Boon and let himself out onto the balcony. When Diane got one of her headaches, she lay low. She wouldn't be able to drive herself to the hospital. She might have been desperate enough to ask her mom for a ride.

Helen answered on the second ring. She listened, then sighed. "Not again."

He heard the telltale puff of air. His mother-in-law was smoking. It didn't matter that Helen was on oxygen, and that if the tank exploded, she'd take the entire place down with her. One of the reasons he didn't like Diane taking the kids over to visit her. They'd argued about it, but he was firm. *You want your mom to spend time with our kids, she has to come here.* Only when he was around and could see for himself she wasn't lighting up.

"Helen, it's different this time. She left the kids behind."

"I don't know what to tell you . . ."

"Let me know if you hear from her."

"Hmm," she said, and Whit knew she'd checked out from the conversation. Probably lighting another cigarette.

"Something's burning," Boon told him when Whit stepped back into the kitchen. Sure enough, the spaghetti was smoldering. Whit dashed the pot from the burner and into the sink. He looked down at the smoking mess. What had he done? What had he done to all of them? "How does pizza sound?"

Boon thought about it. "I guess."

They ate in front of the TV.

Cassie joined them, ignoring Whit's shifting over to make room for her on the couch. Instead, in the armchair, she drew her knees to her chest. She was wearing ratty fishnet stockings and a black, heavy pleated skirt. Her hair hung in greasy hanks. She hadn't washed her hands, either, and he knew homework would never happen. But at least she was eating.

"How was school today, guys?"

Cassie folded a thin slice in half and nibbled the point.

"Kristin lost a tooth. On the bus." Boon tugged a strand of cheese to its stretching point, dripping grease on the couch. "Her second one."

"That so?"

"Everybody's lost a tooth but me."

"Your turn will come."

"When?"

"I don't know, but any day now, I bet. You been wiggling it like I told you?"

"Yeah."

"Well, then it's just a matter of time."

"What if it never falls out?"

"It will."

"But what if it doesn't?"

"Then I'll get out my special tooth puller and take hold of it. That's what I did for your sister and look how she turned out." Cassie lurched sideways so he couldn't pat her head. His hand fell through air.

They watched a nature program about honey badgers, nature's escape artists. It grew late, well past their bedtime. Should he send them to school tomorrow, or let them sleep in? It was almost the end of the school year. What were a few missed hours? But if he kept them home, he'd have an audience to every minute of his day. He decided to play it by ear, see how everyone felt in the morning.

When Boon began to snore softly, Whit carried him into his room and settled him in his bunk. He tucked Wolf beside him. Cassie followed, scuffing her feet, and climbed up the ladder to her bunk. "Good night, honey," he told her, reaching out to give her a hug.

"Don't." She yanked the covers over her head.

He started with Dee's pastor, apologized for the lateness of the hour. "Diane hasn't been to church in months," Gleeson told him. "Let me check with my wife." Mrs. Gleeson came onto the line and gave him the names of other parishioners Diane might have been friendly with. Whit called each of them, got more numbers. He called Dee's phone over and over. He let his messages grow increasingly concerned, then tinged with annoyance. A man whose wife hadn't come home, who had abandoned her children, would be annoyed.

Chapter 10
Sara

Sara preferred cleaning occupied houses to rentals. Even though it entailed more work, there was the extra money Terri had promised, plus there were the other advantages. Sara had worked hard to earn Terri's trust. She knew that Terri came in afterward to spot-check a cleaning job, so she made sure to Lysol the hell out of everything, remake the beds if they looked the tiniest bit rumpled. She never called in sick, and she kept her complaints to herself.

Sara let herself in through the etched-glass door and set down her bucket and mop, listened for a moment. Except for the buzz of the air conditioner, the house was silent.

She started upstairs.

Looked like the husband was sleeping in the den. There'd been some attempt to disguise it, but there were pillows stacked in the top shelf of the closet and a man's electric razor in the desk drawer, the blurred ring of a glass on the side table. The master was tidy, the drapes pushed back to flood the room with light. Family photographs on the wall. Sara had never sat for a family photograph. She didn't even have a picture of her mother. She had only one of her father, torn from the newspaper. It in no way resembled the man she loved.

There'd been a tantrum in the nursery sometime during the night, the ripped pages of a picture book stuffed into the seam between mattress and crib rail, grimy fingerprints on the white wooden railing. A baby bottle lay beneath the dresser. Sara retrieved it and pressed a damp cloth to the carpet fibers.

The oldest kid must be off somewhere, probably college. Silver and gold chains dribbled across the dresser. Mismatched earrings. Papers and school supplies in the plastic bin beneath the bed, a shiny packet of condoms, one end torn. Photographs were tucked around the huge mirror, the same laughing girl in most of them, with her arm slung around the shoulders of girls and boys who looked as safe and unconcerned as she did.

The middle child was a boy, his room reeking of spicy deodorant and testosterone. Dirty clothes on the closet floor, under the bed. Sports equipment in a corner, the dried husk of a towel in the opened gym bag. Nestled beneath the bottle of shampoo and a powdery bar of soap was an opened pint of whiskey. A carefully rolled pair of socks amid the chaos — tucked in the toe of one of them was a plastic bag of white capsules. Uppers, she thought. Worth fifty, sixty dollars on the street. She hefted the bag in the palm of her hand. What would the kid do, report their theft?

Her cellphone chimed. She pulled it from her pocket and scanned the incoming text. She had a meeting.

She drove along the narrow highway, followed the signs for the bridge. It was the middle of the week, so traffic was light, the vacationers settled into their rentals and not thinking yet about the trek homeward. Lounging on the beach or on their decks, contemplating dinner options and worrying too late whether they should have reapplied sunscreen.

It was the first time Sara had been back onto the mainland, and she saw things she hadn't noticed before — fields of shorn crops, billboards offering up Jesus like a delicious dessert or a glass of water for the parched. People needed their emotional crutches. Her father had taught her that.

She turned south, following the coastline. South Carolina lay ahead, maybe a couple hours away. She watched the odometer. When it clicked over, she turned in to the wildlife preserve and rolled up to the guard's booth. "One," she told the elderly man who came out to greet her, handing over a five-dollar bill. "Park closes at ten," he reminded her cheerfully, and she nodded. She'd be long gone before then.

Luis sat waiting for her on a picnic bench set among the thin trees. He appeared to be alone. She parked beside a dark sedan with South Carolina plates, the only other vehicle in the lot. Did they have plates they regularly switched out, or had he borrowed it from the local field office? He wore civilian clothes — shorts and a polo shirt. But his haircut betrayed him, trimmed so close his hair was just a shadow. It was only as she reached him that he looked at her, away from the ocean. He wore dark sunglasses. She couldn't see through the lenses to his eyes.

She sat, rested her elbows on the worn wood. "How come we're meeting here?"

"I had business nearby."

"Relocating another victim?" It pleased her to think of someone else out there, going through what she was going through. They should form a support group. Witnesses Anonymous.

"You know I can't say."

"Where's Nicole?"

"On assignment."

Which told her zero. "I thought you two were partners." She'd studied them during the drive to the Outer Banks, trying to figure out whether they were lovers, whether they even liked each other. Luis wore a wedding ring, but when did that mean anything?

He just smiled, not taking the bait. "The apartment working out?"

"It's Paradise, isn't it?"

"You install a dead bolt?"

She nodded.

"How about work?"

"Barrel of laughs."

"It won't be forever. It's just for now."

She had to hold down a job. It was a requirement of the program. The government expected her to help support herself, like they were parents teaching her a lesson. She could do anything but go back to accounting, they'd told her. She could do anything but the one thing she'd been born to do. The surf was calmer here than up on the Outer Banks, the water glinting smoothly to the horizon.

"We've got a trial date."

She looked back to him, surprised. "When?"

"August fifth."

Just over six weeks. She felt relief that there was an end in sight, and panic that it was so soon. She'd hoped she'd have more time. There were so many moving pieces to keep track of. "How's this going to work?"

"Nicole and I will come get you. Four, maybe five days ahead of time. We'll transport you to and from the courthouse. You won't even have to be in the same courtroom. You can testify remotely."

There would be additional security around the trial. Probably an entire team of people ferrying Sara around. She wouldn't have time to figure out their routines, their weak points. No, if she had any chance of getting away, it had to be here, on the Outer Banks. "If I can do that, why can't I testify from here?" Letting Luis think she was terrified. She'd already gotten word to her former client: she was no threat.

"You know that's not how it works."

"Where will I stay?"

"A safe house."

"You sure it's safe?"

"I am. But we can go the motel route, if you want. Anyone you want to see while you're in town? We can work something out. Supervised, of course."

Who did he have in mind? The neighbor across the street who let her Great Dane pee on Sara's mailbox? The jerk at the bank who insisted Sara show ID for every single transaction, even though he knew damn well who she was? Luis had to know there was no one in St. Paul whom Sara considered a friend, and no one who missed her. Was he trying to provoke her? "Sure," she said. "I'd love for everyone to meet you."

He pulled the sunglasses off, pinched the bridge of his nose. "It's always hard at first, Sara. Everyone goes through an adjustment period."

"How the hell would you know?" He'd probably gone to the same high school all four years. His family likely still lived in the same damn house he'd grown up in.

"Sara —"

"You walk away from your life, then you can talk to me about how hard it is."

"So young to be so angry."

Not so young, and he knew it. He knew the details of her life, thirty-two, single, only child, an orphan now. He didn't give a damn about her. She was just a minnow they were using to trap a shark. She didn't fool herself into thinking otherwise. "You think I should go to prison." Her father had died there.

"Not up to me."

"You do, don't you?"

He looked around the deserted woods. It was growing dark. The ocean glimmered. Finally, his eyes came back to her. "I think people do what they have to do."

His voice rang with sincerity. Maybe he did care about her. She could use that.

"Listen," he said, sighing. "You're in the homestretch. Keep on doing what you've been doing. Get through the trial, then everything will be behind you. Okay? You'll be free."

There would be other trials. The FBI planned to keep tabs on her for the rest of her life. Just like when she was growing up, only then it was social workers checking in, asking questions. Making her feel all the things that were absent in her life. Well, those things were still absent, but she'd gotten used to it.

She'd never be free.

She drove back to her silent apartment, her crappy car shaking and rumbling. She paid close attention to the road and all its various exit points. Next time, she'd drive north and cross the bridge there. The Wright Memorial, it was called, and the one she'd just taken was the Bonner. She would commit both routes to memory. When the time came, she wouldn't be hampered by indecision.

She stopped outside her door. A white crab skeleton no bigger than her thumbnail sat on her windowsill. Where had it come from? It couldn't have scaled up the weathered planks on its own. It seemed unlikely the wind had blown it with such precision to land on its miniature claws. Sara brought the crab inside and set it on her kitchen counter, blank-eyed and frozen midscrabble. It had withstood the ocean and blinding sun, the wind. It only appeared fragile.

CHAPTER 11
WHIT

The police found Diane's car parked in front of the Raleigh bus station two hundred miles away. A scribbled note had been stuck in the visor: *Sorry, Whit.*

The cop handed Whit the note a week later — after it had been fingerprinted and forensically examined or whatever the hell else they figured they needed to do to it. Whit sat in his living room while the cop talked, gripping the pink scrap as though it contained answers. The first few days had been hell. It was clear he was under suspicion. But he'd been at work the day Diane went missing, dozens of witnesses testifying to that fact. Both kids vouched for their mom having been home when they left for school, behind her closed bedroom door nursing a headache. Then there was Diane herself — troubled, damaged Diane, who'd almost killed her son.

"We've pinged her phone, but it's still

turned off." Nothing in the way the cop sat there, composed and contained, told Whit he was still a suspect, but there were her eyes. Cop eyes. Brown and certain. "No cameras outside the station, nothing on the ones inside; in fact, there's no record of her having even bought a ticket. Her car's clean."

"I don't get it. What was she doing there, then? Why go to Raleigh?"

"Maybe she was meeting someone?"

Whit shook his head. "I don't know who. Dee . . . Things have been rough lately. She hasn't been spending time with friends."

"We've spoken with her coworkers. People from church. We understand she's done this sort of thing before."

Adventures, Diane called them. Every so often, Whit would come home to an empty apartment, Diane having decided the kids had to meet Mickey, or see Luray Caverns. They never got very far. She'd run out of gas, out of money, or one of the kids would call him from her phone after she fell asleep. He'd drop everything and go get them from wherever they'd gotten stranded. She may have called them adventures, but he knew them for what they really were. Practice runs.

The cop was watching him. He felt the

accusation of her gaze. "A couple of times. But she didn't take the kids with her this time."

"She mention running into an old boyfriend recently?"

"No." He spoke slowly, processing. An old boyfriend? Had that happened? Diane hadn't mentioned it.

"Was she spending a lot of time online?"

"No more than usual. Look. I know what you're getting at. I don't think Diane was seeing anyone."

She sighed. Then she flipped her notebook shut and tucked it in her shirt pocket. "I'm sorry, Mr. Nelson, but we've taken the investigation as far as we can — further, actually, because you were so worried about her. There's no indication your wife left against her will, no indication she might do herself harm, or harm to others. She even left a note. Unless there's anything else you can tell us . . . ?"

"No. Nothing I can think of." What more could he add? Their lives had been peeled apart, exposed. He unfolded the note, stared down at his wife's familiar handwriting. "I just need to know she's okay."

"Unless circumstances change, we're going to have to move on. We know it's hard to hear, but the thing is, there's nothing criminal about your wife deciding to walk away from her life."

After she left, as he sat at the kitchen table, holding that note that he only imagined carried Diane's vanilla scent, he thought — *There goddamn ought to be.*

By the time he got to the school gymnasium, the kids were already in folding chairs arranged in rows across the basketball court. Families crowded the bleachers. Everyone was listening to the PTA president make her case that they should all feel welcome to become involved in the school and its activities. He found a spot against the wall and searched for Boon's glossy, dark head. It was hard to tell where one class started and the other left off, but the kindergartners were easy to spot. They sat in the very front rows, fidgeting and giggling. This was their big day. A blond girl shifted position and he caught a glimpse of his son swiveling in his seat, eyes searching the crowd. When he saw Whit, he lifted his hand in a delighted wave. He leaned to see who was beside Whit, and then his smile faded. He turned back around. *Do you think Mom will come?* Boon had asked again and again that morning. Whit had taken the coward's way out. *Maybe,* he'd lied. Cassie had shot him a scathing look. The front door had banged behind her.

There she stood now, leaning against the far wall and scowling at the PTA president. She'd figured out how to sign out of class and make her brother's graduation. Good for her. Whit tried to catch her attention, but she refused to look over. She knew he was there.

He had enlisted Cassie's help, or tried to — spreading out the bills and showing her the numbers. She was old enough to understand addition and subtraction, the concept of monthly obligations. *This is our rent — I always pay it first.* Turned out Dee hadn't paid the previous month's rent. They were three months in arrears. Who knew where that money had gone. He'd torn the apartment apart, searching. *This is what we pay for electricity and water, and here's my car payment.* Cassie had crossed her arms and grumbled, but he knew she was paying attention. He brought out receipts. *Groceries, visits to the clinic when you or Boon get sick, the dentist. Clothes, shoes.* God help them if Cassie or Boon needed orthodontia or glasses. Way at the bottom of the list was childcare and saving for college education. So far, the balances of both those accounts were zero.

She'd slumped in the kitchen chair and glared at the papers he was moving around. "Why are you telling me this?"

"I might have to get a second job." There was no public transportation to the Outer Banks. He could earn some extra cash driving the occasional stranded tourist to and from the mainland. It wouldn't be a reliable source of income, but the hours would be flexible. With any luck, he could pick up a job or two while the kids were asleep, be home before they woke in the morning.

"So?"

"So I need you to watch your brother while I'm at work. Grandma will help out when she can, but you know she's got Grandpa to take care of." On top of everything, his father had fallen and broken his leg in two places. He was out of work, and foul-tempered. Until things settled down over there, it was better Whit kept the kids home.

"What about camp?"

"I'm sorry, Cassie."

"This is so screwed up," she muttered. She climbed down from her chair and stalked away.

After the retiring teachers had been applauded, and the orchestra leader had her round of clapping for leading the orchestra to a regional victory, it was time for the kindergartners to receive their certificates and awards. Whit had no idea there were so many kids in his son's grade. They skittered across the stage, fizzing with the importance of the event. The girls wore candy-colored dresses, and the boys were in button-down shirts and long pants. All except Boon. He was in his favorite Scooby-Doo T-shirt, faded from washing and hanging down to his knees. At least his hair was combed. Probably the teacher had taken care of that, or one of the room moms. Murmuring to each other when the kids couldn't hear. *You know, it's just his dad now.*

After the final kindergartner paraded across the stage to scattered applause, everyone was released to the coolness of the cafeteria. Cupcakes sat displayed on tables against the far wall beneath loops of streamers. Yelling, the kids pelted across the room toward them. Parents held up cellphones to take photographs of the grinning graduates. A few stopped to ask how Whit was doing, to let him know they were available if he needed help, daycare, meals, that sort of thing. He smiled and nodded his thanks. He didn't recognize a single one of them. Boon stood beside his teacher, a pretty young woman whose hand rested on his shoulder as she talked to the principal. She'd taken Boon under her wing these past few weeks. Whit was on his way over to congratulate his son and thank the teacher when he spotted Cassie alone in a corner, peeling the paper liner from a cupcake.

She eyed him as he approached. "You were late."

"Hello to you, too. I'm glad to see you made it."

She shrugged. She had a smudge of pink frosting on her cheek. She wore a long-sleeved black shirt printed with a human rib cage and black jeans with silver duct tape running down the seams. Her hair hung in tangles. She looked like a juvenile delinquent.

"You have any trouble signing out?"

"Puh-lease." Meaning she hadn't signed out. She'd just skipped out. He would be getting a phone call later. It had been only after he'd gone to school and pleaded her case with the vice principal that she'd waived the Saturday school requirement and let his daughter finish out the year. *Your daughter has a problem discerning reality,* she'd told him. Why didn't she come right out and say it? *Your daughter is a liar.*

Cassie licked her finger. "You working tonight?"

In so many ways, Cassie was older than her years. In other ways, she remained painfully young. He glanced around for a paper napkin to wipe off the frosting, then stopped himself. She'd be horrified, in front of everyone. "I tried to switch shifts —"

"So, yes."

"It'll be late, after you and Boon are in bed."

"There's no milk."

"We'll stop at the store on the way home."

"There's nothing to eat, either."

There was sandwich meat, bananas. But Boon deserved a little celebration. "I thought we'd get burgers."

"You said we couldn't eat out anymore."

"True, but you only graduate from kindergarten once." Cassie's last day was Friday. The summer yawned before them. "Which reminds me." He pulled a small package out of his pocket, folded into a plastic bag.

She eyed it suspiciously. "What is it?"

"Open it and see."

She unrolled the bag and peered in. "You got me a *phone*?"

"It's so you can reach me. I've got my number programmed into it."

"But you said I had to be thirteen before I could have my own phone."

"You've taken on more responsibility.

116

Seems to me that that should be rewarded."

The look Cassie gave him made him grin back at her. Families surged around them. A few parents had brought flowers for their graduates. Diane would have rolled her eyes. Or she'd have gone in the other direction, decorating the apartment with streamers and balloons, ordering a cake, insisting Whit's parents make the drive, broken leg or no.

Cassie was firing up her phone. Boon was nowhere to be seen.

"Need any help figuring that out?"

"I got it."

"You'll have to keep track of how many minutes you use. It's only for emergencies, okay?"

"Can I play games on it?"

"Sure." He caught a glimpse of Boon through the crowd, still glued to his teacher's side as she talked to Pastor Gleeson and his wife. "Whoa. Looks like Mrs. Gleeson's expecting again." How many kids did that make, four? Five?

Cassie's head was bent, her thumbs flying over her phone screen. "She's such a bitch. *You better watch out or you'll turn out just like your mother.*" Her voice was high and mincing, a pitch-perfect imitation of Mrs. Gleeson's sugary accent.

117

When had the woman said that? "She probably meant that you look like her." The resemblance was there — the way Cassie tilted her head and looked at something out of the corners of her eyes, cognac eyes that were the same color and shape as Dee's. The long spill of blond hair. All Dee.

"Really, Dad?"

He watched the woman standing there beside her husband, her hand high on her rounded belly. Who would say something like that to a child? Whit had always found her husband a real jackass.

So fierce, his daughter. She'd been like that even as a toddler. She'd take a tumble, fall to her hands and knees, and Dee and he would brace themselves for the outburst. Every time, though, she'd right herself and keep on going, her face set with grim determination.

"You know," he told Cassie. "When your mom turned eighteen, she quit her job, packed up her little VW bug, and drove for three straight days until she got to the Outer Banks." Cassie stared down at her phone, but he knew she was listening. She used to love this story. When she was little, she begged Dee and him to tell it over and over. When had they stopped telling it? "She didn't have a job. She didn't have a place to stay. She didn't know a single person here. But she wanted to live where she could see the sunrise every day over the ocean."

"And four years later," Cassie prompted.

"Four years later," he said.

"She met you."

"She met me. And then we had you and your brother. But she didn't know all that would happen when she got here. She took a chance. She was incredibly brave."

They'd always told the story as though there'd been a purpose to Dee's headlong rush to leave home. The truth was, she'd just driven until she'd run out of road.

"Dad?"

"Hmm?"

"I don't want to go back to the Gleesons' church. Ever."

"Deal."

A paper map stretched side to side, all white states and blue water, folded into a floppy piece — one corner burned and powdery, and still smelling of smoke.

CHAPTER 12
SARA

Sara waited for the people working the third shift to drift across the courtyard to their cars and drive away before she quietly let herself out of her apartment. It was just before midnight. The partiers were still out. She figured she had maybe an hour before they returned, tires squealing and music blaring out of car windows, searching for anything that might extend the party. The last thing Sara wanted was some amped-up drunk stumbling over and calling out, *Hey, baby.*

She ran down the stairs and headed toward her car, parked away from the streetlight in a shadowy spot by the swimming pool. She'd already gone over the car's undercarriage, shining the beam of her flashlight into every corner and crevice. She wasn't surprised to find nothing there that shouldn't be. The Feds would be shrewder than that — but it did mean more effort on her part.

She climbed behind the steering wheel, pulled the lever to shove the seat back as far as it could go. The interior of her car was a steam bath, but she couldn't start the engine to roll down the windows. The miserable heat would provide extra incentive to be efficient. She set her tools on the passenger seat beside her — screwdriver, needle-nose pliers, wire cutter, and a roll of black electrician's tape. She tugged her hair back into a ponytail and went to work.

Forty minutes later, she found it. Nestled in the steering column, a small black box the size of her palm with protruding wires and two tiny blinking lights — one red and one green. The same GPS anyone could order online. The Feds probably bought them in bulk. She should have guessed they'd hardwire the damn thing. She loosened the wires and lowered the box to her lap. It would continue to run on backup battery after she clipped the power source. Right now, with the car engine off, it was in idle phase. She detached it, checked the battery, and tucked it into the glove box. She packed everything around the steering column back into place and snapped on the cover. Sweat prickled the back of her neck, collected in the hollow of her throat. She scooped up her tools and climbed out into the night.

Motion seen out of the corners of her eyes made her glance toward the pool. There, a small figure was trudging along the fence, moving in and out of moonlight. A dark-haired boy with his head down, the little one who lived next door. He spotted her at the same time, and stopped. He raised his hand tentatively. She found herself raising hers in response, a stupid reaction — he instantly changed course and headed directly for her. She stood there waiting. She couldn't say why. Maybe it was the way he was beetling toward her, as though he were on a mission. Maybe he needed help. He appeared to be alone.

"What's up?" she asked when he arrived.

He gazed up at her with interest, his hair flopping back from damp temples. The undone strap on his left sandal flapped. He gripped his stuffed dog by one stiff paw, the toy hanging upside down and grinning up at Sara. "You see any copperheads?"

"Snakes?"

"This is their hunting time."

She hadn't given a thought to what might be slithering on the ground at this hour. She glanced around the cracked pavement, then back to the boy. "Shouldn't you be in bed?"

He shrugged. "It's okay."

Did his parents even know he was out here? Maybe they did, maybe they didn't. Either way, it wasn't her responsibility. She told the boy good night and headed toward the stairs. But he fell into step beside her. "My grandma and grandpa live in the woods," he said. "They got *lots* of copperheads. Blacksnakes, too. The blacksnakes *eat* the copperheads."

"Terrific." Sara had never met her grandparents, didn't know if she had any.

"Yeah. But you got to watch out for ticks. They're really, really tiny. You can't even feel them bite you."

"Too bad." Were ticks a problem here, too?

"Yeah. Because then, *pow!* You could smash them."

"You can't smash ticks."

"Yes you can." He peered up at her earnestly. "You pinch their bodies really hard and make their guts squish."

"I'll keep that in mind." Why was she arguing with a kid?

He followed her up the stairs. She was silent, hoping to discourage his company, but he grabbed the railing to haul himself along. He bent his head with determination, panting with the effort to keep up. She relented and slowed.

"You want to come to my birthday party? It's going to be Teenage Mutant Ninja Turtles. We're going to have cake and presents."

"Sounds like fun." Sara had never celebrated her birthday, sandwiched in that dreary period between Thanksgiving and Christmas. To her, it was a day like any other, one to get through. She always felt relieved when she was on the other side of it, as though she'd passed a test and emerged victorious. One year down, who knew how many more to go?

"Lots and lots of presents."

Her father had surprised her for her tenth birthday. She'd come home from school to the apartment they'd been living in to find him sitting alone at the kitchen table. He gestured to the seat beside him and she sat down. Her birthday routine was always very simple — a good-morning pat on the head, maybe an adventure like a movie or hike through the woods, depending on where they were living at the time. But never this, her father sitting there in the middle of the day, clearly waiting for her. *You're old enough now,* he told her, *to start helping out.*

The boy stopped on the landing and

stared up into the darkness. "Look." He pointed. Sara followed his finger, saw the massive silvery web strung from ceiling to railing, and in the center, a fat spider with long, jointed legs. She recoiled, but the boy went right up to the monster, his face inches from its teardrop-shaped blob of a body. Was it poisonous? Should she pull him back? He seemed to know what he was doing. "That's a writing spider," he informed her. " 'Cause it writes a big X in its web and hides behind it."

"Clever." Too bad people couldn't hide behind letters. She backed away, started up the stairs. She had an early morning. She was done talking about ticks and snakes and spiders. Her skin was beginning to itch at the thought of all those crawling, creeping things.

But he trudged along with her. "It's not my favorite spider." He paused, giving her a chance to respond and, when she didn't, went on. "It's not jumping spiders and wolf spiders and brown recluse spiders, either. My very, very favorite is goldenrod crab spiders. Wanna know why?"

She spoke despite herself. "*Crab* spiders?"

"Uh-huh. They sit on flowers and wait for bees to land. Spiders are smart."

"Jesus." North Carolina had a lot of bugs.

She'd never lived in a place so infested. She was always having to work around the exterminators who regularly sprayed the houses she cleaned. She'd taught herself to turn on the light before stepping into the bathroom at night.

"I used to have an ant farm. But it got busted."

"The ants must have been upset." Delighted, more likely. No longer sandwiched between plates of glass, would they even have known what to do with themselves?

"I never saw them again."

He sounded sad. She didn't know what to say. Was he looking for comfort, reassurance? She joked. "Maybe they went to a party."

"Ants don't go to parties. They dig tunnels and take care of each other."

"I see. Well, I guess that's important."

He adjusted his stuffed animal. "That's what my dad does. My dad takes care of us."

And doing a great job, too, letting his needy little brat wander around searching for snakes in the middle of the night.

"Do you have a dad?" he asked, suddenly.

Witnesses were advised to tell people they had no family. In a sense, they didn't anymore. But in Sara's case, it was true.

"No." It had been her and her father. Now it was just her.

"A sister?"

"Nope." She'd never longed for one, either. Sometimes, she thought she might have liked the company, but what if they'd detested each other?

She waited for him to add Mom to the list, but he kept his head lowered, trudging forlornly but resolutely up the stairs. At last, they reached the top floor. She paused outside her door while he banged on his. There was no answer. He pounded again. Sara twisted her key into the lock. Was she supposed to wait and make sure he got inside safely?

Then his door swung open. He turned and waved goodbye to Sara before stepping across the threshold. The door swung shut. There had been no conversation, no exclamation of surprise at finding the boy in the shadows, outside the door.

Two nights later, she met his father.

She stood on the walkway, leaning against the railing and studying the stars, thinking. She heard him before she saw him, footsteps ringing on the metal stairs. Then he appeared around the corner, his white shirt gleaming in the darkness, a suit jacket

128

folded over one arm. She'd seen his SUV pull into the courtyard below, and the headlights blink off. A moment of stillness, then he'd climbed out and closed the car door quietly. Respectful of his neighbors, she guessed, not wanting to wake them, though there always seemed to be plenty of neighbors awake, lights showing around the blinds in windows. He trudged toward her, head down, shoulders slumped. He hadn't noticed her.

"Long day?" She put her cigarette to her lips. She inhaled, felt the catch in her throat and the almost instant dizziness. It had been years.

He glanced up, startled. He was very good-looking, with regular features and dark hair that fell in a wave over his forehead. "You could say that." He looked from her to the door behind her, then his expression cleared. "You must be our new neighbor." He held out his hand, and she shook it. His fingers enclosed hers, warm. "Whit Nelson."

"Sara Lennox. I've seen your kids around."

"Hope they haven't been pestering you. I've had to leave them to their own devices this summer."

Yep. He sure had. She said the polite thing. "Not at all."

He tugged at the knot in his tie. "You do realize the view's *behind* the building?"

She laughed. "I get tired of looking at the ocean." She approved of a man wearing a suit. Her father always wore one when he was working.

"Don't think I've ever heard anyone say that before. Got another one of those?" He motioned to her cigarette.

"Sure." She tossed him the pack.

He fished out a cigarette, used her lighter, and tucked it back into the cellophane, handing the pack back to her. He inhaled. The embers glowed. "What brings you to the Outer Banks, if you don't mind my asking?"

It was her accent that gave her away as a newcomer, she thought. Or maybe her pale skin. She trotted out the usual answer. "Just looking for a change, I guess."

"You find it?"

"I'm working on it."

"Be careful." He rested his elbows on the railing beside hers, the line of his white collar crisp against his tanned throat. He smelled citrusy, a clean scent. "This place has a way of sucking you in. I was just passing through on vacation. Never meant to stay, but here I am. Been fourteen years now."

He sounded wistful. He was telling her a story. She liked stories, both hearing and telling them. Stories gave her control over the ending. "That right? What made you stay?"

"I met my wife. She liked it here, wanted to stay."

Yes, the pretty blonde painting her nails on the balcony that day. Sara hadn't seen her in weeks. They smoked in silence for a while. It wasn't any of her business, but there was something about the darkness closing in around them and the way he leaned beside her, staring up at the distant stars high in the sky, that prompted her to ask, "But?"

"She took off last month."

Women did that, left husbands and kids behind. Marriage was such a fake institution, doomed to failure. Sara had seen it over and over. People changed. No one person could be everything to another person. Expecting otherwise only set you up for disappointment. But this guy sounded genuinely sad. "I'm sorry." Sara wondered if his wife had fallen in love with someone else. Someone richer than this guy. It wasn't likely she'd found someone better-looking.

"I'll survive. It's my kids I worry about."

"How old are they?"

"Boon's almost six. Cassie's twelve."

Boon, Copperhead Boy. Cassie, Balcony Girl. "Boon's an interesting name."

"It's a nickname. Cassie gave it to him when he was little. He loved balloons, was always asking for one. *Boon,* he'd say."

Cute story. She could tell he thought they were too young to be abandoned by their mom. Maybe they were. But everyone had problems. "They'll be okay. Kids are pretty resilient."

"They need their mother." He sighed.

Society seemed to revere motherhood. Sara never understood it. Women got pregnant. They had babies. It was simple biology. Didn't make them saints. "Depends on the mother."

"Yeah?" He looked at her.

She'd said too much. It was the small things that would trip her up. "Wow, it's got to be a hundred degrees out here. Have a good night." She crushed her cigarette on the railing and went inside.

CHAPTER 13
WHIT

Whit found the calendar buried in the dresser drawer. Cassie was marking off the days. He stared at the angry slashes, wondering if he and his daughter needed to talk. Then he shoved aside the socks and slid the calendar back into its hiding place.

"Five minutes, Cass."

He rapped on the bathroom door and went down the hall, knotting his tie. She'd stomped off the night before, banging the bedroom door and locking it, keeping Boon out for hours. Now she had locked herself into the bathroom, keeping both of them out. He was going to have to shave leaning over the kitchen sink, fully dressed. One of these days, he was going to go around and remove all the locks.

He came into the kitchen and saw Boon balanced precariously on a chair, peering into the microwave's lit interior. The air was rich with the smell of bacon fat, and something else, something acrid. Burning plastic?

"Jesus." He hurried over, grabbed his son beneath his armpits, and swung him down. Yanking the door open, he saw the un-opened package sitting on the glass plate, its corners crimped. Smoke billowed out. The smoke detector started shrieking.

He snatched up a dish towel and whipped it around, opened the slider to air the place out, but the air was too humid to do anything but ooze. He flapped the towel more energetically. The alarm silenced.

Boon peered up at him from beneath his bangs, his eyes weepy, his mouth pinched with remorse. "Sorry, Dad."

Whit had wanted the bacon to last a couple of days, at least. Was any of it salvageable? He reached into the microwave and inched the package toward himself. "I know you were only trying to help." He dropped the bacon on the counter, waved his scalded fingers. "But remember you can't use the microwave without adult supervision. It's a safety rule."

"Better pay attention, Boon," Cassie jeered behind them. "At least until Dad changes the rules again."

Her hair was wet, selectively. She'd been patting down the knotted tangles. She wouldn't let him touch it. *Get away,* she snarled every time he so much as approached her with a brush. "Here's another one," he said. "No locking yourself into the bathroom until I'm done in there."

She scraped out a kitchen chair and sat heavily, drawing her knees to her chest. She was wearing those awful fishnet stockings. "You're the one who made me get up."

"I want to make sure you two eat something besides junk. It's going to be a long day." Some days, he could get something into them before he left for work. Some days, he couldn't.

"I'm not hungry."

"You have to eat something."

"Well, I'm not eating *that.*"

She'd always been a picky eater, but lately she hadn't been eating anything but candy. He didn't know where she got it from, but he'd been finding creased wrappers heaped in the laundry basket beneath the dirty clothes. Her go-to dumping ground. He'd hoped the treat of bacon might turn her around, had stood at the refrigerator case in the grocery store and debated the cost before picking it up and dropping it into the cart. Now, he looked down at the plastic shriveled tightly against the Styrofoam. He plucked at a plastic corner and tore it loose. Steam rose. A length of red and white meat

135

came clinging, slid down the face of the plastic. "I'll stick it back in. It'll be fine."

"We'll get cancer."

Where did she get this stuff from? When he was twelve, he didn't even know what cancer was. "People microwave plastic all the time."

"Yeah, and it gives them *cancer.*"

He remembered the sweet three-year-old who slipped her hand into his, who gazed up at him with adoration and believed he knew everything. Maybe she was right, though. The plastic had bubbled, leaving gaping holes. The bacon was raw in places, brittle in others. He set it down, looked over at his son. "How about cereal, buddy?"

"It's all gone." Cassie sounded triumphant.

"Why didn't you put it on the list?" The one he'd stuck to the refrigerator door with a seashell-shaped magnet. He'd been proud when he thought that up — a simple solution to a complex problem. Why hadn't Diane ever done that?

"I forgot."

"If you don't put it on the list, I won't know to get any." Cassie was old enough to understand that. She was old enough to suffer the consequences. "Have a seat, Boon. I'll fry up some eggs."

"Vomit," Cassie said.

"How about French toast?"

"I hate . . ."

"With maple syrup." He pulled out the plastic jug from the refrigerator door and gave it an experimental shake. He had no idea how long it had been there. Syrup didn't go bad, did it? He looked over at her.

She picked at a hole in her stockings. He took this as a yes and twisted open the loaf of bread. "Boon, you want French toast, too?"

" 'Kay."

"Coming right up." He cracked eggs into the bowl, stirred them with the tines of a fork.

"What about the vanilla?" Cassie said.

The way Diane made it. She was everywhere. "We don't have vanilla." Forget the blank sheet of paper fluttering on the refrigerator door. Was there some sort of master list he needed to keep in mind every time he went to the store? "How about cinnamon?"

Boon bumped out the chair beside Cassie. She wrinkled her nose and elbowed him away. "Jezus. You *reek*."

Whit poured the beaten eggs into a bowl, dipped in a slice of bread. "Enough, Cassie."

"But he does."

Whit knew. He'd caught an acrid whiff. Boon had wet himself again. Whit put down the spatula and walked over to where she sat. She glared at the floor. "Look, Cass. I wish you could come with me. But you can't. I need you here, holding down the fort." Who knew what she'd see or overhear?

She turned away, refused to touch the French toast he placed in front of her a few minutes later. Boon stared from her to him, his fork motionless in his hand. "Eat up, kiddo," Whit told him, and Boon lowered his fork to the food. Whit glanced at the clock, dumped the frying pan in the sink. He'd deal with the mess when he got home. "Make sure you put on some clean clothes. Okay? We'll get you into the tub when I get home from work."

Boon nodded, head bent.

Whit would have to put Boon's sheets through the wash, too. He couldn't count on Cassie to do it. "How about I bring home a bucket of chicken for dinner?"

His son looked up, chin gleaming with syrup. "With mashed potatoes?"

"And gravy," Whit promised. Cassie sat there scowling, pointedly staring out the window, making sure he knew how much she despised him. "Call me at twelve," he reminded her. "And again at four." Even if he couldn't pick up, he'd hear the buzzing. "Cassie?"

"Yep."

Patience, he told himself. He paused by the door. He was going to replace that coffee table, move the furniture around. Rearrange the photographs on the wall. Maybe over the weekend, if he had time. "I'll be home as soon as I can."

But that wasn't the point, and they all knew it.

Holly was checking in a guest when he came into the lobby. She glanced up as he walked past and smiled. She found him later, talking to Engineering as they both studied the dripping air-conditioning unit. Moisture pimpled the wall. The carpet had been peeled back. The wood floor beneath was streaked, and the stink of mildew was persistent. The guest staying here had approached him in the hall. *We're not paying you a dime. My husband has terrible allergies. You'll be lucky if we don't sue you.*

"Who knows how long it's been like that," Engineering was saying. "Housekeeping should have caught it before it got to this point."

That was the way it was. Housekeeping

blamed Front Desk when guests showed up early, or not at all; Front Desk blamed Engineering for not responding to guest complaints quickly enough, and Registration for making promises they couldn't deliver on; Room Service blamed Restaurant for hogging the best servers; Restaurant blamed Room Service for cutting into their hours; Engineering blamed Housekeeping for not being proactive; Registration and Catering blamed Front Desk for keeping them out of the loop, and Room Service blamed Catering for stealing the limelight. And everyone blamed Whit because he was the assistant manager. Not the general manager with the nice office and the paycheck, but the assistant manager, who got things done.

"Can you fix it?" he asked.

"It'll have to be replaced. Second one this week. I'm telling you, we need to overhaul the whole damn system."

"Let's see if we can hold out one more season."

"Can't you talk to the GM? I got better things to do than babysit air conditioners. I found a rodent nest in the elevator shaft this morning."

Holly pressed her hands against her ears. "Don't tell me that!" Pure earnestness, with her scrubbed-clean, oval face, brown hair neatly parted down the middle and pulled back into a knot. No makeup, not even lip gloss. Sometimes, it was a relief to look at her and know there was nothing hidden behind her eyes.

"I'll bring it up again." He knew it wouldn't do any good. Thompson tracked every penny. His cheapness was probably why he'd gotten the job as general manager. It was a shortsighted approach, and if they didn't watch out, they'd all end up in the toilet with him. He crouched and rubbed his fingers across the planks. Dry. But the carpeting was damp. "Set up some fans in here. Let's see if we can save it."

"Sure, but I think it's a lost cause." Engineering picked up his tool chest and thumped away.

Holly lowered her hands. "Please tell me we're not talking about rats."

"Mice. They're long gone, but they might have done some damage."

"Yikes."

"Engineering's on it."

"I hope so." She toed the carpeting. "Why don't we just replace the padding? And use air freshener?"

Would mold creep in unchecked? Thompson would be quick to hold him accountable. Whit couldn't lose this job, not until he'd lined up something else. He'd put out a few feelers, but had heard nothing back.

Holly misread his hesitation, pushed the point. "It's at least worth a try. We can get the room back into circulation sooner, too."

He rolled the carpeting back another foot or so. "We have an extra pad in storage, don't we?"

"I'm sure we do, from last year's renovations."

He stood. "All right. Good call."

She beamed, her cheeks turning pink. Her eyes were bright. "I'll handle everything."

"It's all yours. But I'll have to check the room before we put any more guests in here."

"Sure."

His phone buzzed, and he pulled it from his pocket. Cassie, right on time. He thumbed a quick text and slid the phone back into his pocket.

Holly was watching him. "How are things going?"

"We're hanging in there."

Her face softened. "No news?"

He shook his head, held open the door for her. "You got someone picking up the family in 212 from windsurfing?"

"All taken care of. And the kitchen's packing a picnic lunch for the reunion."

Twenty or so midwesterners who came every year. They liked to assemble on the shore and brag about fishing back home. He and Holly paced down the hall. The flower arrangement on the console across from the elevator had been pushed into the corner. He stopped to recenter it, then jabbed a finger into the foam to make sure it was still damp. Flowers were expensive. They didn't need them dying before they were due to be replaced. Holly had eagerly suggested early on that they switch to fake flowers — *There are some really good silk substitutes out there, you wouldn't believe —* and he'd had to remind her that their guests didn't pay for substitutes. They paid for real. He'd tried to be gentle about it, but she'd reddened, clearly embarrassed. It was weeks before she approached him with another suggestion. That time, she'd hit a home run — working with local vendors to offer small goodie bags to guests checking in. He took it to Thompson, who approved of the plan. The next day, he came in to homemade brownies. *You said you like peanut butter,* she told him, presenting the paper plate.

She bent to pick up a water glass someone had left outside a door. "I heard you need a ride to Raleigh. I can drive you, if you want."

"You sure? I don't know what time I'll be getting out of here." He tried to arrive before Thompson and leave after he'd gone home for the day. Sometimes Whit suspected Thompson delayed his departure deliberately.

"Sure. It'll be fun. Text me when you're ready." She turned away.

Holly was a great front desk manager. Always going the extra mile.

She chattered the whole way, talking about her family and childhood in Baltimore. *You ever been?* she asked, and Whit told her he hadn't. She drove slowly and cautiously, glancing frequently at her rearview and side mirrors before changing lanes. She nosed her car to the guard booth. A uniformed man sat inside, visible through the barred window. Holly glanced at Whit. "Want me to wait?"

"I'll be fine. You should hit the road. It's a long drive back." He climbed out of the passenger seat, leaned in to look at her through the open window. "Thanks again."

"See you tomorrow." She turned her car around and grumbled away, bumper riding inches above the gravel, held in place by lengths of duct tape.

He talked to the cop in the booth, showed

him his driver's license. The man came out to let him into the padlocked yard. The lot was filled with a United Nations of vehicles, every make and model, every color. He followed the cop down a few rows. A white stretch limo sagged across three spaces. He wondered how it had ended up here.

The cop looked around, pointed. "There."

Diane's bright red Focus turned muddy beneath the streetlight, dwarfed by the SUVs flanking it. But there was no mistaking the scrape across the driver's door from when she'd once backed out of a space without checking first. She'd bashed the side mirror, too; it had dangled like a loose tooth until they could get it fixed. Fingerprint dust smeared the door handles. The trunk was cracked open. Whit automatically raised it. The carpeted space inside was empty. He slammed it shut. On the fender beneath was the bumper sticker Cassie had brought home from second grade. I'M THE PROUD PARENT OF A JAGUAR!

"Everything we found inside the vehicle is in a bag on the front seat. You want to check to make sure it's all there?"

Whit shook his head. How could he know? Diane drove her car. He drove his.

The cop extended the clipboard. "Sign here, Mr. Nelson."

He dashed off his signature, handed back the form. The cop tore off a copy and gave it to him. "You know your way out of here?"

He folded the flimsy sheet of paper. What was he supposed to do with it? "That's it?"

"That's it. Drive safely, Mr. Nelson." The cop waddled away.

Whit sat there for a minute in the gloom. The car smelled of nothing in particular. He wondered whether it made sense to hold on to it until Cassie was old enough to get her license. After all, there were the taxes to worry about. Insurance.

He put his hands on the steering wheel, where Dee's hands had rested. Her lovely hands, always in motion. He stared at his own hands. The scrapes from that night had healed, become invisible to everyone but him. The plastic bag gleamed beside him. He undid the tie and looked inside — a crumpled tissue box, a tube of ChapStick, a few mummified French fries. A fashion magazine with furled corners, an empty can of soda, wrinkled receipts, loose change, a bent straw. Cassie's purple earbuds. Boon's flip-flops, the ones they'd been looking for and given up on. The precious bits and pieces of a family.

Diane had been gone twenty-seven days.

He turned the key, and the engine

coughed to life. He backed out of the lot and headed home to his kids.

CHAPTER 14
HANK

Three different times a week, more frequently on school holidays, Hank drove around: through the two stoplights that anchored the small downtown, then up and down the back roads that cut through rocky fields and tapered off to a stop in front of a farmhouse, or a barn. An abandoned gas station, the dilapidated building still standing, and the concrete block where the pumps had been. Been that way ever since Hank had moved to town, thirty-one years before.

Not much changed in this town buried among the foothills of the Appalachians. The population hovered around the same number; the same quarrels rose and fell among the town leadership. Same houses, same streets. Same mountains bumping along the horizon. The bakery still served cinnamon rolls that were ambrosial the first half hour after they emerged from the oven and after that were hard as rock; the movie theater continued to show two films each weekend six months after they'd been released everywhere else. Used to be every house up and down these streets had an American flag out front — now it was those ridiculous nylon squares of Easter bunnies and Christmas trees and autumn leaves, or nothing at all. Hank and Barb had dreamed that their son, George, would settle down nearby with his family, but that had never happened.

But since things around here didn't change, it was easy to spot what had.

Hank had just turned onto the landfill road when he noticed a teenager traipsing along the sidewalk ahead, head bent, hands in his pockets. It wasn't the safest part of town. Hank slowed his car to a crawl. The boy didn't take notice.

He rounded the corner. Hank followed, turning away from home. He didn't know the boy. One by one, the younger generation was moving away from Hank. This one would be somebody's grandson, somebody's great-grandson. His legs lanky, his sneakers overlarge. Middle school, Hank estimated. Not yet high school. Boys his age usually hung in packs. Where could he be heading? Not to the park on the other side of town, or the creek that carved across the nicer neighborhoods. Downtown was in the other direction.

The boy ambled along, head bobbing to whatever music he was listening to. Not a care in the world. The way it should be. The way it wasn't. A couple men lurked in a doorway, watched Hank coast by. A woman sat in a plastic chair, legs crossed, watching the world go by as she finished her cigarette.

At the corner, the boy let himself in through an iron gate. It clanged behind him as he strode up the front path. Right, right. The family that lived there had had relatives move in with them. Hank had overheard something about it at the diner. The boy jogged up the porch steps and into the house. The screen door clapped behind him.

Hank's biggest case had been the bank robber who shot the guard and then locked himself inside the bank with seven hostages. Hank could still see him now, his oversize T-shirt hanging down like a flag, his baggy pants, pacing nervously behind the smoked glass, waving his gun around. Nine-thirty in the morning, before everyone had settled into their days and had their wits about them, least of all the moron hopped up on speed who decided life owed him something. Hank got him out without any of the hostages getting hurt, a bullet in his leg for the trouble of it, and a street named in his honor. Two years later the mayor regretted that decision, but by then the ceremony had been held and the metal plate nailed to the post. For a while, a petition circulated. Now people took potshots at it. Last time Hank passed by, the sign was pockmarked and hanging at an angle. He should take it down himself and put it out of its misery. But it was a reminder, wasn't it? Hank had been a good cop. He'd loved his job. And this town had wrenched it away.

He reached for the flask in the glove compartment, window rolled down a few inches, engine running. Watching closely, listening. Making sure.

CHAPTER 15
SARA

After that, she seemed to see Boon everywhere.

"Sara!" he would screech, tearing across the courtyard toward her as she carried down her trash. He'd be heedless, not glancing right or left to check for cars. People flew into this parking lot; they angled their vehicles every which way across the sprawl of concrete that had no painted lines. It was more like bumper cars than a parking lot. He'd arrive at a panting stop in front of her, ask her where she was going and could he please, please come along? He wanted to show her a fallen leaf frilled like a cupcake liner, another one like a witch's hand with long, bony fingers. A bullet-shaped acorn. Was it real? he wanted to know.

"Hi, Sara!" he'd yell as she walked past the dead fountain in the center of the courtyard. "Sara!" she'd hear, a distant voice, and she'd look up to find him standing at the railing and waving down wildly at her. Had she told him her name? She didn't think so. Maybe his father had.

Coming home from work one hot afternoon, Sara heard laughter from the swimming pool area tucked into the far corner of the complex. The sun was unrelenting. Even behind a thin scrim of clouds, it was piercing, driving through polyester and sunglasses, dashing off metal surfaces and glittering sidewalks, bouncing against the invisible droplets in the humid air. It blinded her, consumed her, baked her shoulders, seared the part in her hair, the tops of her cheeks. It chased her to and from her car. The wind did nothing to relieve the intense heat, but at least it drove away the bugs. She couldn't remember a time when she'd been able to walk outside in warm weather without slapping away mosquitoes and ferocious horseflies.

She found an empty lounge chair along the fence and snapped her towel at the pollen that lay like yellow chalk dust over everything. The woman in the chair beside her didn't even glance up from her gossip magazine. An older couple sat silent at a table beneath an umbrella, while two girls in matching hot-pink bathing suits carefully went down the pool steps into the water, their faces averted to avoid the splashing of the older boys in the deep end. Their dark pigtails fanned out behind them.

Sara sat down and unscrewed the cap of her water bottle. She'd brought a book with her, and as she was reaching for it, she sneezed.

The woman beside her said, "Pollen." She had bleached frizz and dark roots. Her bikini struggled to contain her cleavage. The thin straps of her bikini bottom cut deeply across her hips.

"It's horrible."

"Every year, same thing. Least it only lasts a week or so."

"Good to know."

"You just move here?"

"Last month."

"Sara!"

It was Boon, waving from the pool. He clambered up the ladder and pelted across the pavement to stand dripping before her. His hair was plastered to his skull, wet and sleek. His Batman swimming trunks drooped. He hitched the waistband with one fist. "Hi, Jasmine," he said to the woman sitting beside Sara.

Jasmine set down her magazine. "Good Lord. Is that a rash?"

The boy squinted down at his torso. "It's okay."

"It most certainly does not look okay. Come here."

Obediently, Boon shuffled closer, and Jasmine peered at his ribs. "Does it itch?"

"It's okay," he repeated.

Jasmine sat back and shaded her eyes with her hand. "You here by yourself?"

"No, ma'am. Cassie's here." He pointed. Sure enough, there was Balcony Girl, sitting on the edge of the hot tub, dangling her skinny legs into the water. She was watching the teenagers clustered beneath a patio umbrella, climbing and sliding off each other's laps.

"You go on and play now."

"Yes, ma'am." He took off across the slick pavement.

"Least the skin wasn't broken." Jasmine picked up her magazine. "I'd have yanked my girls right out of that pool. Who knows what kinds of diseases that child might have."

Diseases? He was just a little kid. On the scrawny side, sure, but that was all.

"Watch me, Sara!"

Sara looked over. Boon had reached the ladder at the far end of the pool, standing with his toes curled over the tiled edge and clasping the aluminum handrails. When he saw she was paying attention, he lowered himself gingerly into the water. The water reached his chin. He let go and went under. He popped back up with a noisy splash and bobbed, coughing. His eyes sought Sara. He waved.

Jasmine uncapped a tube of sunscreen. "He banged on my door the other day, asked my girls to come to his birthday party. Got them all excited. There was no party, of course. Went all the way up to the fourth floor to find that out. He just wanted a toy, of course."

Cassie had climbed out of the hot tub and was spreading a towel across the pavement in a patch of sunlight. Her bathing suit was turquoise, not black. But the moody cloud hanging around her was black. The teenagers had moved to a vending machine beneath the overhang, and Cassie was watching them from the corners of her eyes and pretending not to. Boon was paddling in a circle with the other boys.

"Marco."

"Polo!"

"How do you know?" Sara asked.

Jasmine smoothed sunscreen over her plump arms. "How do I know what?"

"That he made it up."

"Because I know them, that's why. That woman is unstable. Those kids were in trouble long before she took off. She'll be back, of course. Acting like nothing happened and hopping on her high horse when the rest of us don't want anything to do with her."

"Marco."

"Polo!"

One of the other boys darted toward Boon and smacked him on the head. "You're it!"

"No fair! You peeked!" Boon's face was pink with fury.

"Did not!"

"Did too!" Boon paddled around to look beseechingly at Sara. "Did you see, Sara? Did you?"

Sara closed her eyes and tipped her head back. "Sorry."

But Sara saw everything. How her neighbors came and went at certain times, like the tide; who locked their front doors, climbed into which cars and drove away, who strode down the sidewalk to wait at the bus stop. She noticed the hours that held the most activity, and when the courtyard of the Paradise echoed with emptiness. She saw how the sun breached the rooftop and stripped everything bare, knew when shad-

157

ows would claim certain corners of each day. She sat on her balcony and watched the houses below and the white-tipped surf beyond.

She saw how Terri counted out the bills and slid them into an envelope before handing over Sara's pay, the way she locked the small metal box afterward. How she held the clipboard and twisted her mouth as she tapped the pen against the paper, decided who got which houses to clean that day. She saw the cobalt-blue vase spotlighted in the window of the antiques shop downtown, mislabeled Ming and really from the Qing dynasty and far more valuable. She saw how there didn't appear to be an alarm system in the store.

The FBI was good, but they saw the world laid out in a grid. Sara knew real life was convoluted, waved up and down and folded back in on itself.

Sara had taken the GPS out of her glove box and left it on her kitchen counter. Luis phoned within the hour, pretending to be checking in. Sara knew he was wondering why she wasn't on her way to work. "I got a ride today," she told him, steering her car down the highway. He didn't contradict her. She'd learned a few critical things: they weren't tracking her with a drone flying so high she couldn't see it, and they had access to her work schedule, which meant they'd hacked Terri's computer.

It started to be a game. She'd let a day go by, then leave the GPS at a park, tucked among tree branches. "I went for a walk," she told Nicole. She'd leave it at one rental house, return at the end of the day, after she'd cleaned two others, to collect it. "Car trouble," Sara lied when Luis called. She was sitting on a bench across the street, playing solitaire on her phone. "But it's okay now."

She drove across the bridge onto the mainland and kept going. Ten miles, twenty. With each passing mile, she picked up speed. Buildings blurred. Fields stretched out and lengthened. Could it be this easy? At fifty-five miles, her cellphone rang. The Director. Just checking in, he said, making sure she was settling in okay. "Fine," Sara said, pulling to the berm and catching her breath. "Just picking up a lamp off Craigslist." So now she knew how short her tether was.

Six weeks became five, shrank to four. There had to be a weak spot. She couldn't find it.

She spent the Fourth of July cleaning vacation homes for time and a half. In the evening, she ventured out of her apartment to look down into the courtyard, where a couple of guys were setting off fireworks, standing up the cardboard tubes and stumbling back as sparks shot high into the darkness and exploded to scattered applause. Kids sat cross-legged on the ground, faces tilted. Instantly, one of them waved. She lowered her wineglass and squinted through the drifting smoke. Sure enough, it was Boon, pushing himself to his feet and grinning up at her. Someone reached for his arm and yanked him back down — Cassie. Sara didn't see their father in the crowd. She pivoted on her heel and went inside to lock herself in and splash cold water on her face over the kitchen spigot.

Her dad had once rented a cabin up north. They stayed there for weeks. It was the tail end of the season, when the weather was cool but not quite freezing. School started without her. There weren't many people around, just fishermen who kept to themselves. She'd had to duck her head to avoid the low branches of the crabbed pines as she walked from the cabin down to the beach and the brown water that lay smooth and still. When it stormed, the misted rain crept toward shore, dappling the water. No one knew they were there.

At night, her dad would build a bonfire in the pit outside the cabin and they'd sit in molded plastic chairs, hoods pulled over their heads, feet socked and hands tucked into their sleeves to ward off the mosquitoes that swarmed and could bite through denim. Or through cement, her dad joked. The fire smoked, the wind nudging it this way and that. The stars came out. Her eyes burned and her ears rang from smacking away the bugs, but she wouldn't leave her father's side. He told her about being orphaned, his face ruddy in the firelight, his voice soft. He didn't want her to grow up like he did. He was sorry about her mom, but Sara had to know her leaving had nothing to do with Sara. With all her heart, Sara wanted to believe him.

Late one evening, a terrible storm howled across the lake. Sara huddled inside the small pine cabin and watched waves lift the docks and crash them into pieces. Boats rode high. Rain pooled around the windows and ran down the walls. When it was over, a fishing boat lay mangled against the shore. Strangers appeared, from the cabins, from the campground, to help lift it back onto the water. Compelled by an emotion she couldn't name, Sara pushed open the screen door to join them when her father put a

CHAPTER 16
WHIT

"Thompson's cheating on his wife," Holly confided as they walked together to the front desk. Then she blushed. Holly was usually careful, Whit had noticed, not to make comments on other people's marriages.

"How do you know?" he asked, letting her know it was okay to talk about it.

But before Holly could answer, Housekeeping radioed.

"Mr. Nelson? We have a problem on two. Don't take the stairs."

He reversed direction and got into the elevator, pressed the button for the second floor. A photographer was coming out to take shots for the website, and Catering wanted him to stop by and meet with a VIP bride. The doors slid open to reveal three housekeepers crowded together outside the utility room where they'd stowed their carts the night before. The hallways on either side of them were lined with mattresses stripped of their bedding and pushed together. He could see dirty footprints where people had tromped on them to get to the elevator. Only the space in front of the elevator had been left clear. "Jesus."

"We found it like this. Must've been that tennis guy, him and his people. They're gone. I think they checked out early this morning."

"What do the rooms look like?"

The head housekeeper's face was shiny with sweat. "We don't know. We can't move these things by ourselves."

"No, of course not. I'll call for help." There were some burly guys in Engineering. He toed off his shoes and pulled out his cellphone to take photographs. "Why don't you go get extra linen? Let the Front Desk know no early check-ins."

"Yes, boss."

He took off his jacket and tie, rolled up his cuffs, went down the hallway and checked each room. The tennis pro had rented out the entire floor. At the time, Thompson had been pleased. He'd insisted that diversifying their clientele in this way was exactly the sort of thing that kept them afloat. As Whit poked his head into each disheveled room and took photos, he wondered what Thompson would say now. Whit wondered if he should rope in Robineaux. Maybe Thompson's position as GM wasn't as strong as he'd figured it was.

Holly radioed as he was kneeling to examine a king-sized mattress. A corner had been slashed, which meant it would need replacing as soon as they could get to it. For now, they'd have to double-sheet it and hope it held together. "Someone's here to see you," Holly said in a low voice.

The photographer. She couldn't start setting up until he'd had a chance to get guests to sign the waivers. "Ask her if she can come back at noon."

"It's not that."

A guest then, needing something. He didn't mind. Distraction was good. It had, in fact, become necessary. He looked around, found his jacket hanging from the back of a chair.

As he rounded the corner, he saw a brown-haired woman at the front desk talking to Holly. Both turned as he neared them. Robin, Diane's social worker. She had the usual bulging canvas bag hooked over her shoulder. Privately, Whit had taken to calling her the Bag Lady. "Here he is," Holly said brightly.

He shook Robin's hand. It had to mean

something that she was here. She'd never stopped by the Seaside before. She couldn't know anything. Diane wouldn't have confided in her. She wouldn't have wanted to raise any flags. "Everything okay?"

She smiled a smile that meant nothing. Robin smiled at everything, even when delivering bad news. He had to look beyond the smile to try to figure out what she was really thinking. "I was hoping you had a few minutes to talk."

He didn't, but of course he couldn't tell her that. She cupped the fate of his family in her hands.

They walked to the patio restaurant. Servers were setting up, the clatter of silverware, muted laughter. One brought two glasses of iced tea. "How much time do we have?" Whit asked him, wanting to let Robin know there was a deadline. The server flickered a glance at him, read between the lines. "We have a reservation for this table at eleven-thirty," he said, adjusting the umbrella over their heads. Twenty-five minutes.

"White linen," Whit reminded him, thinking of the photography shoot. The server nodded.

"It's such a gorgeous day. Nice to be outside." Robin opened her folder and set it on the glass-topped table. "How are you?

How are the kids?"

She'd printed his name on the top of the page. His, not Diane's. He blinked past the surprise. "We're okay. We're adjusting." Just enough sincerity to keep her off guard.

She didn't look up as she jotted a note. "Who's watching them while you're at work?"

Robin didn't know he'd been driving people around at night. He'd done it only a couple of times, but every cent went to paying down their credit card debt. He'd scrutinized the statements, trying to decipher what Diane had bought online because it sure as hell wasn't in the apartment, until he realized it was a hopeless business. "My folks help out. Every so often, I leave Cassie in charge."

Robin paused and studied him over the tops of glasses striped in red, orange, lime green. "How often does that happen?"

Cassie was legally old enough to watch her brother. Still, he hedged. "My mom takes them when she can."

"Is that where the children are now?"

"They're home." Cassie and Boon knew the rules. They had to stay on the grounds of the Paradise. If they wanted to go to the beach, they had to go with an adult or wait for him to come home. No using the stove or oven — and now the microwave. If they went anywhere with anyone, Cassie had to text to let him know. But so far, that hadn't happened.

"Oh. They didn't answer the door when I stopped by."

"You stopped by?" Diane hated it when Robin dropped by unannounced. She complained that she felt spied on. She claimed Robin had an uncanny ability to visit when one of the kids was out of sorts or the apartment was a disaster. Whit told her she was being paranoid, but now he found himself thinking, Was it suspicious that he'd shoved Diane's makeup into a drawer? That he'd started taking over her side of the closet?

"I just came from there."

"Hold on." He pulled out his phone. He texted Cassie, waited a moment. Her answer popped right up. He showed Robin the screen. "They're at the pool."

"Okay." She made another note, upside down and indecipherable. "I'll try again later this week, next week at the latest."

This wasn't the last visit, then. "I thought our case was closed."

She glanced at him. "I'm sorry. I know it's not easy having someone checking in on you. I get that. I really do. But I'm hoping you'll consider me as someone who can help you, not just an interloper you have to put up with. There are county resources I can help you access. There are ways I can help the children adjust, make sure they've got the support they need. I care about you and your family. I want the best for you."

She worked closely with the cops. They were friendly. She might say something to them that would bring their attention right back to him. It wasn't hard to look worried. "You have to understand how hard this is on Boon and Cassie. Every time you show up, they think it's because they did something wrong. I try to explain that it has nothing to do with them, but they don't believe me. I'm concerned about the long-term effect."

"Of course you are. I really think it would help to bring in a therapist, someone the children can talk to. Have you done any more thinking along those lines?"

It was the last thing he was going to do. Who knew what they might say? "I've talked to the kids, but Cassie refuses. If she won't go, neither will Boon."

Diane had balked at taking Boon to the therapist after he'd been released from the hospital. She hated sitting in the waiting room, paging through old magazines, while the other moms eyed her. But most of all she hated not knowing what Boon was saying to the guy. *Kids exaggerate,* she reminded Whit. *They always make things sound worse than they are.* And as soon as the court-ordered sessions were over, she'd stopped taking Boon. It didn't matter what Robin said. If a judge wasn't making her, Diane wasn't doing it.

Robin looked thoughtful. "How about if I talk to Cassie about it? And if she agrees, I'll drive her. That okay with you?"

"Sure. I appreciate it." This woman could talk to Cassie until she was blue in the face and Cassie wouldn't hear a word. She hated Robin. And it was true what he'd said about Boon. His son followed Cassie's lead.

"We'll get there, Whit. You're doing everything you can to keep your family together. I consider you one of my success stories. I really do."

Eventually she'd ease her grip on his family.

Robin set down her pen, but the folder lay open. He tried not to think of all the other folders she had on them, back in her office. He hadn't always been around when she'd talked with Diane. But the way Robin was looking at him, with sympathy instead of judgment, confirmed for him that Diane had kept her mouth shut. "Maybe she'll call."

Robin knew about Dee's adventures. The subject had come up more than once. Robin had talked to her, tried to explain how confusing and disruptive it was to the kids to be suddenly uprooted without explanation. Robin had proven to be unexpectedly helpful. She'd explained this to the cops, told them that Diane must have finally listened to her advice, gone off without hauling the kids along. "Maybe."

"If she does, I'll need to know."

There it was, that threat. Robin reminding him she still had control.

"Whit? You'll let me know?"

She sat there with her canvas bag stuffed with folders, her genuineness and concern wrapped around her. The sun had moved, slanting over the edge of the umbrella and gilding Robin's arm and hip as she reached for her glass of melted ice. All her probing questions, her smarmy smile. The way she studied the kids, Diane. Now, him.

A heavy jar of slippery orange jelly, the
dust wiped off the glass sides so it sparkles
in the sun.

Chapter 17
Sara

More and more, Terri was assigning her occupied houses. *One of my girls called in sick,* she'd say when Sara came into the office in the morning. *Can you cover for her?* Or, *I just got an emergency clean — could you handle it?* An encouraging smile. *You work so fast.* Then, frankly, *The owners have requested you back.*

Sara had been careful. Homeowners checked, she knew, just as Terri used to when Sara first started working for her. They wanted to make sure they could trust her, so they laid traps. Sara was skilled at sidestepping them. The few dollars casually tucked under some papers, the laptop left open, the tempting half bottle of wine chilling in the refrigerator. As they lowered their guard, they started leaving out the more interesting things — credit card bills, a mortgage statement. Keys.

Terri was lowering her guard, too. She

chatted with Sara at the end of her shifts. She talked about problems with the other girls who worked for her, the difficulty she had collecting on outstanding invoices. When Sara suggested Terri set up a prepay system, she helped Terri compose an email to notify customers of the change and installed the software. In order to do that, Sara needed access to Terri's computer and business files.

To celebrate, they went out for drinks. Terri talked about her crappy luck with men. Her first husband cheated on her. Her second was an addict. She was still looking for Mr. Right. She knew he was out there, somewhere. The secret, she realized, was not to hold on so tight.

Sara came out one day to find her car tilted strangely on the asphalt. She walked around the vehicle and saw it right away: a tire had gone flat. She must have driven for days with it slowly seeping air and not noticed. She opened the trunk and removed the spare. The sun was broad and hot as she worked, and she stopped often to sip from the bottle of water she always carried. Seagulls circled overhead. One landed and strutted past, jet-chip eyes brittle with curiosity. "Sorry, this is mine," she told it. This was what she was reduced to — talking to birds.

Terri was sympathetic when Sara finally got back to the office, said the guy she was dating was a mechanic and could take a look to see if the tire could be repaired. The next day, Ron spent some time studying the treads, shining a bright light onto the black rubber and reaching in with a pair of pliers.

"Here's the problem." He held up a shiny piece of metal. "Roofing tack." He tossed the nail into the trash can. "Won't take me long to fix this. You can wait in the office. When was the last time you had the oil changed?"

"Don't worry about the oil," she said. He wasn't trying to pad the bill, was he? She poured herself a cup of tepid coffee from the glass pot and sat in the waiting room thick with the smell of rubber. It was a small shop, and busy. Customers came and went. Ron joined her a short time later, wiping his hands on a rag so filthy it was hard to tell it was once orange. "All done," he said, cheerfully. "No charge." She insisted on paying him, but he shook his head. "Buy me a beer sometime."

She smiled, and he smiled back.

After work, Sara walked downtown. She passed a café, bookstore, hardware store.

Couples strolled hand in hand. A pack of giggling teenagers jogged across the street to the protest of car horns. A woman in a sequined fairy costume stood outside a toy store blowing bubbles to the delight of the children clustered around her. Everyone smiled here. Maybe it was the sun.

She crossed the street to the five-and-dime.

"Hullo," called the man behind the counter. He was busy preparing a milkshake for a customer. He didn't seem to expect an answer. Sara unhooked a large canvas beach bag from a spinning rack and got in line.

She glanced around the store. People browsed the aisles, or sat around small marble-topped tables and chatted. She didn't expect to see anyone she knew, but there was Boon, spooning ice cream from a bowl into his mouth, his cheeks glistening with chocolate. Cassie sat beside him, jerking a straw up and down through the plastic lid of her cup. Sara's gaze settled on the brown-haired woman with them. Robin, the social worker. Two days before, Sara had come home to find a business card slipped beneath her apartment door, a smiling face sketched on the back. *Sorry I missed you,* Robin had jotted in looping letters.

Robin didn't see Sara. Her gaze was

focused on Cassie. Sara knew Robin was trying to appear as though she was listening intently, but in fact, she was mentally running down a checklist, ticking off items one by one. Neglect? Abuse? Nutrition? Exposure to unsavory influences? Amount of sleep? Adjustment issues? Regression? Therapy? Medication? All the questions a worried mother with a troubled child might ask herself. Robin might be a mother herself.

"What can I get you?" The guy behind the counter grinned at Sara.

She stepped close to the counter and lowered her voice. "Do you sell phones?"

"Sure. Right over there." He jerked his chin to the display of preloaded phones hanging behind the register.

"Not that kind of phone."

He studied Sara. He nodded. "I go on break in twenty."

"Okay." A group of teenagers had come up behind Sara. They stood there, elbowing each other and giggling. "I'll take an iced tea." Sara put the beach bag on the counter. "And this."

The clerk handed Sara a cup and took the bills she held out. "Help yourself to lemon over there."

Boon was running his spoon around the

inside of the bowl. Cassie stared out the window, looking bored.

Sara's first social worker had been a thin guy with dreadlocks who arrived while the police were still milling around the house, boots thumping and radios blaring. The officer who'd been sitting with Sara looked up at the newcomer with open relief and stood. *Hey, Skinner.*

Skinner had scraped out a chair. *Hey.* He'd rested his elbows on the kitchen table and smiled at Sara, his honey-colored eyes crinkling at the corners. Sara had almost smiled back. For a moment she'd believed he was there to take her to her dad. What he did was take her to a farmhouse where the wind blew through the pine planks and snow collected heavy on the steep roof and had to be pulled down with long-handled rakes. She shared a room with three other girls and rode a clattering bus to school. The foster mom made her bologna sandwiches and the foster dad drove her to the doctor when she broke her elbow. There were two more foster homes after that, and then Skinner went away.

She was reassigned to a caseworker named Mrs. T. *What happened to Skinner?* Sara had demanded, shoving her hands into her pockets to hide how they trembled.

Mrs. T's answers were vague and unsatisfactory. *He gave up social work. He moved out of state. He went back to school.*

Sara was fourteen by then, and angry. She was angry at the weather, at the way her jeans were too tight or too loose. She was angry when the other foster kids nagged her to play games with them, and enraged when they excluded her. She was furious that Skinner had gone away without saying a word to her and she was stuck with lumpy Mrs. T, who always had food stuck in her teeth. Sara would lean back to avoid a close-up view, and Mrs. T would only lean forward and ply her with questions.

This caseworker was doing the same thing, a pen poised in her hand. Social workers were like chiggers. They burrowed. Mrs. T was the one who'd broken the news to her that her father was dead. By then Sara was on her fourth foster family.

Robin pushed back her chair, and the two kids climbed to their feet. Apparently, their allotted time was up, and she was probably mentally preparing herself to move on to her next case. Sara turned away, not wanting to draw attention to herself as they trooped past. Robin led the way like a mama duck.

Cassie lingered by the cash register, eyeing the display of gums and candies. Without looking, she reached over and dipped her hand into the tip jar. It was such a smooth and practiced move that if Sara hadn't been paying attention, she'd never have noticed. Certainly no one else seemed to.

The bell over the door tinkled, and the three of them were gone.

The Liars' Club, her father called it. He made it sound fun, like something anyone would want to join. He would hum as he got ready to go to a meeting, grab her hands and whirl her around in a little dance. Sara would imagine games and frosted cupcakes. *I want to go, too,* she would say with a pout. He would smile and pat her shoulder. *Your time will come,* he'd promise, smoothing his brown hair and tugging at the cuffs of his starched shirt. *Appearances count,* he always told her. She'd stand by the window and watch him stride off into the shadows of the busy street. After he was long gone, she'd venture into the bathroom and climb onto a stool to study herself in the mirror. When the time came, how would her weird red hair and freckled cheeks count?

If he didn't make it back by the next morning, she'd get herself ready and walk to school. She usually had a quarter for milk, and if there wasn't any food in the house, she'd steal a pinch of tobacco from her dad's stash. She'd unknot the bandanna and spread it wide, and offer it to the boy who offered the best trade — lefse smeared thickly with butter and sugar and rolled into a soft cylinder, a pudding cup.

When Skinner asked her how long she'd lived there with her father, she couldn't tell him. She didn't know. There had been the house on the corner with a porch swing hanging from rusted chains, the basement apartment that smelled, the huge empty house with shining wood floors that she raced endlessly across. The house they shared with another family that had a baby that cried all the time. That one had been in a row with other houses and they all looked exactly alike. Sara would stand outside and wonder which one was hers. Then the baby would shriek and she'd follow the sound.

No matter where they lived, there was always the Liars' Club.

At home that night, she poured a glass of wine and took it out onto her balcony, thinking of what she'd seen Cassie do. The moon hung there, drifting up through smoky wisps of clouds. The roofs below took on detail, the linked gutters and careful arrangement of tiles. The surf was lace unfurling across the sand.

They had beautiful night skies here, spreading to infinity. The stars were so clear. Her father had taught her the names of the constellations. The Big Fat Wheel. Pinocchio's Nose. The Lady Sitting on Her Rump. Every one had made Sara giggle. *Really?* she had pressed her dad. *Really,* he'd assured her with a straight face. Not all the lies her father told hurt people.

CHAPTER 18
WHIT

The apartment was dark when he got home, not even the TV playing. The place stank of cooking grease. A covered dish sat outside the front door. Meals had been appearing with regularity — one of the bus-stop moms had been dropping off a casserole with a chatty note taped to the lid. *Hope everything's going ok! Let me know if you need anything!* Her phone number scrawled beneath her name. Looked like lasagna, one of Cassie's favorites, but she wouldn't touch it.

He picked up the dish. The kids had walked right past it. "Hey, guys," he called out. "I'm home."

There was no answer. He hung up his jacket, then flipped on the overhead and sent the ceiling fan whirring. Food wrappers fluttered on the coffee table beside a dirty drinking glass. The cushions had been punched into lumpy shapes. A blanket puddled on the floor. He put the dish on the counter. "Boon? Cassie?"

Kitchen cabinets hung open. Sandy footprints collected in front of the refrigerator. So they'd made it down to the beach at some point. Boon must have liked that. He was always begging to go to the beach. Whit opened the fridge. They were out of juice. He brought out the egg carton. Empty. A frying pan sat on the stove, half an inch of grease congealing in it.

He walked down the hall. A damp towel hung over the side of the tub. Pots of eye shadow lay scattered across the counter, tubes of mascara. A bottle of hairspray. Cassie insisted it was stuff her friends lent her. He suspected she was lying but had no way of proving it.

He found Boon sitting in his closet, thumb in his mouth. "Hey, buddy. What are you doing in here?"

Boon lowered his thumb. "Nothing."

He held Wolf in his lap. It did look like he'd been doing nothing. "You guys went to the beach, huh? That must have been fun."

"I guess."

I'm not going anywhere, he'd told Boon over and over. "You guess? What's the matter? Didn't you find any shells?"

"No."

184

"It's always better at low tide. Listen, I'll try and take you sometime before work. Just you and me, kiddo. What do you think?"

" 'Kay."

Dee was the one who took him to the beach. "Where's your sister?"

"Um . . ." He scratched an arm.

Boon always did that when he was nervous. It made him break out in rashes. Whit squatted, so that his eyes were level with his son's. "Hey, pal. You're not in any trouble."

Boon chewed his lower lip, then nodded. But still, the scratching. Whit put his hand on his son's, stilling him. "When did you last see her?" He'd called Cassie on his way home, but she hadn't answered. Maybe her phone had run out of battery, though she was pretty good at keeping it powered up. They could run out of cereal and juice, but her phone would be fully charged.

"Don't know."

Boon probably didn't. He couldn't tell time. He gauged events by meals and television programs. It was getting on nine o'clock. "You've got to be starving, buddy. Come on. I'll heat us up a Magic Casserole." That was what Boon called them. He delighted in their appearing like magic on their doorstep. As Whit straightened, the doorbell buzzed.

185

Joy flared across Boon's face. He thought it was his mother; he wanted it to be. The kid lived in that pocket of hope that every time the doorbell sounded or the phone rang, Diane would be on the other end of it. "I'll get it," Whit told his son. "You get started picking up your toys."

Whit swung open the front door. Ted stood there, gripping a writhing Cassie by the arm. "Let go of me, perv!"

Whit winced. "Hey. Come here." He held out his hands. Ted released Cassie, and she stumbled free, rubbing her upper arm. Whit rested his hands on her shoulders — when had she gotten so tall? "Hey, Ted. Want to tell me what's going on?"

Sweat ringed the collar of Ted's T-shirt, sagged beneath his armpits. His cheeks were an alarming red, and his breath came in pained gasps. "Caught your kid going through people's cars, opening doors, looking in."

"He grabbed me, Dad. He gave me *bruises*. Look." Cassie shoved back the cuffs of her black flannel shirt and thrust out her arms.

She was so thin. She wasn't eating. Dressing in those ridiculous dark clothes only emphasized how pale her skin was. Whit sighed. "What were you doing going through people's cars, Cassie?" All he wanted was a beer and bed.

"I wasn't doing anything! I was just minding my own business!"

"People have been complaining, Nelson. Graffiti by the pool area, dumpsters tipped over, trash scattered everywhere. That's not all —"

"Hold on," Whit interrupted, feeling his temper flare. "Go inside," he told Cassie. She started to protest, then saw the look in his eyes and obeyed. Whit stepped outside and closed the door behind him. "That doesn't sound like Cassie. None of it." Was this some ploy to up his rent? Ted was no fan of his. Back when Whit was dealing with the horrible aftermath of Diane forgetting Boon in the car, Ted had stopped him in the courtyard, not to express sympathy but to demand to know how long the reporters were going to hang around the Paradise.

"Yeah? What would you know about it? You ever here?"

"You want to talk about the lights in the courtyard you promised to install? The fountain that still isn't running? How many times this summer have you had to close the pool?"

"Look. One of the ladies reported her wallet missing. She swears your kid swiped it from her at the pool."

"That right? Then why didn't she say something then?"

"Your kids are out of control, Nelson. You need to rein them in."

"Or what? I have a lease."

"Read your fine print, Nelson. I have a waiting list for these apartments."

It could be true, this time of year. It'd be impossible to find another apartment on such short notice. Moving in with his folks was out of the question. Ted smirked. He knew exactly what Whit was thinking. Lazy fuck. Whit exhaled, smoothed out his features. "I'll talk to my daughter."

"Sure." Ted held up his hands. "That's all I'm asking."

Whit let himself back into the apartment.

The kids sat in front of the TV. Cassie turned and shouted at Ted through the closing door, "I'm gonna sue your ass!"

"Enough!" Whit barked. "Turn off that TV."

Boon scrabbled for the remote. The canned laughter died. Cassie wrapped her arms around herself, defiant.

Whit sat down on the coffee table and faced her. "He says you stole someone's wallet."

"No way. He's a liar. He's a big, fat —"

"Enough." Now she wouldn't look at him. She tugged on a loose button, picking at the black thread. She'd drawn on the inside of her wrist, a jagged lightning bolt. Who was this child? It was like his sweet Cassie was disappearing before his eyes, turning into someone Whit didn't know. "You have any idea how serious this is?"

Cassie shrugged, rolled the thread around the tip of her forefinger, twining it tight. Whit put his hands on her knees, gripped them. "Cassie. Are you listening?"

The tip of her finger was turning red. "I didn't take it, Dad."

"Just tell me the truth, Cass." All he could see was the uneven part in her hair. He felt the pulse in his temples. "Please."

"I am."

She wasn't even trying. He closed his eyes briefly. This was on him. All of it. "Get the wallet."

"I don't have it. You can go see."

He hesitated. She sounded so convincing. He was raising a thief who knew to get rid of the evidence. Where had she learned this? "Where is it, Cassie? What have you done with it?"

"Nothing! I didn't touch it! I swear."

Boon had pressed himself into the sofa cushions, Wolf squeezed tight. Did he know

189

what his sister had done? Whit had the horrible thought he might have helped her. "Cassie. Honey. Look at me."

She raised defiant eyes to his. That matted mass of hair. Her mouth caked with black lipstick. He drew in a breath. "Cass, I know you're upset. I'm sorry. I really am. But you can't do this kind of thing. You can't. Do you understand?"

"I didn't —"

"Stop."

"You never believe me."

"You can't steal things. You can't break into cars. Those are serious crimes. You'll be punished. I won't be able to protect you. Please tell me you understand."

"Whatever."

"Do you understand, Cassie?"

"Fine!"

"Say it. Say, I understand."

"I understand!"

Whit looked at his son. Boon's eyes were huge. He clutched Wolf to his chest. "Do you understand, Boon?"

His son nodded, mute and miserable.

"All right. Both of you. Go wash your hands for dinner."

After they'd gone to bed, he nuked the few inches of coffee still left in the pot from that morning. With any luck, someone would need a ride to the mainland — an easy hundred bucks or so. He stepped out onto the balcony to the muted pounding of the surf. The air was thick with humidity. He stood at the railing, watched the pale surf. Things had to change. He had to pull his family back together.

A car drove into the alley below, headlights fogged. The engine silenced, and the doors opened. He found himself waiting for Dee to climb out, to glance up to see him watching, to smile and give him that flirty little wave of hers. That's what he missed, the small things. The way she curved up one corner of her mouth, or chewed her lower lip when she was thinking hard. The silken hairs at the nape of her neck, the skin on the crooks of her elbows. Her sudden laugh.

The lights came on next door, spilling over the clutter of furniture on the balcony. Two plastic lawn chairs, a red plastic crate upended to serve as an end table. Same crap the former people had. What was his new neighbor's name again? Sara. *Depends on the mother,* she'd said, like she knew all the answers.

CHAPTER 19
SARA

Terri lived in a box-shaped cottage painted pea green, with a screened porch slapped onto one end and an outdoor shower slapped onto the other. Cars were parked out front. Seagulls pecked the scrubby dirt and squawked. Terri met Sara at the door and took the six-pack Sara carried. "You didn't have to bring anything, sugar," Terri said, standing back to let Sara in, but she looked pleased.

They walked through the paneled living area crowded with mismatched furniture to the kitchen, where platters of food sat on the counters. One of Terri's roommates was getting married in September, Terri said, and moving out. The room was Sara's if she wanted it. Only one bathroom, iffy cable connection, but the rent was reasonable for an oceanfront. Terri faced Sara, her eyes wide and serious. Surely Sara was looking to make a change. Terri had remembered

192

why the Paradise had sounded so familiar. It was where Diane Nelson lived, the mother who'd left her kid in the backseat of her car for hours and almost killed him. It had made the national news. Had Sara caught the coverage? Sara put it together: Diane Nelson was Whit's missing wife, Boon the kid who'd almost died. Did Sara know the family? Terri asked, and Sara thought about the blond woman painting her nails on the balcony, the little boy wandering around the apartment complex late at night. She shook her head.

She followed Terri outside, where people stood around holding red plastic cups, talking and laughing. Beyond them, the promised ocean — at the end of a long wooden walkway that wound through the tall saw grass and across the dunes down to the spangled water. Sara promised Terri she'd think about taking the room. She planned to be long gone by then, though of course Terri didn't know that. Still, it was a great location — not another house in sight.

Terri introduced Sara around. Neighbors, Terri's roommates and their dates, a friend of Ron's from work named Jim. Terri's boyfriend stood manning the Weber, his shirt unbuttoned and tight around his biceps. Ron scraped at burgers with a long-handled spatula and told Sara he was glad she could make it. It had been an impromptu invite. Terri had texted Sara that morning while Sara was cleaning a rental, asked if she was free that evening. Sara had thought about it while she mopped a game room floor sticky with tequila and lime juice. She liked Terri, and it had been a long while since she'd done anything social. Still, she was torn. Did she really want to spend an evening with a bunch of strangers making small talk? She caught herself. She was turning into some kind of a social recluse. She'd always been good at adjusting herself to fit a new space. Those were skills she needed to keep sharp. *Sure,* she texted Terri. *Thanks!* She thought about it, then added a second!

It seemed a friendly group. Sara did the math. Jim was there to meet Sara, or she was there to meet Jim. Lanky, blond hair buzzed short. Pale blue eyes. Late thirties, Sara estimated. There was a wary hopefulness about him. He'd had bad luck in relationships, Sara guessed. Or maybe no relationship history at all — which was worse. He offered to get her a beer. She and Terri watched him walk over to the cooler. "Jim's a great guy," Terri said. "Little on the shy side, but once you get to know him, he's a lot of fun."

"Hmm," Sara said, noncommittally. Sounded like a lot of work. Sara wasn't interested in anything that required effort. She liked her relationships loose and comfortable. Ron stood talking to Jim, who held a couple cans of beer in his hands. Ron clapped Jim on the shoulder, then turned back to the grill. Jim made his way back to Sara, held out a can. He'd already opened it for her. She thanked him, and he settled by her side.

They ate barbecue off paper plates, a dozen or so people clustered around Terri's small backyard heatedly debating the merits of ketchup-based sauce versus vinegar-based sauce. Sara nibbled at the pork, kept her thoughts to herself. Let others get loud with their opinions. She hated both, actually. She drank beer to wash away the sour saltiness that filled her mouth.

Paper lanterns hung along the leaning wooden fence, their gentle colors growing more brilliant as the sky turned dark. Terri told the story of how she and Ron met. She'd been on a Tinder date and had gotten stood up. But Ron was there, sitting at the bar. "Love at first sight," Terri said, hooking her arm through his. She was getting tipsy, swaying a little, losing the ends of her words. She pressed her cheek against Ron's shoulder. He was solidly built, thick through the shoulders. Sara imagined the smoothness of his muscles, warm beneath the cotton of his shirt. She imagined him scooping her up into his arms, effortlessly.

Jim hovered by Sara. She felt the weight of his attention, his need. She summoned a smile, asked him about himself, listened to his answers, which came haltingly. He hadn't always been a mechanic. He'd done a stint in the Army, been in Afghanistan. Before that, he'd trained as an EMT. He was a helper, Sara decided. Kind, soft-spoken, and way too nice. He would never be tempted, never stray. The path of his life lay straight. It matched the woman Sara was working to portray. Reliable Sara, the hard worker, deeply interested in other people but too modest to talk much about herself. All of it a lie. Well, except for the part about talking about herself. She'd never liked sharing her own story. It felt too much like peeling away her skin.

The talk turned to the hurricane. "What hurricane?" Sara asked.

"It's not a hurricane yet," Jim told her. "It's a storm system. But it's starting to strengthen."

Sara glanced toward the ocean. It seemed

calm to her.

"It's nowhere near here," Jim said. "It's still down in the Caribbean. But the weather-people figure it's headed our way."

Sara had had no idea. She hadn't opened her laptop in days. When she got home at night, she was too exhausted to do anything but shower and go to bed. Was she depressed? she wondered. "What does that mean?"

"Well, it could make landfall in a couple days," Jim said. "Or it could turn out to sea and amount to nothing."

"What do you think will happen?" Sara asked him, interested for the first time in what he had to say.

He shrugged. "I think it's going to hit us."

"Seriously?" Sara couldn't believe that he was just standing around, drinking beer. He seemed so relaxed. They all did.

"Yeah." He nodded. "We're due."

Terri laughed at Sara's expression. "We get a couple hurricanes every year. Most of them are only Category One. Arthur was Cat Two, and even that was nothing."

"Lost the highway for a couple days." Ron drained his beer. "No big deal."

But it seemed like a big deal to Sara.

"Just make sure you have water and food, batteries," Jim warned. "That sort of thing."

Sara looked around the group. "You wouldn't leave?"

"And go where?" Terri squeezed Ron's arm. "I hope they do evacuate. Then it really is paradise around here."

Someone put on music. People started to dance. Sara excused herself before Jim could get any bright ideas and wandered down the sagging wooden walkway to the ocean.

She had only pretended to listen to Luis's and Nicole's admonitions that she could never tell the man she was involved with who she really was. She had nodded and told them she understood, while inside she had laughed at their naïveté. She had no intention of staying with the program. Their rules meant nothing. But now, she was beginning to realize that they'd been right all along. She could never reveal the truth about herself. She could never say, *I broke the law and was caught; I was put into Witness Protection and I escaped.* She would have to carry those things along with her, always. Maybe she was doomed to end up with someone like Jim, who would never question too deeply. Who would be satisfied with whatever she could give.

She stepped onto warm and yielding sand,

bent to remove her sandals. She wriggled her toes, skirted prickly clumps of saw grass, and made her way down to the water, carrying her shoes.

She wasn't surprised to see him, standing in the silvery surf, staring out across the waves. Maybe he'd been waiting for her. Maybe she'd been looking for him. She should have turned around, gone in the other direction, but she didn't.

Ron looked over as she approached. Starlight touched the points of his jaw, his shoulder. His eyes were lost in shadow.

She tugged a strand of hair from her mouth. "Where's Terri?"

"Not here."

They began to walk along the shore. The sand was smooth and cool, the air warm and briny. It coated her skin, stiffened her hair. The music behind them grew faint, overtaken by the sounds of the surf. She felt transported back to a simpler, primordial time.

"How's the tire?" he asked.

"Fine."

The tide swirled around her ankles, thick with broken shells and bits of seaweed, unseen creatures swimming with claws and tails and antennae. House lights glimmered in the distance. The ghostly gray shape of a pier emerged, jutting out over the water. They could keep walking, cross beneath the wooden struts and come out on the other side. A town would be there, marked by beach houses and lifeguard stations. Then a blank sprawl of beach before the next town began. Every town would look the same from the water. Anonymous. Sara could lose herself. She could be anyone she wanted to be.

He caught her hand. She turned in to his arms. Her lips found his.

Sara drove home. The numerals glowed on her dashboard. Three A.M. Her cellphone hadn't rung once. She'd been searching for a loophole in the Feds' surveillance. She'd found it.

The moon rose. The dark houses stood tall against the night sky. The ocean flashed silver between them, a distant orange flicker of a bonfire. All those families, tucked in and sleeping.

CHAPTER 20
WHIT

Cassie locked herself in the bathroom and refused to come out. She wasn't a thief, she yelled through the door. When Whit threatened to take away her cellphone permanently, she unlocked the door and stormed into her bedroom.

Now she sulked in the backseat, arms folded against her chest. She'd insisted on wearing a long-sleeved shirt, despite the heat, and a knit winter cap pulled low over her ears. Boon sat next to her, talking softly to Wolf. He had refused to climb into the car until Whit agreed to lower the windows an inch. Still, it was progress. Just last week, Boon wanted all the windows wide open, which made Cassie clap her hands to her ears and yell that the wind was messing up her hair. Whit had glanced in the rearview mirror and seen how she'd pushed her bangs to one side and shellacked them oddly in place, but wisely made no comment.

"Stop acting like it's the end of the world, Cassie." Whit braked for the stoplight and knotted his tie. He was going to be late again for work, but with any luck, Thompson wouldn't notice. "I'll be back to get you Sunday afternoon."

"We can go crabbing with Grandpa," Boon volunteered, hopefully.

Cassie loved crabbing. She wasn't the least bit squeamish when it came to tying the string around the chicken neck. She leaned so far over the side of the boat to search for movement that Whit had to warn her to sit back.

She snorted. "How, dumb-ass? Grandpa can't even *walk.*"

"Don't call your brother names," Whit said, automatically. "He can play cards or games. He can tell you stories." It sounded weak, even to his ears. His father wasn't the most talkative man.

"Oh, boy. We can hear all about what it was like to grow up without a real toilet, just a hole in the ground."

Patience, he reminded himself. He adjusted the airflow vents, aimed them in her direction. She had to be burning up. The light turned green, and he accelerated through the intersection. "How about the mall? You could look for a new bathing suit." She'd been asking for one for weeks.

"With Grandma? Gross."

Just yesterday, Whit had caught her standing in front of the mirror and studying herself unhappily. He'd backed away, out of his depth. Now, he tried a joke. "Well, I guess you could always help clean the house."

Not even a chuckle. Silence filled the car from window to window. He gave up. They rode the rest of the way listening to news and weather and traffic reports.

Whit's mother held open the front door, and Boon ran into her arms. "Well, well, look who's here." She was still in her green scrubs, her graying hair scraped back. Her face looked naked, scoured clean, the tip of her nose and the points of her cheeks ruddy, dark smudges of fatigue beneath her eyes. She looked tired, as if she had barely the energy to stay on her feet. "Just in time for breakfast. You two have any requests?"

Cassie gripped a plastic bag stuffed with her clothes. "I just want to go back to sleep." She stalked off down the hall. A moment later, a door slammed.

His mother gave Whit a rueful look and patted Boon's head. She leaned back and eyed her grandson. "What on earth is that?"

"A Spider-Man Band-Aid," Boon said. "I made it myself."

Whit hadn't noticed the bandages dangling from his son's kneecap. Boon had colored on them with what appeared to be Magic Marker. The black squiggles ran over the flesh-colored strip and leaked onto his skin.

"I see." Whit's mother crouched, examining the injury. "Looks a little loose, sweetheart. There might be some dirt under there. I bet I have another Spider-Man Band-Aid around somewhere. Or the Hulk. Do you like the Hulk?"

"Uh-huh."

"We'll take care of it right after breakfast. What do you think about pancakes and bacon?"

"I like pancakes and bacon." Boon was so serious. Normally, the mention of bacon made him jump up and down.

"Why don't you go get out the eggs? You can help me mix up the batter."

Boon shuffled off down the hallway, dragging his bag of clothes after him, his green flip-flops smacking the linoleum. His shirt was pink. It hung over his shorts. Probably one of Cassie's castoffs. Probably had PRINCESS in sequins across the front.

His mother looked after Boon. "Where's their suitcase, Whit?"

It took him a second to answer. "It's with Diane."

"Oh. Right. Of course." She put her hand to her forehead, let out a soft breath. "Want some coffee? I just made a pot."

He glanced at his watch, shook his head. "I have to get to work."

His father sat like a stone in the living room, staring out into space, his casted leg propped on the old footstool in front of him. It had been a bad double break. His mother was doling out painkillers.

"How are you feeling, Dad?"

His father tapped the rolled-up newspaper against his thigh. "You can see for yourself."

"Do you need help around the house? I can deal with it when I get back —"

"Like you dealt with your own?"

Letting Whit know just what he thought of him. His mother broke the silence, patting his arm, an effort to lead him away. "You'd better get going, honey."

His father's profile was granite. He'd cut off his entire family when he was in his early twenties. Whit never knew why. Water under the bridge, was all his father would say. There were no photographs. His father never spoke of them. His entire childhood,

Whit had waited for him to do the same to him. Cut him off.

His mother followed him outside into the wall of heat. "Everything's going to be fine, Whit." She was talking about Diane. "You'll see. Everything's going to work out."

Whit said the same things to his kids. But he didn't know if any of it was true, and neither did she.

Thompson was irritated. His wife had shown up with their three kids to drag him to the restaurant for lunch. "We never see him anymore," she said, smiling at Whit to apologize for the interruption. She was deeply tanned, with frizzy blond hair and faded blue eyes. The kids had her coloring.

"Of course not." He smiled back and shook everyone's hand, even the youngest, who put her sticky hand in his, then tugged it away and buried her face shyly against her mother's leg. Everyone laughed. He wanted them all to leave. The bride and groom had just swept into the lobby, their entourage with them. Whit needed to go over and shake the fathers' hands, greet them with the relaxed confidence that didn't reveal his primary concern was that they and their forty-two guests were gone by three-thirty, when the next wedding party arrived.

"Why don't you head on over, honey," Thompson told her. "I'll join you in a few minutes. I need to talk to Whit about something."

What this time? Last week, it was the Mattress Incident. Turned out the tennis pro had a million Twitter followers. The hotel was getting slaughtered on social media for billing him for two mattresses and a shattered antique mirror. The guy called it slander, said he had an image to protect. Thompson demanded that Whit fix things, but he hadn't yet figured out how. He'd tried phoning the guy to offer a free stay and gotten the runaround. The wedding party had swept onto the patio, where they were posing for pictures.

"No, no." Mrs. Thompson curved her hand around her husband's elbow and smiled up at him. "I know what'll happen. Some emergency will arise, and then another one, and the kids and I will be sitting there for hours." She tugged his arm playfully. "Come on. Please. The kids are so excited."

They didn't look excited. They looked confused, shifting their weight from foot to foot and glancing around. To Whit's knowledge, they'd never been in the place before — only their mother had, breezing in occasionally to check on things. Whit couldn't help but wonder how Diane would have fit the role.

We need to plant something bright over there, Mrs. Thompson would tell him, pointing to the beach entry. He'd politely pretend to agree. He couldn't have anything that might attract stinging insects. *Avocado and crab are so popular,* she'd tell the head chef, who'd come to him, annoyed. *You know there's no profit in that,* she'd grouse, and he'd calm her down. *Add crab to the gazpacho, and double the price.*

No, he decided. Diane would have stayed far away. She would have wanted nothing to do with the hotel and its operations. The bridal party had moved out of sight, probably gone down to the shore, where the arch was set up in front of rows of white chairs. Good thing the weddings were today. He'd just caught the tail end of a weather report on his drive over from his parents' house. Something was brewing a couple hundred miles offshore. Too soon to know whether it would amount to anything. But the weather was looking iffy for the weekend.

Thompson sighed, shook his head. "I can never say no to you."

"Secret to a happy marriage." Triumphant, she led him away, leaning against him and looking up at him, their children bobbing around them. Something Thompson said made her laugh. It followed Whit like tinkling glass across the lobby to where Holly stood frowning behind the front desk. "He is *so* cheating on her," she muttered.

"You're imagining things." Whit would go down to the beach in a few minutes, talk to the bride and groom there. "Is the hashtag still trending?" #SeasideSucks tweets had been raining down on them for days. His phone rang. He pulled it from his pocket and glanced at the screen. His mother. She knew not to call him at work.

Holly typed a few keys. "Look at the way he's acting all solicitous, hanging on her every word, holding open the door for her."

Whit watched over her shoulder. The screen bloomed. "He loves her."

"Ha. That's not love, Whit. That's guilt, pure and simple." She tracked down the page.

His phone was still ringing. "Hold on," he told Holly and put the phone to his ear. "Mom? Everything okay?"

"The kids are gone."

"What?" Gone where? Where was his mother calling from?

Holly looked at Whit with surprise.

"Whit, I'm so sorry. I woke up from my nap and there was no sign of them. Your father was supposed to be watching them, but those pain meds really knock him out. I —"

"You sure? They're not just playing in the woods or something?"

"Their clothes are missing."

"Call the police. I'll be there as soon as I can."

His parents' driveway was empty. No police cars sat out front. Whit thundered up the porch steps, banged on the door. It swung open beneath his fist.

"Mom? Dad?"

No one called back. He spun in a helpless circle, pulled his cellphone from his pocket, called his mother. Thompson had been beeping in. Whit had sent every call to voicemail. He stepped out onto the small porch as it rang, looked up and down the sunbaked street, searching for two small figures, one taller than the other, with flyaway hair. He saw his mother's tan Buick turn the corner and speed toward him. She sat behind the wheel, her face gray. Whit's father sat beside her, staring grimly ahead through the windshield.

She lurched into the driveway and braked hard. She opened the door and climbed out, ran over to clutch Whit's hands in her strong grip. "No sign of them yet. But don't worry. We've got all the neighbors out looking. We'll find them."

"What do the police say? When did you last see them? Have they issued an Amber Alert?"

Whit's father was trying to get out of the vehicle, poking out a crutch and cursing. Whit went around to help him, and he waved Whit away.

"Didn't call them," he grunted.

Whit stared at him, uncomprehending. "What?"

"You want that damn social worker to hear about this? You're as big an idiot as I always thought you were."

Whit couldn't speak. Two hours. His kids had been gone two damn hours. Anything could have happened. He was still gripping his phone. He started dialing, and his mother grabbed his arm.

"Wait, wait. Your father's right. Think about it. Let's keep the police out of it. For now."

"Call them. Call them right now, Mom." He put the phone to his ear. *Answer,* he hissed. He'd spoken out loud. And, as if by magic, Cassie's voice was there. "We're lost," she said, flatly.

"What the hell were you thinking?" Whit fixed on Cassie. She was the decision maker. She was the one who should have known better. He had found his children almost three miles away, waiting on the grassy shoulder with their bags of clothes beside them. Cassie stood, arms folded. Boon was crouched, picking dandelions. Cars had whizzed by at terrifying speeds. Any one of those cars could have hit them. Any one of them could have stopped. "Do you know what happens to runaways? Do you?"

"Like you care." She slumped on the pullout couch, gnawing viciously at her thumbnail, her eyes narrowed. There sat Diane in miniature, rigid and obstinate. Her brother huddled beside her, staring at Whit with huge, scared eyes, his thumb in his mouth again. He was six years old, for Christ's sake. Old enough to protest. Old enough to know that just because his sister said jump, he didn't have to. Old enough to stop sucking his fucking thumb.

Whit's parents were in the kitchen. He heard the clatter of dishes, smelled onions frying. "Because I have to work? Is that what this is about?"

"You never listen to me."

"Stop with the attitude."

"Why? Does it offend you, *Daddy*?"

He wanted to smack her. "One more word out of you and I'll take away your cellphone. Get rid of the TV."

"Poor me. No more cartoons. Wah wah wah."

"Give me your phone. Now."

"No!" She scrabbled back against the cushions, her backpack clutched in her arms. "You can't have it!"

He grabbed hold of the backpack straps. She flailed at him, kicking, her bare feet pummeling him. She was a small tornado, whirling and shrieking, and out of control. "Don't touch me! Don't touch me! I'll tell Robin. I'll tell her *everything*!"

He released the backpack. She fell back, her face raised, defiant and young, her chest heaving. Boon had casually mentioned that Robin had stopped by the other day. Whit had been just as casual. What fun thing had they done with Robin? What did she want to talk about? But when he wanted to know what Cassie had said in response to the woman's questions, Boon's eyes had slid away from Whit's. *Nothing,* he'd mumbled and clambered down from the chair and run off, swinging Wolf like a pendulum. Now

Whit looked at his daughter and believed her.

"You want Robin to take you away? That's what'll happen. You'll end up in foster care, Cassie. Boon, too. That's if you're lucky. Chances are there won't be any openings, so you'll have to go to a state institution. You'll sleep in a big room with lots of other girls, and share a bathroom. There won't be any trips to the mall, or take-out pizza, or hanging by the pool. If you want to watch TV, you'll have to take turns. Boon, too, but he'll be in a different place." She had to understand. He needed to make her understand. Boon was sobbing, rocking back and forth, his arms wrapped around his bent knees. For an instant, Whit felt like his kids were strangers. "That's what they do with kids your ages. They'll separate you. You'll never see each other. You'll be there until you're eighteen. Boon won't even remember you by the time he gets out. That what you want?"

Cassie refused to look at him. But she'd heard him. He saw the color drain from her cheeks. "Answer me, Cass. Is that what you want?"

"I. Hate. You."

"Take off that damn hat."

She ripped the cap off her head, flung it

across the room.

It was a silent drive home. Every time he glanced in the rearview mirror, he saw Boon staring out one window and Cassie glowering out the other. His kids. All Whit had ever tried to do was protect them.

The wind had picked up by the time they pulled into the Paradise.

Diane's Focus sat parked over by the row of bushes, hidden from view. In the morning, he would place an ad on Craigslist and prop a For Sale sign on the dashboard. At some point, he'd have to start making decisions about the rest of her things.

CHAPTER 21
SARA

The next morning, the storm had a name. The weather maps showed a churning circle wavering out in open water. It was too soon to know whether it would amount to anything. It might head north, toward the Carolinas. Or it might collapse under its own weight.

Sara drove to work. Did she imagine the riffling of distant palm trees?

Terri told Sara that if she wanted the overtime, she could pick up a few extra houses. Two girls had called in sick, and she'd already started to hear from renters planning to leave early.

Sara watched Terri. Was she imagining it, or was Terri acting slightly chilly? "They're saying it might be a big one."

"They always say that." Terri studied the clipboard, made a few notes. "Everyone gets worked up, then it all peters out to nothing."

Terri couldn't possibly suspect anything, not unless Ron had said something. But he didn't seem the type. At least, that's what Sara hoped. "What if they order an evacuation?"

"If that happens, we'll have to close for a day. Maybe a week. Depends on how bad things get." Terri fingered out some crisp bills and slid them into an envelope.

No, Sara decided. Terri wasn't her usual cheerful self. "Everything okay?"

Terri sighed, looked at her. "Ron didn't stay over last night. He said he had to get to work early this morning, but I think that was just an excuse."

Sara and Ron had returned to the party separately. Sara had helped Terri clean up the kitchen, while Ron hung out in the yard with Jim. Sara hadn't glanced in Ron's direction, but she felt the heat of his gaze on her every time she passed by Terri's kitchen window. "An excuse for what?"

"He doesn't like it when I drink."

"But everyone was drinking." Why did women do that, automatically blame themselves? If anyone should be blamed, it should be Sara. But had she really done anything so bad? Terri had implied she and Ron had an open relationship. Terri had flirted with the other guys at the party.

She'd hung on Jim's arm, laughed at his jokes. Well, it wouldn't happen again. It was just a physical thing. Nothing more.

"I know."

"You told me it was better not to hold on too tight."

Terri handed Sara the envelope. "And you believed me?"

Sara tucked the envelope into her bag, took the keys for the houses she was to clean that day. She *had* believed Terri. But she knew better than anyone: people always believe what they want to.

She was driving home that afternoon when her cellphone chimed. It could be only one person. She thought of the days when her phone would be alive with texts, Facebook updates, Instagram. Now, just this. She braked at the stoplight and picked up her phone to text back. The light turned green, and she continued on her way home. Luis wanted to meet at the Paradise. Sara wondered why. Maybe the trial date had changed, but if it was something like that, a phone call would have sufficed.

When she pulled into the courtyard, she didn't immediately see him. She circled the lot, looking for the telltale government vehicle. She got out of her car and shaded her eyes. People were at the pool, laughter and splashing filling the air like bubbles. Someone was grilling, the rich smell of roasted meat rising. The office door stood propped open for some reason. Maybe the air-conditioning had failed. She glanced up, saw a few neighbors on the various walkways, carrying laundry or standing in groups, talking. Everything appeared utterly normal. She wondered if that might be about to change.

She crossed the courtyard toward the stairs, and that's when she spotted him, standing back in the shadows as the sun slanted down hard. He was wearing a tan polo shirt and shorts, a baseball cap pulled low to hide his eyes.

She couldn't read his expression. "What's going on?"

"Let's go upstairs."

His voice was mild, but she sensed a restless energy about him. Maybe he'd been driving all day, needed to stretch his legs. She thought about the other witness he was working with, the one in South Carolina, and felt a twinge of jealousy. It reminded her that she was nothing more than a job to him. There was nothing sexual between them. He was just one of a few people who knew who she was. Why did she want to

220

matter more to him than she did?

They reached the fourth floor. Luis moved with ease, but she knew he was paying attention to the neighbors they passed.

"Want a drink?" Of course, she hadn't been expecting company. She wasn't the best housekeeper. Dirty dishes sat on the counter, an opened box of pasta. A tilting pile of books on the floor beside the couch.

"Sure. Whatever you're having. Mind if I look around?"

It bothered her. What did he expect to find? "Go ahead." She took down two glasses and turned on the kitchen faucet. The glass rattled against the spigot, and she adjusted her grip. She watched him as he walked around, then went into her bedroom. She filled both glasses, sipped the tepid water. It tasted metallic.

They talked on the balcony. It was uncomfortably warm despite the breeze. The surf shifted restlessly beneath the milky sunshine. They sat on the two plastic chairs.

Luis set his glass on the milk crate between them. He hadn't tasted it. Maybe he'd wanted something stronger. "How's everything going?"

"Same old, same old."

"Meeting people?"

Sara rubbed her shoulder. She'd washed

windows that morning. "Cut it out. Tell me why you're really here."

He turned his mirrored sunglasses toward her. "We've decided to move you."

It was a blow. Sara concentrated on breathing. "Why?"

"The storm. We have to get you out of here before it hits."

"But it might not come anywhere near us." She wished he'd take off his glasses, let her see his eyes. A power move, hiding behind them. She'd used it, too. Where was her wall now?

"We can't risk it."

"But I'm settled here." Something had tipped off the Feds. What? They'd never move her unless they had reason to suspect she'd been compromised. Sara had the sensation of pieces being shuffled around, tacked down and lifted up again. The guy she was supposed to testify against knew she was keeping her mouth shut. Unless he hadn't believed her. "Has there been a leak?" She kept her voice steady.

"No, no. Nothing like that. You're safe, I told you. We just want to get you out of the storm's path."

It was her, she realized. They hadn't called her the night before to check on her because they'd had eyes on her the entire night.

While she and Ron fucked on the beach. Her guard down, her raw self exposed. Nothing was private. Nothing was hers anymore. That was why Luis had searched her apartment just now. He'd been looking for signs of male company. Meet people, hadn't he urged her? But he hadn't meant it.

It was the small things she had to watch for. *There are two kinds of people,* her dad used to say. *Some people make their choices. Others have choices made for them.* "All right," she said, leaning back and crossing her legs. "When?"

That night, she called Terri. "Sorry to wake you," she said when Terri answered the phone.

"No problem. What's up?" Terri listened while Sara explained the problem she was having with her car. It had been sputtering every time she pressed the accelerator. Now it was stalling and she was having difficulty getting it to accelerate. "Hold on, hon," Terri said. "I'll ask Ron." Good. He was there. Sara heard voices talking, then Ron came on the line.

"Hey." His tone was warm. He'd carried the phone into another room. "How are you doing?"

Sara abandoned the pretense of sudden car trouble. Her car had been a problem from the beginning. "I need a favor."

"You've come to the right place."

She could hear the smile in his voice. He thought she meant sex. Of course he did. She stood on her balcony, looked out over the rooftops to the dark, restless water. If there was a hurricane out there, Sara couldn't see it. "I need a new car. Something reliable."

"Sure." He sounded puzzled, trying to work out her intent. "I can help you."

"It's tricky. I don't want my name on the title."

A long, heavy silence. Sara waited it out. Then he said, "You know I can't do that."

"I bet you could if you wanted to."

Another silence. This one was stiff. He'd heard the threat in her words. "When do you need it by?"

"As soon as possible. Tonight?"

"Can't do it. Make it tomorrow."

"Fine. Tomorrow. I'll be by first thing."

"No. Don't come to me. I'll come to you."

She hesitated, then agreed. She gave him her address.

"You owe me," he said. This time, there was no smile in his voice.

Sara turned to go back into her apartment. Someone sat huddled on the balcony next door. The girl, Cassie. She was curled up on a chair in the shadows, her arms wrapped around her bent legs, her pale face turned toward Sara, letting Sara see her. Letting her know.

CHAPTER 22
CASSIE

Her mom had been gone for weeks. Her absence peeled back the soft tender layers to reveal a world Cassie hadn't known, sharp with claws and biting teeth. Breathing hurt. Monsters followed her into her dreams. Days were worse — she saw herself in every reflected surface, her mom's own face staring back at her. Nothing helped. She'd tried everything. Beer, weed, sex. But she couldn't drink enough beer to blur the edges. She only ended up vomiting all over herself. Weed made her suspicious of everyone, certain that they were watching her as closely as she was watching them. And sex, well, that had been a big fucking disappointment. Danny had shoved himself inside her, his eyes rolled up toward the ceiling. One, two, three, and it was over. It was messy, too. But it had made Danny like her. It had changed everything between them. Now she was the one who stood back. She was the one who decided. The girl she'd been before would have been crazy with happiness, but the girl she was now felt nothing.

Still, when Danny texted to ask if she wanted to hang out, she didn't hesitate. *OK,* she texted back. She'd just gotten up. He'd been texting for hours.

Danny came to get her, clomping up all those stairs and knocking on the door. It was part of the new Cassie. She didn't hang around the courtyard, watching every car pull in, chewing on her fingernails and try-ing not to look desperate. No, this Cassie calmly waited inside her apartment, took her time applying makeup. She was still figuring out how to keep eyeliner from seep-ing into the corners of her eyes; she was still getting used to the heavy mascara that made her eyelashes feel like spiders whenever she blinked. The black lipstick never washed off. She had to wait for it to fade. Lexi had shown her how to draw the shape, leaning close, her nose red around the tiny silver hoop stuck through, her warm breath puff-ing across Cassie's face, and her eyes intent on Cassie's lips. Cassie could see every clot-ted lash, the crooked, inky lines of Lexi's eyeliner. *Be careful not to get it on your teeth.* When she stood back, Cassie looked in the mirror. She didn't see her mom. She saw a girl who looked like the others. She saw a girl who belonged.

Boon was playing with Lego on the rug. He was a disaster — his hair hanging oily over his eyes, his shirt inside out, the insides of his elbows and his tummy covered with a rash. He'd been scratching again. At the sound of the knock, he scrambled to his feet. He thought it was their mom. He knew nothing.

"It's for me," Cassie said and went to the door.

"You're leaving?" Boon wailed, gripping Wolf by the belly, the animal's furry head drooping like his neck was broken, his dirty pink felt tongue curled and coming loose, one eye creepily dangling from a thread. That stupid thing. Boon was going to get torn apart in first grade if he didn't stop carrying it around everywhere and pretending it was real. Cassie had told him a million times — first grade isn't like kindergarten — but he refused to listen. He just wrapped his arms tighter around Wolf. Fine. Let him learn for himself.

"I'll be back."

"But Dad said —"

"I know what Dad said." He'd said it over and over. He'd threatened her with foster care. He'd even thrown Boon into the threat

— trying to find the switch that would make Cassie snap back. But that girl was gone. There was no switch. She slung her new purse across her chest. "Don't burn down the place," she told Boon and opened the door.

Danny was leaning against the railing. His hair fell over his orangey brown eyes as he looked down at her. You have to do tricks, Lexi had helpfully told Cassie. You can't just do *it*. Cassie had nodded at the wisdom even as she wondered what Lexi was talking about. Cassie didn't know any tricks. For now, *it* seemed to be enough.

He slung his arm around her shoulders as they walked down the stairs. He always did that, or slid his hand into the back pocket of her jeans, which she didn't like. If they didn't match their steps exactly, she'd be yanked back if she went faster. And if he went faster, his fingers cupped her rear and dragged her along. Today, she was spared that. She was wearing a sundress over her new bathing suit, the one she'd found during Crazy Days, when all the store owners rolled their sale racks outside and lined them up along the sidewalks. Cassie had raked through the hangers, stopped at the bright pink bikini, and lifted it clean off and away, pushed down into her bag in one seamless motion. Lexi had shown her how to sew cut-up socks to the insides of the bra cups to fill them out. *Otherwise, when Danny feels you up, he's going to know.* Lexi thought she knew all about Cassie now. She thought they were friends.

Lexi sat behind the steering wheel of a big white car. She'd just gotten her learner's. They were going to celebrate. "Hurry," she told Cassie and Danny. She wore huge black, circular sunglasses. They made her narrow face look like an insect's. "Parking's going to be a bitch."

Cassie climbed in back with Danny. Mikey P sat in the front passenger seat. Bruno was home, helping his grandma grocery shop. She was worried about the hurricane. Lexi turned up the music, all the windows open and the wind rushing in. Mikey P was smoking a cigarette. He turned around and passed it back. Danny took a puff. When he held it out to Cassie, she shook her head. Smoking was disgusting. Danny's breath tasted horrible after he had a cigarette. His clothes smelled, his hair. He was always having to find a place to light up. He complained constantly about the expense. Cassie had no intention of smoking — ever. Besides, she saw what it had done to her grandma Helen, having an oxygen tank tethered to her like a heavy dog lumbering along.

Lexi slapped the steering wheel, steered with her knees. Mikey P said something, and she giggled. Danny was holding Cassie's hand, drawing circles on her palm with his thumb. He was trying to find the switch, too. *Sorry about your mom,* he had said. Everyone always said sorry. They all wanted to know how Cassie was doing. They didn't care about Cassie. They were just nosy. They wanted to split open her heart and take a good look.

They rocketed down the highway, swooping this way and that. The rushing air whipped Cassie's hair around, made the trash in the car go fluttering. Fast-food bags, old receipts. Lexi yelped as a small piece of paper lifted up from the console. "Grab that!"

Danny snatched it out of the air. He held it up, tantalizing. "What'll you give me?" he teased Lexi as she scrabbled for it with one hand, the car swinging from lane to lane. A blast of horn from another driver, his angry face. "You'll see," Lexi promised, and Danny handed her back her learner's. He grabbed Cassie's hand again. She let it lie in his, limp.

"Look!" Lexi bumped off the road and

into a parking lot. "Primo, baby!" She slid the car into a space and turned off the engine. "We've only got till three. I have to get the car back before my stepdad gets home."

Cassie sat up in the backseat, brushed back her hair from her eyes. The sprawling white building was surrounded by perfectly manicured shrubs and colorful flowers. The wide semicircular entrance, the valets' stand tucked beneath the overhang. The lot wasn't completely empty. There were still plenty of cars around. "Here?"

Lexi glanced at her in the rearview. "Sure. We'll pretend to be guests. It'll be a blast."

Everyone else climbed out. Danny looked down at Cassie, still sitting in the backseat. "Coming?"

He didn't know her. None of them did. They didn't know this was where Cassie's dad worked. She looked around. Something was wrong. She couldn't figure it out. Then she got it. There wasn't a valet standing out front, hands clasped behind his back. No bellmen, either. And Lexi was right: it was amazing they'd found a parking spot. Usually, the lot was jammed with cars, every spot assigned to a guest. She eyed Mikey P with his half-shaved head, thinking no one would ever mistake him for a guest, then shrugged. "We can't go through the lobby."

They wandered along the wide sweep of the main building, cut through the outdoor restaurant to the beach. This time of day, every table should be filled, servers hustling around with coffeepots and leather-bound menus. But there were just a few families and only one server, who huddled by the water station, talking on her cellphone. Cassie frowned. If her dad caught that the server would be fired in a heartbeat.

Clear gray water washed back and forth, turning up seashells and chunks of sea glass. They found four lounge chairs lined up in a row on the hot sand.

Cassie peeled off her dress and stretched out. She looked down the length of her body, making sure her bra cups were lined up. She closed her eyes. The sun fell like a warm blanket across her face. The world turned red behind her eyelids. The surf whooshed.

Her mom didn't like the beach. She wanted to live somewhere cold. *The heat gets to me.* It made her headaches worse. It made her go into her room for hours, sometimes days. If Cassie tried to hug her, she went, *Ow.* It was like her whole body was hurting.

Mikey P was telling a story. Lexi giggled.

Danny sang a fragment of a song. He had the best voice and he knew it. Lexi passed around a box of crackers. Cassie flipped over onto her belly and put her head down on her folded arms. There was noise nearby, people calling to their kids to get out of the water, *Right now.* Probably lunchtime.

Then a familiar voice. "Cassie?"

She lifted her head without thinking, then wished she hadn't. Her dad stood there, staring down at her. He had his jacket off, his shirtsleeves rolled up. He glanced to Danny, Lexi, and Mikey P, and he frowned. "Who are you?"

"Who wants to know?" Danny asked.

"I'm the manager here and that's my daughter."

"It's a public beach," Lexi said.

"They're my friends." Cassie sat up. "Leave them alone."

"She's *twelve,*" her dad said, as if that meant anything. Cassie felt her insides shrivel. "Cover up, Cassie. For Christ's sake."

"Be cool, man," Mikey P said, raising his palms, like he thought her dad would hit him. "We're leaving."

"Not with my daughter you're not. Get out of here. Leave my daughter alone. I see you hanging around her again and I'm calling the cops. Got that?"

Cassie wanted to die. She wanted to die right then and there. "Stop it, Dad! It's not like that."

"I know exactly what it's like. Go home, all of you. Don't you know we're being evacuated?"

Holly drove like an old lady, both hands on the wheel, slowing before lights turned red, looking both ways before creeping across an intersection. She had a clot of air fresheners dangling from the rearview mirror and long acrylic fingernails, deep pink striped with silver that sparkled every time she turned the wheel. "The hotel's been crazy all morning. Boarding up the windows, bringing everything inside. Guests are pissed about having to check out early."

Cassie and her dad had fought about Holly driving her home. Her dad said Cassie wasn't getting back into Lexi's car; she wasn't grabbing an Uber, either. He was going to drive her, goddammit, even if he got fired, and she was going to stay put. Was she a toddler that needed watching every single second? Where was her brother; had she even thought about his welfare? She was turning out just like her mother.

Into that shocked, breathless gap, Holly

had unexpectedly stepped forward. *I can take her home, Whit.* The way she said it, her cheeks glazing pink. Cassie had given her a nasty look, but here she was sitting in the passenger seat as the streets rolled past.

"Hard to believe a hurricane's coming."

Cassie shrugged. Her phone buzzed with another text. This time, it was Danny. *What an asshole.* He meant her dad. She turned off her phone, dropped it into her bag.

Holly glanced at the long line of vehicles on the other side of the highway. "Your dad says you're not evacuating."

"We never do."

"Really? I'm from Baltimore. We don't get hurricanes up there."

"We do down here." People who evacuated were sorry when they came back and found their homes broken into, and their houses flooded. It had happened to her third-grade teacher.

"My folks are really freaking out. They want me to come home."

"So, are you?" Cassie pulled forward a length of her hair and began tightly braiding it. Sometimes, she'd make hundreds of tiny braids, and when she undid them, her hair would ripple out in a fan. It never lasted, though. She didn't have her mom's curly hair.

236

Cassie, when I found out I was pregnant with you, I ran all the way to where your dad worked to tell him the news. I forgot my shoes. I forgot my purse. I even forgot to put on my bathrobe. I ran the whole way in my night-gown. Good thing it was only two blocks.

"I don't know. They're saying it's going to be Category Three."

You can't talk to Robin, her dad had told her. He'd put his hands on Cassie's shoulders, crouched to look her straight in the eye. *You can't tell anyone anything. If you need to talk, you come to me.* Cassie's chest had ached from holding her breath. The apartment had hummed and flickered with light. *Talk* to him? She couldn't even *look* at him.

Honey, can you light the grill? her mom would call. Her dad would chase her mom around the kitchen with the tongs. She would giggle as he tried to kiss her.

Holly braked in front of the Paradise. She turned to Cassie with a timid smile. "Here we go. Will you be okay until your dad gets home?"

Did Holly want to come in and make mac and cheese for them, play Lego with Boon? Cassie picked up her bag from the floor. "Your parents are right. You should go home."

Holly blinked. "Really?"

"You're wasting your time, you know. My dad's really not that into you."

Cassie got out of the car and slammed the door. She felt Holly's hurt eyes following her into the shadows. Her dad didn't even see Holly. The only person he'd ever seen had been her mom.

CHAPTER 23
WHIT

His little girl lying there, every rib showing, her hip bones jutting out — that boy hunched over her, trailing his fingertips along her narrow arm. Like he owned her.

Whit wanted to punch him. He wanted to keep punching him, smash the smirk right into the kid's face, bundle a towel around Cassie. Where the hell had she gotten that bikini? Everyone was in motion, the kids shoving themselves to their feet, Cassie's face raised challengingly — so challengingly — to his. Holly had placed her hand on his arm. *I can take her home, Whit,* she'd suggested, yanking Whit back to the present.

Now he paced the silent hotel, checking doors and windows, unplugging appliances, drawing drapes, plunging everything into darkness. He was alone. He'd spent the afternoon assisting staff in hauling in patio furniture, taking down hanging plants, clearing off balconies and stripping the pool area, hammering long planks across the expanses of glass. Holly had returned from dropping off Cassie, asked if she could leave early. She'd decided to get on the road — was that okay? Thompson, focused only on hustling his family into their minivan and driving north, had left, too. Whit let himself out the entrance, locked the door behind him and pocketed the keys. Clouds were starting to roll in. The surf was a dull drumbeat.

By the time he pulled into the courtyard, the clouds had thickened. The Paradise stood hunched against the gray sky, windows blazing here and there. The parking lot was half empty. He unloaded the trunk and made his way upstairs, carrying three bags of groceries, dodging a family of four frantic to maneuver their suitcases down the stairs past him. The apartment was dark. He elbowed on the overhead and kicked the door closed. "Cassie! Boon! Guys! I need your help."

The store's shelves had been picked over. Whit had gotten what he could. When he'd scraped his credit card through the reader, he held his breath to see if it got accepted. He lowered the bags to the kitchen floor, cans rolling away.

The back bedroom door opened. Boon

stood there, clinging to the doorknob and clasping Wolf by one paw. The thing was beat to hell. It was no longer recognizable as a dog.

"Hey, buddy. Come see what I got for you."

He shuffled over. His bare feet were dirty. His hair was too long and covering his eyes.

"Look. It's a flashlight. You can stand it up like a lantern. It doesn't use batteries. You have to shake it to make it work. See?"

"That's cool."

"I got one for your sister, too."

Cassie was standing in the doorway, arms crossed, scowling. He was relieved to see her. She looked so young. It wasn't too late, he told himself. It had been a bad day for both of them. They'd figure it out. "There you are, Cass. Wait until you see how much junk food I got." He piled packages on the table. Doughnuts. Marshmallows. Popsicles. "Peanut butter cereal. No milk, though. They were all out." He set out cans of pasta, a bag of apples. "Not bad, right? Why don't you two start putting it away while I make dinner." The skeletal remains of a sandwich sat in the sink. Boon's probably. Cassie refused to eat the heels. "I'll put on a pizza."

Boon glanced to Cassie, checking, as always, for her response. She moved zombie-like toward the pantry with a box of pasta. Whit winked at his son. She'd cut it out sooner or later. She couldn't keep up the silent treatment for much longer. "I'll take that as an *Oh, boy, Dad. Can't wait.*"

They ate off paper plates. He sliced the pizza into rectangles. Boon reminded him his mom always sliced it into triangles. Whit told him he was getting good at his shapes. "You guys remember the last time we had a hurricane?"

Boon nibbled a circle of pepperoni, then shook his head.

"We roasted marshmallows over the burner."

"That's right." Whit grinned at Cassie. He'd known she'd come around. The kid just needed time. That had been a great couple of days. Everything around them shut down, the Paradise mostly empty, and it had been the four of them, playing board games and making a picnic over odds and ends from the fridge. He and Diane had shared a bottle of wine after the kids went to sleep. At dawn, still a little tipsy, they'd ventured out, walking barefoot down the street heaped with sand. *Better than Disney World,* he'd murmured to Dee, and she'd kissed him. For a while after that, things had been good between them.

After dinner, while the kids got ready for bed, he pulled open the sliding glass door and stood on the balcony. The surf was building. He dried his hands on a dish towel. "Want to go to the beach?"

"In our PJs?" Boon was doubtful.

"So what? Grab a jacket, both of you. It'll be cooler down by the water."

They walked along the shore, his flashlight beam dancing in front of them. Maybe the cops were right. Maybe Diane had been seeing someone. It could explain her behavior, maybe where the money had gone. He went down the list. He couldn't help himself. The pastor, some guy she'd worked with. Jesus. Maybe one of the other fathers at the kids' school. The ones Dee thought could fill her life with magic. The ones who believed they could.

The water rushed in, unexpectedly cold. Boon squealed, thrilled. How long had it been since he'd walked on the beach with his kids? He handed Cassie the flashlight, and she sprinted recklessly ahead, dashing the beam over the frothing surf, the scattered shells and tangled reeds. He took Boon's small, wet hand in his and tightened his fingers around it.

School would start in a few short weeks. Maybe it was time to think about moving inland, to a different district. Out of Robin's jurisdiction and away from her prying. More job opportunities on the mainland. He could find a three-bedroom place that allowed dogs. Boon was desperate for a dog. What they all needed was a fresh start. Enough time had passed. No one would think anything of it.

The jangling of the phone dragged him out of sleep. He fumbled, dropped his cell, glanced at the screen. "Dad?" He cleared his throat, swung his feet to the floor. "What's up? Everything okay?"

"That tree out back just went down, landed on top of the septic. It's busted the cover off the manhole. I told you we should have gotten to it."

"You kidding me? The winds haven't even started."

"What can I tell you?"

Whit rubbed his forehead with the heel of his hand. "Is the plumbing still working?"

"Think so. Christ knows how long that's going to last."

The rain would fill the tank; worse, the electricity might go out, forcing sewage into the house. "I'll be right there." No way his father could handle this alone, not with his leg in that cast. "I'll pick up some lumber

244

and plastic, see if we can cover it up for the time being —"

His father disconnected.

The apartment was still dark. Just before six in the morning. He heard nothing from the kids' bedroom. They'd slept through the call. He tossed down his phone and went into the living room, tugged open the blinds. The wind gusted across the road, stirred up sand and debris. Treetops shuddered. He grabbed the TV remote. The hurricane was out in open water, indecisive. The newscasters kept yapping about projected paths and wind speed. Looked like it'd be late afternoon before she made landfall. If she headed inland at all. He veered into the kitchen and turned on the light. He started a pot of coffee.

He cracked open the kids' bedroom door, stood looking in. The lower bunk was empty, blanket dragged across the floor like an oil slick. Boon was curled in the closet. Cassie lay in the top bunk facing him, her eyes closed, her hand curved against the pillow. He'd have to leave them behind. What if they overheard — or worse — saw something? Boon was naturally observant and Cassie was out of control. She'd defy his command to stay inside just to show she could.

He scribbled a note and stuck it to the fridge. The coffee had finished dripping. He filled a thermos and grabbed his windbreaker from the closet. He wouldn't be long. An hour there, an hour back, maybe an hour helping his father. Three hours all told, four at most.

When he got home, he and the kids could make breakfast together, watch the storm roll in.

CHAPTER 24
SARA

Sara paced, smoked the last of her cigarettes and wished she had more.

Just after nine, there was a loud pounding. She froze, turned to the door. It couldn't be Luis. Maybe, just maybe, it was Ron. She peered through the peephole. The apartment manager stood on the other side, his face rounded and distorted by glass. She unlocked the door. "Hey, Ted."

"Ms. Lennox." He held a clipboard, dappled with rain. His black windbreaker flapped around him like crows' wings. The sky behind him was churning. "I'm going around, checking with everyone. You staying or going?"

Going. Definitely going. But she couldn't let him know that. "I don't know."

"Better make up your mind before they close the bridges."

"When will that be?" The reports differed. It was going to be the storm of the century.

It was going to be nothing.

"Depends."

She'd given Ron the number for her new cellphone, the one the FBI didn't know about, but she didn't have his. All she had was the number of his garage, which she'd been dialing since dawn. She got the same recording every time: *Shop closed. Call back during normal business hours.* Well, those hours had arrived and no one was answering the damn phone. She told herself that Ron was on his way. His lot was filled with cars waiting for repair. All he had to do was pick one.

Ted glanced at his clipboard. "Just so you know, the owners can't be responsible if you stay."

Yes, she understood that. She closed the door, drove the dead bolt home.

We'll be there by noon, Luis had told her. *Be ready.*

She snatched up the cigarette pack from the counter, shook it as though the action would magically refill it. She dropped it in disgust.

Every TV station showed a reporter clutching a microphone as their coat flapped sideways and their hair whiplashed into comical shapes. The hurricane had reached Category 3 status. Apparently, the last time a hurricane of that magnitude smacked into the North Carolina coast, it almost wiped out Topsail Island. Topsail wasn't that far north. A couple of the places she cleaned were on the southernmost tip of the Outer Banks, not all that far north of Topsail. All the houses there had seemed brand-new because they were.

Someone was being interviewed who refused to leave. The reporter asked, "You have a death wish?" The homeowner shook his head. "Nah. It's just a decision I made. I gotta protect my stuff."

Sara knew about tornadoes and straight-line winds, which sprang up suddenly and tore past in a matter of minutes. No time to think or plan. But she didn't know how to deal with a lumbering giant that took its time getting there.

She stood staring out the window. The sky was boiling with clouds. The waves thrashed, higher than they'd been the day before, sending sheets of foam to the shore. It was the storm surge that killed the most people. What if she got stuck here, waiting — doing the one thing she hated the most, placing her life in other people's hands? Where the hell was Ron? What if the race wasn't between him and Luis getting there, but with the hurricane beating them both?

She filled the bathtub with water, stoppered the bathroom sink and the kitchen sink, and filled them. She unloaded the few items in her refrigerator into a Styrofoam cooler and cracked the cubes from the single tray that had come with the place on top. As if they would suffice to keep anything cold. She filled pots with water, searched for the can opener, set out candles and matches, slotted batteries into a flashlight. She pressed the switch to make sure it was working.

A few minutes past eleven.

The TV tracked a sluggish line of vehicles crawling bumper to bumper along the highway that ran just a few hundred feet from the Paradise. An accident had shut down one side of the road. Police were directing people around it and into the opposite lane. Was Ron stuck in that mess? Luis would just hold up his badge, be waved around the long line of cars and pickups. He'd put on his flashing lights. Nothing would stop him. She tried the garage again. She heard the same telltale click that told her the call had been forwarded to an answering machine. She disconnected.

The rain picked up, a stinging spray whipped by the wind. Debris pelted the glass. Something came loose on the roof, banged up and down. Someone screamed, over and over, rhythmically. Sara stopped her pacing to listen. The screaming changed, soared higher, and she understood the scream wasn't human. It was the trees.

She texted Luis: *ETA?* She stared at the display, waited for a response. None came.

She unlocked her door. It blew open, smacked against the wall. She pushed into the wind to peer down into the courtyard, sheltering her eyes against the whirling sand. There were fewer parked cars than there had been just an hour before. She saw her own small sedan by the fountain. No car pulling into the lot.

The streetlights flickered. She hurried back inside and slammed the door against the wet. Her jeans clung to her legs. Her cuffs dripped. Not worth it to change clothes. She'd only get soaked again. At the sliding glass door, she squinted through the driving rain. The ocean had surged closer, charging across hundreds of feet of sand. Now it lapped around the row of houses below. A deck sagged on a single stilt that looked like it might buckle at any moment.

Luis still hadn't replied. She called Terri, was swamped with relief when she answered right away. "Hey, Terri, it's . . ." Sara almost blurted out her real name, caught herself. "Me."

"You're not at the office, are you? Because we're closed." Terri sounded cheerful.

"No, but I'm wondering if you've heard from Ron. He was going to help me with my car —"

"Oh. Right. He said something about that. Hold on."

Sara heard Terri's muffled voice, then the low rumble of Ron's. She stared at her phone with disbelief, then saw a text from Luis: *Hang tight. 30 mins out.* Terri came back on the line. "He's swamped right now, hon. Everyone's hollering for a tow. Can you hang in there until things calm down?"

Ron wasn't going to help her. He'd never intended to. Sara longed to make good on her threat, let Terri know just what kind of man Ron was.

"Are you stuck somewhere, hon? Do you need me to come get you?"

"No, I'm good," Sara replied. "Thanks." When they hung up, Sara knew they'd never talk again.

She lifted the canvas bag, bulging with the things she couldn't leave behind. Luis would have noticed it the afternoon before, sitting on the floor of her closet, but he might not remember having seen it. She toppled a kitchen chair, threw a glass against the wall, and tore the kitchen blinds to the floor. She left her two black suitcases lined up by the front door, neatly packed with her belongings. When Luis and Nicole got here, they would find an apartment that looked as though Sara had been patiently waiting for them, been surprised by an intruder while sitting at the kitchen table. With any luck, they wouldn't look too closely at the lining of the larger suitcase. Even if they did notice Sara's careful stitching and ripped open the seam, they wouldn't find anything. Sara had already removed the two keys hidden inside — one sturdy and square, the other small and brass. As soon as she got a chance, she'd hook them onto her key ring.

She left the door open.

Rain drove at her sideways.

She hurried down the stairs treacherous with spray. She opened her umbrella, a cheap thing she'd bought on sale. The wind tore it instantly from her grasp. She ran, hunched and splashing through ankle-deep puddles. A plastic chair sailed past, newspapers, palm fronds. Something struck her shoulder, whirled away. A siren started up in the distance. She reached her car and slid behind the wheel as thunder boomed.

A silver deluge slammed into the windshield as lightning flared, obscuring the apartment building in front of her, pockets of light glowing here and there. Would the Paradise still be standing in twenty-four hours?

She opened her glove box and removed the GPS. Rolling down her window, she hurled the black box into the storm.

Rolling the window back up, she fumbled the key into the ignition. Rain drummed on the roof. She was drenched and shivering. Without warning, the Paradise vanished. The entire building went black behind the wall of rain. She was surrounded by darkness, only her headlights tunneling through the semidarkness. The ocean was coming. It roared, unseen. At any moment, it would swamp the building, reach around it to flood the courtyard where she sat parked. She shoved the car into reverse and pressed the accelerator. Water sprayed. Another slash of lightning. Sara would never know what made her look up. She'd been so hell-bent on getting out.

CHAPTER 25
WHIT

His parents' house stood among the trees on the narrow road, windows blazing in the gloom. His mother came down the porch steps the moment Whit pulled into the driveway. He climbed out and slammed the door as she ran over. A fine rain had started. The wind whipped at her clothes, dragged hair across her face. She cradled a pair of boots in her arms. Her greeting was a moan of disbelief. "Oh, Whit. What a mess."

She'd aged these past weeks. They all had. "I know. Don't worry. I'll take care of it. Get inside, Mom."

"I found an old pair of your father's waders." He took the dusty pair of black rubber boots and rubber gloves. Leaves came flying, skittering across the glass and sticking. She slapped them away, peering into the backseat. "Where are the children?"

"Sleeping." He bent to yank the boots over his shoes. They were too big, his feet slipping around, but they would do. He jammed the gloves into his pocket, yanked the hood over his head and tightened the string. "I'd better get going. You got a flashlight?"

"Your father's got all of them."

"Where is he?"

"Where do you think? I couldn't talk him out of it."

"Do me a favor, Mom. Could you go back inside, maybe put on some coffee? I could do with another cup."

"You're just trying to keep me busy."

"Is it working?"

Her smile flickered dubiously. "Be careful, honey. Things are flying around." She patted his wet cheek.

A chain saw whined through the trees. An unfamiliar cluster of lights bobbed among the branches. The rain was starting to pick up, tapping all around him. Whit skidded down the muddy slope, catching at branches to slow himself. At the bottom of the yard, he spotted his father's tall, angular form bent awkwardly over the broken half of the dead tree. Standing with one crutch anchored beneath his armpit, his father worked the blade of the chain saw through the wood. The saw skipped and bounced in his grasp.

Whit moved into his father's range of sight

and waited. Wouldn't take anything for his father to lose his balance. His father glanced up, then turned off the saw. As the sound stuttered to silence, the roar of the wind rushed in to fill its place. "Took you long enough." He had a plastic bag duct-taped around his cast.

"Traffic." Whit pushed in among the web of branches as close as he could. His father had twisted snake lights around various branches, aimed their piercing beams toward the twisted mass on the ground. Chunks of concrete lay in the puddled muck. He couldn't tell if the riser beneath was intact. This was an old system. Who knew how sturdy the metal would be? "The hardware store was closed."

His father snorted.

Whit heard the *I told you so.* "How about I take over?"

"Why don't you try and figure out how the hell we're going to cover this thing up?"

Whit found three old truck tires in the shed, a box of heavy-duty garbage bags. He pulled the nail gun from the wall. His father bent and straightened as Whit rolled the tires across the grass, rain falling in curtains. His father glanced over as Whit landed the first tire. "Watch the hell where you step."

"How's it look?" With any luck, the cover

had taken the brunt of the impact.

"Don't know." His father limped around the tree to tackle it from the other side. He'd opened a thick wedge in the fallen tree. His face was wet and gray with fatigue. His leg was hurting, Whit could tell. Whit started to tell him to get inside, bit it back. He knew he'd be wasting his breath.

The rain hammered down as Whit rolled the final tire into place. He was soaked to the bone. He started to run a forearm across his forehead and stopped himself. Who knew what had splashed up onto those branches he was standing among?

His father shut off the saw. The wind shrieked. "Try it now."

Whit worked his way to the chiseled point bisecting the blackened wood. He gripped a thick bough and pressed with all his weight. It held. He repositioned himself, tried again. With a loud crack, the dead tree half dropped the final foot. His father hobbled closer, thrusting the flashlight at him. Whit directed the beam through the branches. The putrid stink of raw sewage made his eyes burn. He tried to breathe through his mouth. He thought of his kids, home sleeping. Safe. "You think any of the cover landed inside?"

"Probably. Put the damn light over there."

Whit redirected the beam. "Riser looks intact."

They both stepped back.

They worked quickly and in silence, throwing the garbage bags over the gaping hole and anchoring the corners with the tires. Wind buffeted the slick plastic surface. Rain slashed, streamed along the chopped-up ground.

Whit eyed their handiwork. All it had to do was keep out the rain. "Think it'll hold?"

His father yanked off his work gloves and thrust them at Whit. "It'll have to."

On crutches, he made his way to the back door, shrugged off his jacket.

Whit rinsed both pairs of gloves beneath the outside spigot, did the same with his boots, shrugging off his windbreaker at the last. Everything needed to be soaked in bleach, but that would have to wait.

"Whit!" His mother's voice sailed to him, shrill with fear.

He looked up. She stood on the deck above, clutching the railing and leaning over to look down at him. He saw her face, and thought — Dad's fallen. Had a heart attack. He's gone.

"There's been an accident. They've closed the Bonner Bridge."

"What about Wright Memorial?"

"I don't know. Whit —"

He turned and ran to his Explorer. Two hours north to the Wright Memorial, along back roads, and another hour or so to the Paradise. Traffic onto the island would be nonexistent. He might be able to make up some time there.

He shot north on narrow roads that zigzagged along the coast. For long stretches, he was the only vehicle on the road. He floored it through swaying red lights, took turns too fast. The sky lightened and the winds calmed. The rain eased. Maybe the storm had stalled. Or shifted away from the Outer Banks. But he got CALL FAILED every time he tried Cassie's cell.

The road curved east. The sky darkened again. Signs for the bridge appeared. He made the final turn, swerved to a sudden stop. A line of police cars, light bars flashing, blocked the bridge entrance. He squinted past them to the wide bridge extending over the churning water. The roadway was clear. It appeared traversable. A cop in yellow rain gear approached, head bent against the wind. Whit powered down the window. Rain shot in, along with the howl of the ocean.

"Bridge is closed, sir."

"My two kids are over there. You have to

let me through." On the opposite side, a pair of headlights glowed fleetingly over the low rise of the bridge, heading away from the island and onto the mainland toward him. They swung right, heading west. A small blue car, a woman behind the wheel. Whit pointed. "It's still open."

The cop glanced over his shoulder, then back at Whit. He shook his head. "Last car we're letting through. Sorry, sir, but you'll have to turn around. There's been flooding —"

"The Bonner's already shut down. Please. They're just kids." They had to be scared out of their minds. The storm had come up faster than predicted. It would have woken them. Boon would be terrified.

"They alone, your kids?"

"Yes. I've been trying to call —"

"Phones are out. Let me see if I can get someone to check on them. Address?"

Whit gave it. The cop thumbed his radio, brought it to his mouth, and turned away. Waves surged against the side of the bridge. Whit had never seen the water so high. He climbed out of the Explorer, squinted. The more northern side of the bridge was a better bet. He'd be driving on the wrong side of the road, but the bridge was empty.

The cop turned back around. "Sir —"

A shout. The cop looked behind him. The ocean had broken through, spewing a flood tide of water across one empty lane, then the other. Helpless, Whit stared over the writhing waves to the faint shadow of land a mere mile away, where his children were, alone. It might as well have been a million miles.

CHAPTER 26
SARA

Sara gripped the steering wheel. Rain pounded the roof. The wipers thudded. Branches somersaulted past — trash cans, a lawn chair. Every hurtling thing made her wince. Any instant, she expected to feel her own car lift into the air and spin away. She had no confidence in it holding itself together. Other vehicles crept in front of her, one disjointed, snaking line. People had to let her in. They had to. A grudging gap formed, and she pressed the accelerator. They jolted forward. "Try him again, Cassie."

"I did. He's not answering."

The cell towers must be down. The kids didn't know where their father was. He couldn't be at work. The hotel must have been evacuated. The only people on today would be emergency responders. He couldn't be out getting supplies. Nothing was open anymore. Cassie kept calling him, without luck. Whit must have gotten caught in traffic, or had car trouble. Maybe he was just an asshole out on a bender. A mailbox bounced past. Something struck the car roof. She flinched, repressing a curse. "Are your seatbelts fastened?"

A shadowy hulk reared up in front of them. A vending machine. She jerked the steering wheel. They bumped onto the shoulder. Water shot up.

"Cassie!"

"Yes!"

The wipers cleared brief arcs. Sara fought to read the highway signs. They drove through town after town, all of them invisible behind the rain and flying objects. Treetops bent sideways. Water streamed across intersections. A man stood on a corner, braced against the wind, his arms opened wide and his face lifted. The billboard above him teetered. The radio sputtered words that droned in and out of focus. Sara crept close to the red blur of taillights in front of her.

"Call your dad again." She should have left him a note. Why hadn't she thought of it? Because they'd been in such a panic. The kids had flung things into backpacks as Sara stood in the doorway and hurried them on. That moment in the courtyard when she'd glanced up at her rearview mirror and glimpsed the two small and solitary figures standing at the railing, looking down — she'd climbed out of her car without thinking. She'd known they were alone. Somehow, she'd absolutely known. She couldn't shout up to them, not over the keening trees and wind's howl. She'd had to run up all those stairs and pound on their door, bent over and gasping for air. Boon had flung his arms around her knees and buried his head against her stomach, his narrow shoulders shaking. *It's okay,* she'd told him, biting back *Where the hell is your dad?* She'd helped them into their raincoats, and Boon had yanked down a coat hanging in the closet for Sara to put on. He'd insisted. Sara had found herself reaching for the silver coat and sliding it on. Underneath, her clothes were drenched.

Somehow, they reached the bridge. Police cruisers and fire trucks seemed to be everywhere, lights spitting sparks of color through the rain. Two state troopers dragged a heavy chain across the bridge. A firefighter approached, waved his flashlight at her. She skewed to a stop and rolled down the window. Rain and wind whipped into the car, and she heard Boon whimper.

The firefighter bent, his face hawklike

beneath his helmet. "Sorry, ma'am. You're going to have to turn around. We're closing this bridge."

"But we have to get across." She wasn't turning around. She wasn't about to be trapped on this narrow spit of land. *30 mins,* Luis had texted. Which meant he and Nicole could have reached the Paradise. The cops would have let the agents through. They could have already searched the lot, issued an APB for her car. At any second, one of these cops could pull a radio closer to his ear, then turn scowling toward Sara.

"You're going to have to go back."

"I've got *kids!*"

A light dazzled her eyes, then darted away, leaving her blinded. "Oh, Christ. Go on, lady. Stick to the middle of the bridge." Was it her imploration, the sight of the kids huddled together in the backseat? Boon's tearful face because oh my God, he wouldn't stop weeping? Whatever it was, it worked.

The firefighter stepped back, waved to the cops. She rolled up the window, touched the accelerator. They skidded forward.

The bridge stretched out before them, four lanes arcing over the water to the distant mainland. More emergency vehicles parked at angles, headlights pulsing through the gloom. Officers in black rain gear waved their flashlights. *Hurry, hurry.* The ocean was now pooling across the roadway. A motorboat toppled over the edge and onto the bridge, twirling in lazy parabolas across the concrete expanse before tipping over the other side and splashing into the water. If the wind could lift a boat that size, what the hell was keeping them from leaving the ground? Why were the police officers still standing? Sara glanced into the rearview mirror and saw that the slick black raincoats had vanished, hidden by the swell of the bridge.

"Try your home number, Cassie. Maybe your dad's there by now."

"I don't know it."

"How can you not know your own home number?"

"Why should I? I never use it."

"I guess we can look it up."

"Good luck. It's unlisted."

"Are you sure?"

"Yes, I'm sure," Cassie mocked. "We were getting calls."

"Mean calls," Boon contributed, sniffling. "Really, really mean. They made Wolf mad."

"Wolf doesn't get mad, stupid," Cassie said.

"Yes, he does!"

"Oh, my God. You are such a moron."

"You're a moron!"

"You don't even know what a moron is."

"Yes, I do, 'cause it's *you*!"

They swept around a long, flat curve. Theirs was the only vehicle on the bridge. Had Sara made a mistake, insisting they cross? The wind buffeted the small car. Rain fell harder. The wipers couldn't keep up. She struggled to see the wavering yellow line spooling out in front of her.

An SUV waited at the opposite end of the bridge, headlights glowing. The driver was talking to a police officer. Another officer waved her through. She held her breath as she drove past. No one even looked over. Her car exited the bridge and coasted through a series of dead stoplights, swaying and bouncing overhead. The traffic had increased. They were on the mainland now. Early afternoon and it was dark as night, rain falling steadily.

"What are we doing?" Cassie demanded. "Where are we going?" Someone's foot thumped the back of Sara's seat.

"I'm looking for a shelter." Sara would follow the cars in front of her. They were looking for safety, too. Surely they would know where to go.

"What's that?" Boon asked.

Rain thundered on the car roof, nearly

drowning out his words. "Shelter's a place where you can stay until the hurricane passes."

The first shelter they came to had lost power. The second one was full. The aid worker turned them away apologetically. *Everyone was caught off guard. Hurricane came in so fast. I'm so sorry.* The woman didn't know where another shelter might be. She had to finish processing the family in front of Sara, but if Sara wanted to wait, she could try to find someone to ask.

But every moment that passed meant another bed was being taken somewhere else, another space filled. Every moment that passed meant a police cruiser might spot her parked car in the lot. Sara wasn't about to waste another second, hoping for information someone might or might not have.

She couldn't tell the woman that. She'd lie, tell her instead that she'd appreciate whatever help she could give. While the woman fussed with her papers and her clipboard and answered her walkie-talkie for the hundredth time, Sara would make some excuse about needing something from the car and leave the kids standing here, then drive off instead. They'd be fine. The aid worker would deal with them.

The aid worker was still waiting for Sara's response. She was committing Sara's face to memory, even if she didn't realize it. The second Sara drove away, she'd call the cops. She'd give them a description. The report would feed through the system. The Feds would hear about it. They'd know Sara had been here. They'd start scouring video feeds.

Sara sucked in a breath. She put on a regretful smile. "That's all right," she said, clamping hands on the kids' shoulders. "We'll just keep going."

"Ouch," Cassie complained, wrenching away from Sara's grasp.

They ran through the rain to where the car was parked at the far reaches of the lot, splashing through puddles, all of them soaked and shivering. Sara didn't look at the sky as she steered her car back onto the crowded highway, but she felt the storm pushing them along. Maybe the kids felt it, too. Their squabble fizzled out. They were finally silent as she drove away.

A head, clustered lights pinpricked the gloom. Sara had blasted the heat until their clothes dried. The car interior smelled damp.

"Sara?" Boon said.

"What?"

"I have to go."

Sara felt a spark of irritation, then realized the kid had sat uncomplaining for hours. "Okay. Hold on." She swung into the parking lot of a sprawl of businesses and parked outside a family restaurant. "Come on. We'll all go in."

The place was loud and bright. Cassie crisply directed her brother toward the men's room and disappeared into the women's. Sara waited in the hallway. It was okay that they were in there alone, wasn't it? Were there rules about how old a kid had to be? People walked past, shaking rain from their coats, closing their umbrellas. No one glanced at her. Still, she took off the borrowed raincoat and folded it inside out, concealing the memorable silver fabric.

Boon pushed open the men's room door, halted in the doorway, then scurried over to Sara, shoelace flapping. "You need to tie your shoes," she told him, and he nodded but didn't move. He had his eyes locked on the entrance to the women's room. A giggling trio of girls in pink sports uniforms streamed out, a gray-haired woman with a walker. Cassie appeared, hesitated, then strolled over. "You can't keep that," she told Sara, meaning the raincoat.

Boon tugged on her sleeve. Sara looked

down at him. "I'm hungry," he said.

Sara glanced to the windows. A rainy afternoon, but the wind had died down. Maybe the hurricane had reached as far inland as it was going to. She could use a cup of coffee, decide what she was going to do with the two of them. "All right," she said. "Let's find something to eat."

The server ushered them to a table in the back. They were lucky, the woman wheezed. Her tan uniform strained at every seam. There was a spatter of flour on her apron. It had been superbusy all morning. They should let her know if they wanted any pie because it was going real fast. They were out of chowder but still had some chicken noodle. The meatloaf was long gone, so were the sirloin tips. She stood there, smiling down at the kids. For a second, Sara saw them through a stranger's eyes: an earnest little boy with round, pink cheeks clutching a bedraggled stuffed toy; a sulky teenager wearing oversize clothes that hung on her skinny frame. When coaxed, Boon admitted in a whisper that he wanted a cheeseburger. Cassie ordered chicken nuggets.

The waitress nodded, jotted a note. "What about you, Mom?"

No one had ever mistaken Sara for a

mother. Cassie snorted, eyes bright with contempt, but said nothing. Sara ordered a cup of coffee. The woman nodded and lumbered away.

The TVs over the bar showed identical Doppler radar images of a huge, swirling white blob. The hurricane had stalled. The governors of North Carolina and Virginia had declared states of emergency. More were expected to follow. It was loud in here, every table filled. People waited at the entrance, rumpled, damp, and impatient. Rain tapped against the glass in static bursts. Maybe they hadn't outrun the hurricane. Sara shivered. Her feet were ice, soaked from the dash across the parking lot. She couldn't remember being so exhausted. "Cassie, what about your grandparents?"

"What about them?" The girl slouched in her seat, shredding her napkin. Boon was coloring the paper placemat, frowning fiercely, giving the princess a purple face and making the sky orange. His stuffed animal leaned against Boon's arm, watching with plastic eyes, one dangling. The toy was grimy, its fur matted and stained. Sara was too tired to tell him to take the thing off the table.

"Where do they live? Is it far? Maybe I could drive you there."

"Their house is white. It has gray shutters." Cassie was distracted, watching people at the other tables. Her damp hair hung down her back. She had her finger in her mouth, gnawing at the cuticle. Sara longed to smack her hand down.

"Okay, well, don't you know the address?"

"Nope."

"You really don't know the address?"

"I really don't know the address," Cassie mimicked. She picked at her thumbnail, scraped off a flake of polish.

Well, maybe she didn't. "What about the town they live in?"

"No clue."

Sara eyed her, turned to Boon. "What about you? Do you know what town your grandparents live in?"

He gripped a black crayon by its neck, drawing wavy lines around the girl's face, boxing her in. "Um. They have a turtle sandbox."

Sara drank weak, tepid coffee, as if the machine hadn't even tried. "What about their names?"

"Grandma and Grandpa."

"No, their real names. Cassie?"

The girl shrugged. "Grandma. Grandpa."

"You don't have a last name?"

"Same as ours."

"Which is?"

Cassie smirked. Did she think this was a game? Sara reached out and grabbed the girl's wrist, her fingers easily encircling the thin bones. "I asked you what your last name was."

Startled, Cassie raised light brown eyes to Sara's. "Nelson."

Boon was staring at Sara, eyes wide, crayon loose between his fingers.

Right. Whit had told her. *Whit Nelson*, he'd said, shaking her hand. A common name. Too common. Sara released the girl's wrist, took a breath. "Do you know their phone number?"

Cassie leaned back, rubbing her wrist pointedly. "No."

"You don't have your grandparents' phone number?"

"No. Just my dad's. See?" Cassie thrust out her phone to show Sara the screen, triumphant.

Why the hell did people even want kids?

The food arrived. Boon eyed his plate, waiting for something. Permission? "Why aren't you eating?" Sara asked.

Cassie splatted enough ketchup onto her plate to feed a small nation. "He's scared of you."

Sara sighed, tapped the boy's placemat.

"Go ahead. Eat."

Obediently, he picked up his burger with both hands. Melted cheese glopped down onto the plate.

Sara watched the people around them, leaning close to talk to one another, or riveted by the TV screens. Over by the hostess stand, a woman in a brilliant emerald sari jiggled a howling baby, her hand cupped against the back of the child's head. The restaurant door opened, admitting a blast of cold wind and a cluster of dazed-looking senior citizens. No one glanced back at Sara. No one stood out as anything but a wet and frazzled refugee from the storm.

"What about your caseworker?"

"Who?" Cassie said around a mouthful.

Sara searched for the name. "Robin." Caseworkers wouldn't be listed by name on the county directory. Sara would have to call the main number and hope someone could help her. Not now, of course, but as soon as the office reopened. She wondered when that might be. Days, probably. The TVs were showing palm trees blowing sideways. "Do you have Robin's phone number?" The caseworker would have given it to Cassie, pressed the card into the girl's palm and told her very seriously that she could call her anytime, day or night.

The girl dragged a chicken nugget through the pond of ketchup, lifted it drenched. "Not with me."

The waitress slapped the bill on the table. "I'm real sorry to hurry you folks along, but we're closing. Raleigh's getting wind gusts up to seventy."

They'd just driven through Raleigh. Sara looked out the window. Headlights swept through slanted rain. She dreaded getting back into her car. "Of course. No problem. Do you know how the roads are?"

The woman adjusted the headband above her shiny forehead. "Ninety-five's shut down both ways. Far as I know, Forty's still open. At least I hope it is. That's my route home." The lights flickered and she gasped. "Oh, Lord. I'd better check on my other tables. You folks be real careful now."

They wrapped Boon's cheeseburger and Cassie's chicken nuggets in paper napkins and dashed across the lot through the cold rain. Sara opened the driver's door, then belatedly realized Boon needed help with his rear door. Rain drove hard against the hood and shoulders of the silver raincoat as she swung open the door for him. He seemed to take forever to climb inside and swing his legs free of the door. She slammed it behind him and ducked into her own seat.

She shook off the raincoat and tossed it on the seat beside her.

"Where are we going?" Cassie demanded.

"I don't know." Sara turned the key in the ignition. The engine coughed, then caught. She pulled her car out of the parking space and eased into the queue of vehicles waiting to enter onto the highway choked with slow-moving traffic. Everyone, it seemed, was headed west. She couldn't leave the kids at a rest stop. There'd be cameras, aimed at the parking lot, fixed to stoplights. Even if she managed to avoid detection, her car wouldn't. Damn it.

"What do you mean you don't know?"

"Just that."

"So we're just driving around? I thought we were looking for a *shelter.*"

"We were." She peered through the foggy rain. Her headlights flickered. She was driving blind. Literally.

"But we're not now?"

"I doubt there are any shelters out here." She needed to get off the major arteries, find someplace off the beaten path, where she could hole up and figure out how she was going to get hold of a new car. She couldn't do that with two kids. She should have left them at that shelter or at the restaurant, taken her chances. But here she was.

"This is crazy. We don't even know you."

"I didn't have to take you with me, Cassie. I could have left you at the Paradise." Without warning, the pickup beside them swerved into their lane. Sara swung the steering wheel to avoid a collision. A rooster tail of water sprayed across her windshield.

"No one asked you to!"

Sara flicked the wipers to a higher speed. "You haven't said thank you. Not once."

"Thank *you,* Sara. Thank *you* so very much. You're amazing. When I grow up, I want to be just like you."

"Jesus, Cassie. No wonder your mother left you. If I was your mother, I'd have done the same thing."

A shocked silence, then Cassie muttered. "Wow, what a bitch."

Boon was staring at her in the rearview mirror, his eyes starting to fill. She'd frightened him. Again. Did she have to watch everything she said? Had she been that thin-skinned as a child? She doubted it. Her father would never have stood for any emotion that slowed him down. They'd been a team. She'd prided herself on that. Sara took a soft breath and pushed down her irritation. "We're going to have to play it by ear. Maybe your dad can meet us some-where. Okay?"

Boon clutched his stuffed toy, eyes on her face. He nodded. Cassie was scowling out the window at the lashing rain, deliberately mute.

"Try your dad again, Cassie." The man would answer his phone. He'd be desperately looking for his kids, wondering where the hell they were.

Chapter 27
Whit

"Cassie's a smart girl." His mother struck a match and held it to the burner beneath the pot. The kitchen leaped with shadows. They'd lost power hours before. Candles stood here and there. The wind shrieked outside. "She'll figure out something."

He was bone-tired. Did he imagine the faint stench of sewage hanging around him? His hands ached from gripping the steering wheel. His left eye twitched. He'd been driving into the storm instead of out of it. It had taken hours to retrace his steps. Three o'clock in the afternoon. Felt like the middle of the night. "Cassie's just a kid." Playing grown-up in a skimpy bikini, hanging out with kids way too old for her. Beneath it all, a little girl. But she knew to stay clear of the windows, didn't she? He tried to push away the image of something crashing through the glass, spraying the kids with jagged shards.

"She's been through storms before. She'll sit tight."

"She won't know what to do if the power goes off."

"For all we know, honey, the power's still on."

They knew nothing. They sat in the dark as the storm battered the windows. They were almost fifty miles inland. It would be far worse on the Outer Banks. Boon would be sobbing. Cassie would be helpless with fear. He picked up his phone and pressed redial. Nothing.

"The Paradise has been around for years, Whit. It's withstood plenty of hurricanes. And they're on the top floor. There's no way the water could reach that high."

The Paradise wasn't a fortress. The windows could explode. A gas line could break. He pinched the bridge of his nose, sucked in some shallow breaths, tried not to think of them trapped in a fire. Four stories up — what would they do?

"Bet you one of your neighbors took them in." His mother ladled soup into bowls, set one on a tray. His father had reinjured himself that morning, tripped as he came into the house, going down hard on the kitchen floor. He wouldn't let her near enough to check how bad. He'd taken a couple aspirins and hobbled off to the back bedroom. From time to time, she went to check on him, returned with her lips pressed in a tight line.

Who would think to check on his kids? They didn't know their neighbors. It wasn't that kind of community. Whit had stood staring at the water raging across the bridge until the cop had yelled at him to get back. He'd checked the shelters, waited with hope lodged in his throat while aid workers thumbed through index cards and scanned clipboards, only to look up at Whit and shake their heads. One of them had rested her hand on his arm. *What about you, Mr. Nelson? Where are you staying?*

"The police are aware of the situation, Whit. As soon as they can, they'll check on them. And then they'll let you know." She placed a bowl in front of him. "Eat."

He looked down. Tomato soup. His kids had dry cereal, marshmallows, junk food. His stomach clenched.

"Please, honey. You need to keep up your strength."

He had no strength. It took everything he had to pick up the phone again. He called the number the cop on the bridge had given him. It rang endlessly. Maybe everyone was out dealing with the hurricane. Maybe the phone line had been knocked out of service. He turned off the phone, set it back down.

She sat and clasped his hands between icy fingers. Her face sagged. She looked so old. She was worrying, too, he reminded himself. "We'll know more soon," he made himself say, feeling like it was a lie when she glanced up at him, startled.

His entire life, his mother had cast out reassurances that meant nothing. *Your father will come around. He just wants the best for you. Stick with it, honey. Hard work always pays off. Believe in yourself.* Meaningless words. It was when she didn't say anything — that long, gasping silence — that Whit felt his stomach curdle with true terror. That night six weeks before, he had pressed the phone to his ear, terrified and heartsick, and waiting for her to say something, anything. Finally, she had said, *Come here. Your father and I will help you.*

And she had, hadn't she? They had. Here they were, the three of them, bound together by ties that went against all nature.

"Honey." His mother's voice was gentle. "You need to stop torturing yourself."

A horror flick, that tide of water shooting across four lanes of highway. He'd left his kids unprotected in that. When would the bridges be traversable? Would anything be left of the towns up and down the Outer Banks? Something occurred to him. "I'll take Dad's boat."

"Don't be foolish, Whit. It's a fishing boat."

"I can't just sit here."

"You can't put that boat in a hurricane. Be realistic, please."

"It's only a mile of open water. I'll take it slow."

"Think it through, for pity's sake. Something happens to you, where will your children be then?"

"Nothing's going to happen to me."

"Wanting that to be true doesn't make it so." She stood abruptly, picked up the tray, and went down the hall.

He thought of the note he'd left the kids. He had signed it *Dad.* Nothing about love. Just last week, he'd forgotten his own son's birthday. Cassie had texted him at work, accusation vibrating through every typed word, and he'd hurriedly stopped for an ice cream cake on the way home, gone into the toy section and blankly looked at the shelves. He couldn't remember what Lego sets Boon already had. He didn't know if his son was too old for Play-Doh, too young for a telescope. That had been Diane's domain. She had prided herself on knowing exactly what to give their children, what was the latest thing and where to find it on sale.

Whit had tried everything. He'd worked to control his temper. He'd stuck by Diane, even after she almost killed their son. He'd swallowed insult after insult to hold on to a job to provide for his family. But in the end, the ugly truth was plain. He had turned out exactly like his old man.

Whit shoved his chair back, went to the window, pushed aside the curtain. The trees thrashed against the sky. Down at the bottom of the hill lay the fallen tree, not visible from this vantage point. Next door, a man in a flapping windbreaker ran up his porch steps. The front door quickly opened to admit him. Whit imagined the man's family welcoming him home. They'd been worried for his safety. They'd pummel him with questions. When would the power resume? Would they lose the roof? Their normal lives.

What Whit wouldn't give to go back to a normal time.

What if that night hadn't happened? All the mistakes he'd made. He was the worst kind of father.

"Whit!" his mother called. "Your father's not in the bedroom."

Whit spun away from the window, hurried toward her urgent voice. In the hall, her face was stricken, shadows leaping from the flashlight she carried. "Where is he?"

"I don't know, Whit. I didn't hear him leave."

"He's gone to the police."

"No. He would never do that."

"That's exactly the damn stupid kind of thing he would do."

"Oh, Whit. No. Don't say that."

"How did he do it? Did someone pick him up?"

"Who, Whit?"

It was true. His father had no friends. But he had people who owed him, which he considered better than friendship. *Can't count on a person's good side.* He'd said it more than once. *But you can always count on their bad side.* People told lies for all sorts of reasons. Whit's father collected them like currency, trading them in when it suited him. He must have decided that it was time to turn Whit in. Teaching him a lesson, maybe. Showing him who was boss.

Whit was already yanking on his boots. He grabbed his jacket from the closet, opened the front door. The wind lashed in. He shook off his mother's clutching hand, stepped onto the porch.

He had to get to his kids. Steal a boat, find a way around the police barricades.

He'd get to his kids and then he'd figure out what to do. His father only thought he knew what had happened to Dee.

CHAPTER 28
SARA

They wound up at the fourth place Sara tried, a dismal little two-story motel in the Appalachian foothills. Sara had given her name, shown her driver's license. But when the woman at the front desk then asked for a credit card, Sara explained how she'd left the house without her cards. Any chance she could pay cash? The woman had started to shake her head just like the other three desk clerks had. But Sara had glimpsed that instant of hesitation. She'd glanced meaningfully to Boon crouched over the gumball machine and Cassie leaning against the wall, her arms crossed as usual, and murmured, *My husband . . .* The clerk had straightened, looked at the children, then back at Sara. *I'll give you a room in the back. You can't see it from the road.* Joyce, her name was. She owned the place, she said. Sara had spotted the sign from the highway, almost swallowed by overgrowth. The Step

On Inn. Joyce patted Sara's hand after she passed along the old-fashioned metal key, feeling a kinship that wasn't there. Sara had felt the surge of relief that came with finding her footing. She hadn't lost her skill at spinning straw into gold. And these two kids were very much straw — bedraggled, irritating bits that clung to hair and skin, dug beneath fingernails.

Sara fit the key into the lock and turned. She swung open the door to the smell of must layered with bleach, reached in to switch on the overhead light. The room sprang into dimension — two sagging beds, cheap wood-paneled walls, an ancient TV squatting on the dresser. No one had stayed in this room for a long time. No one would be looking for her here.

Cassie shoved past Sara, digging her with the sharp point of her elbow. She'd done it on purpose, Sara knew — getting back at her for the wrist incident. The girl raced to the bathroom, screeching, "Dibs!" The door banged behind her. The lock turned with a decisive click.

"She always does that." Boon dumped his backpack on the floor, shrugged off his windbreaker and let it drop. He kicked off his sneakers and, holding his stuffed dog by the scruff, walked it around the room as if giving it the grand tour. Wolf peered into the closet, crawled under the bed, opened the desk drawer and sniffed around, noisily.

Sara turned on the air conditioner to clear out the mustiness, then slumped down on one of the two double beds. She kicked off her shoes and settled back against the headboard. The pillows were thin. She reached for the remote. The hurricane was inching up the Carolina coast. Virginia was braced for impact. Hundreds of thousands were without power. Damage estimates were mounting. Homes had been washed out to sea. People were feared lost. The weather forecasters were reveling in the chaos of it.

Boon climbed up on the bed and pressed beside her. He smelled of rain. He held out his precious dog, stiff-legged and rank, improbable pink tongue now gray and dingy glued to an open mouth. "You want to hold Wolf?"

Did she look like someone who cuddled with toys, especially one so threadbare? She'd never even had a doll, though she remembered a brief time when she'd longed for one. She'd dropped hints her father never picked up on. "No. But thank you."

"Okay." He stared at her uneasily, then reached up and traced a tentative fingertip along her chin. It wasn't unpleasant, not exactly, but Sara wasn't a fan of being touched. "Did that hurt?"

"I don't think so. I don't remember how I got it." The scar had always been there. She no longer saw it when she looked in the mirror.

He tilted his chin and showed her his matching scar. "We're twins."

"How did that happen?"

"I fell."

She probably had, too. Had she gotten stitches? She would never know. He cradled Wolf under his arm and stuck his thumb in his mouth. His hand was as filthy as his toy, the fingernails rimed with dirt and ketchup. Sara tapped his wrist. "Better wash that hand first."

" 'Kay," he mumbled but kept his thumb firmly in place.

She had to shake him awake when Cassie finally emerged noisily from the bathroom in a blast of scent. She wore the same black flannel shirt she'd worn all day, hanging to her bare knees. Flecks of mascara dotted the tops of her cheeks. "We're out of shampoo," she announced blithely.

Perfect. "All right, Boon. Your turn in the shower. Use bar soap to wash your hair."

Cassie stood in front of the closet door,

opened to reveal a smudged full-length mirror. She dragged her fingers through her damp, clotted tangles, scowled at her reflection. She licked her finger, rubbed beneath her eyes. "You have to run him a bath."

Sara looked at the boy, half asleep on the edge of the bed. She'd never given anyone a bath. How did this work? Was it wrong for a stranger to bathe a young boy? Would their father be okay with it? "Come on, Boon. A bath sounds like fun." Had that been the wrong thing to say? Did it smack of creep?

But Boon followed her docilely into the bathroom. The small space looked like the hurricane had been through there instead of outside. Wet towels puddled on the floor; a container of shampoo dribbled in the tub. The hair dryer sat on the side of the sink, trailing a coiled black cord. Wadded tissues overflowed the trash can. Sara cleared out the tub, retrieved the towels, and shook them out before hanging them back on the rack. She kneeled to turn on the water. Boon perched on the toilet seat and watched her. She shut off the water, dipped in a finger. "This feels good to me. What do you think?"

He leaned forward to test it solemnly with the tip of his finger. "Too hot."

She ran cold water into the tub. "Try again."

"Too cold." He shivered dramatically.

"This isn't like Goldilocks, you know." She ran some more hot water in and swirled it all around. "It's fine now. Can you get into the tub by yourself?"

"Uh-huh."

"And your dad lets you?"

"Uh-huh."

"All right. This is what we're going to do. I'll leave, and you get undressed. I'll wait right outside. Call me if you need any help."

" 'Kay."

He watched her go without moving. She closed the door behind her and heard the firm click of the door lock. Too late, she thought about what he'd put on when he climbed out of the tub. "Do you need your pajamas?" she called. He didn't answer. "Boon?"

"He's not supposed to be in there by himself." Cassie was still studying herself in the mirror, inches from the glass, her chin tilted, eyes narrowed, judgmentally.

"He's not?"

"He splashes water on the floor."

Sara shrugged.

"He splashes *a lot* of water on the floor."

Sara rapped on the door. "Boon, open up."

"I'm 'kay" came the cheerful call.

"Your sister says you're not supposed to be in there alone."

"Yes, I am."

Did all kids lie? "Boon."

"I'm taking a bath."

Sara glanced at the clock. Eight P.M. "Try your dad again," she told Cassie.

"I told you. He's not answering." The girl draped herself across the bed and changed the channel to a reality TV show featuring a bunch of chefs running around banging pots onto stovetops. She didn't seem the least bit worried about her father. She was surely old enough to understand the gravity of the situation, but there had been no tears, not a single anxious question. Well, that was what happened when a mother took off. Sara's own mom had left thirteen-month-old Sara on a church pew and walked away forever. Sara had never missed what she hadn't known. She'd had her father, and he had been enough. He had always been there for her, except at the very end, when he couldn't. Still, Sara had understood early that in order to survive, the only person you could ever truly count on was yourself. "The cell towers are probably down."

Cassie shrugged.

"You have no idea where your dad went?"

Cassie's phone hadn't rung. Had their father tried, only to find himself without service? Had he even made it home to find his children vanished? It was possible he was trapped by the storm. Or worse, hurt.

"No. I told you." Cassie raised the remote. Now Sara found herself watching two naked people with blurred body parts tromping through a jungle. Their faces were smeared with mud, their skin bumpy with bug bites.

What kind of father left two kids alone in a hurricane? Well, Sara's own dad had left her alone plenty of times. And she'd been far younger than Cassie.

The bathroom door slammed open. Boon stood there pink-cheeked and very wet, towel bunched around his waist. He stood contentedly as Sara dried him, bashing the empty bottles of shampoo and conditioner at one another, a soggy Wolf tucked under his arm. Apparently, the toy had gotten a good soak, too. Sara dug in his backpack for his pajamas, and he pulled them on before climbing happily into the bed beside his sister. Cassie complained loudly that he'd better get his stinky feet away from her or else. Groaning, she rolled onto her side and dragged a pillow over her head.

"What are we doing tomorrow?" Boon sat cross-legged with Wolf in his arms, watching Sara as she looked around for her bag.

She found it on the chair by the desk. It was damp from rain, but water hadn't reached inside. Her laptop was okay, and so were her clothes. "Well, hopefully we'll reach your father."

"Then what?"

"Then he'll come get you." Sara retrieved the remote from the floor where Cassie had dropped it and switched off the TV.

"What if he doesn't?"

"He will."

"What if he doesn't?"

"Then I'll take you to the authorities." She'd have to figure out a way to manage that. Not here. Not in this little town where Joyce at the Step On Inn would helpfully tell the local cops all about the desperate mother hiding from her husband. She'd have to bundle them into the car, drive a couple towns away. She'd leave them a block from the station and get on the highway as quickly as possible. She'd have some time while the police questioned the kids and tried to figure out how they'd gotten there. Fifteen minutes, maybe thirty? The cops' first reaction, as Sara knew from her own childhood, was to assume a kid had things wrong. *Not your mom,* they'd repeat. *How did you get here?* they'd ask. The kids knew only Sara's first name. Chances were good they wouldn't be able to describe her car. They certainly wouldn't have memorized her plate number.

"What's the . . . 'thorities?"

"The police."

"But I don't want to go!"

"Why not?" Didn't they teach kids that cops were their friends? They certainly had when Sara was in school, though it had been a lesson her father had quickly revised. *You ever get in trouble,* he told her, *you come to me. Never the cops.* If he were still alive, he'd be furious with her. He wouldn't listen to her explanations that she'd had no choice but to work with the Feds. He'd jeer at her plans to outwit them.

Boon shrugged. He wouldn't meet her eyes. He scratched his arm. The rash looked angry. Should she put something on it?

"No one's going to arrest you. You're not in trouble."

"I know." He scratched more furiously.

"Well, it's the only way you're getting back to your dad. And will you stop scratching, for God's sake. You're making yourself bleed."

He let his hand fall to his lap. "Can't we stay with you?"

"Absolutely not. This isn't a vacation, you know."

Boon considered that, started to scratch, then lay down and put his small, rounded back to her.

Sara turned off the light. The room settled to the cough and wheeze of the air-conditioning unit.

She went into the bathroom and closed the door. The tiles were puddled with water, the sink inexplicably stoppered and brimming. She dragged a towel across the floor to clean up the worst of it, and drained the sink. As the water gurgled down the pipes, she pulled on a nightgown, brushed her teeth. She flipped off the light and came back into the room. She heard a stealthy sound behind her and turned to see Boon crawling on his hands and knees into the closet. What on earth was he doing? Sleepwalking? The door closed slowly behind him.

"Leave him alone." Cassie's voice was muffled.

Sara walked over and opened the closet door. Boon lay curled inside, his knees drawn to his chest, Wolf beneath his chin. His eyes were open, gleaming in the darkness. "Hey, what are you doing in here?" she asked softly.

"Nothing."

"Come out and go to bed."

"I'm okay," he insisted and gripped Wolf closer.

Was it all right to let him sleep there? Should she try to force him back into bed? Cassie had hoisted herself up onto an elbow, watching her. "I'm not moving him," Sara told her, hearing the edge in her voice. Cassie flopped down, glaring. Ignoring her, Sara removed the blanket from her bed and the extra pillow, and tucked Boon into the folds, settled the pillow beneath his head. "That good?"

"Uh-huh." He closed his eyes. He did seem perfectly content. How did parents deal with the upheaval? Why the hell would anyone *want* to?

She climbed into bed and pulled the thin sheet up to her chin. She couldn't remember ever being so tired. Was it still Friday? It felt like years since she'd driven away from the Paradise, but it had been only hours before. She'd lucked out finding this place. She'd be safe tonight. Fifty-six hours to go before the bank opened Monday morning.

She sighed, searched through the darkness for sleep. Seemed like she'd been running her entire life.

CHAPTER 29
WHIT

Rain sheeted down. The loud rumble of an engine. Whit halted on the porch. He looked up toward the road. Headlights bounced between the fogged trees. From this distance, he couldn't make out what sort of vehicle it was, but it was headed toward them with purpose. His mother came out to stand beside him, dragging her coat around her shoulders. Together they watched the headlights coalesce into high-mounted bulbs. Then a huge vehicle appeared, rearing up out of the downpour and turning in to the driveway. Tires tall as a man, box-shaped cab perched on top. It lumbered off the pavement and sank into the soft earth of the side yard, shifting side to side, crackling branches and churning up mud. As the backhoe rocked past, Whit caught a glimpse of the driver: his father, sitting high and working the gears, his cast stretched out before him, his face obscured beneath the brim of his cap. Whit watched in disbelief as the backhoe disappeared around the side of the house into the thin trees beyond.

His mother patted Whit's arm. "I better put on another pot of coffee."

By the time Whit joined his father, maples and poplars lay strewn like matchsticks on the sodden ground. His father labored between them, struggling to heave up the tires Whit had rolled down the hill to anchor the plastic sheeting, now whipping freely. The wind drove the rain through the branches to strike his head and shoulders. He tightened the cord around his hood and knotted it.

His father put the backhoe in neutral, leaned back on one hip. He had his leg propped to the side, his bare toes peeping out above the mud-spattered plaster. "What the hell are you doing here?"

Whit could ask him the same thing. "Both bridges are closed. I couldn't get across."

"So you left your kids." His father snorted. "Came running home to Mommy."

Growing up, Whit had admired his father as much as he'd feared him. No one pushed the man around, not a demanding boss, not some smart aleck in a bar. With all his heart, Whit wanted to be the same, tried to be strong the way he thought his father was.

When Cassie was born, he suddenly understood that what he'd once considered strength was obstinacy, what he'd seen as power was in fact cowardice. Now he told himself not to rise to the bait. "I thought you were resting."

"Sure. Let this mess take care of itself. Like you always do. The sheeting was already coming loose."

It was a fairly new machine, in pretty good condition. Not a rental. Then Whit got it. "You took that from the site?"

"They won't miss it."

A roll of plastic sheeting stood propped against the split pine. A cement cover and riser lay off to the side, atop a mashed bed of dead leaves. Probably stole that, too. Another scattering of raindrops. Branches thrashed. The storm was getting closer. "You shouldn't be doing this. You're getting that cast wet." His mom didn't need the worry.

"Who else is going to do it?"

"I will." Whit could at least remove the tires.

His father's mouth curved in a sneer. "You don't know the first damn thing about driving one of these things."

It didn't look that complicated. A lever to operate the bucket, a steering wheel. "I could give it a try."

"Yeah, sure. And we'd be here all night."

A screen door clapped. Whit glanced through the trees to the house next door, didn't see anyone. "Someone's watching."

"Let 'em."

"You're a stubborn bastard."

"You're one to talk. You've been bad luck since the day you were born."

"Yeah, you were doing so well before I was born." He'd been barely making ends meet, his temper keeping him from holding down a steady job. Whit was the reason his mother went back to school for her nursing degree.

"You always figured you were better than me." His father slammed the backhoe into gear. The huge wheels sank in the mud.

"Hold on." Whit grabbed the roll of plastic, flung out a few yards, spread it down behind the tires. "Try it now."

His father spun the steering wheel. The machine groaned, heaved itself backward, spattering mud. A branch crashed to the ground. "Get that crap out of the way, unless you're scared of getting dirty."

"Fuck you, old man." Whit yanked the branch in a deluge of dripping leaves.

His father grunted. "When we're done with this, I never want to see you again."

"Fine by me."

That night, Whit had paced his apartment, then snatched up the phone and called his parents. His mother had listened without interrupting as Whit told her Diane was dead. *It was an accident,* he said brokenly, needing her to understand. A horrible, unbelievable accident. *Come here,* his mother said. *Your father and I will help you.*

The bucket swung through the trees. Whit leaped back. His father sniggered, lowered the swaying bucket to the churned ground, everything in him channeled down into that deep, dark, stinking hole where Whit and his father had worked sixty-five days before to push Diane's body, her long blond hair going last, a fishtail of beauty slithering over the riser's edge and sinking into the filthy septic tank below.

His parents had gone to bed. The house was dark and cold. Rain rapped on the roof. Trees shivered in the wind. Unable to sleep, Whit was on his way to the kitchen when flashing lights filled the hallway. He moved to the window and saw the source: police cruisers, two of them, parked outside, light bars spinning. A uniformed officer was already thumping up the porch steps. Whit's first thought was that they'd found his kids.

He flung the door open. The officer standing there held up a brass badge. "Whitfield Nelson?" His face was grim.

In that moment, seeing how the officer stood with his hand near his gun, how the other officers behind him peered over Whit's shoulder into the darkness of the house beyond, Whit understood instantly the police weren't there about his kids. They were there for him.

Three looped lollipops from the bank —
purple, red, and green — in shiny wrappers pressed flat. Only one is cracked in
pieces.

CHAPTER 30
CASSIE

Cassie didn't know how she'd ended up in a crappy motel room with the Bitch lying in the bed beside hers. Well, of course she *knew.* She'd been there when the Bitch banged on the apartment door that morning; she'd been the one to shine that idiotic flashlight their dad had bought across the room as Sara stood in the doorway, rain blowing in and puddling. The legs of her jeans were soaking wet, her red hair plastered against her cheeks, her mean eyes. *You can't stay here alone,* she'd said, and in the space of those few words, Cassie had heard so much more.

She'd gone down those rain-slicked stairs on her own two feet behind Sara, clutching fast to the railing so the wind didn't scoop her up and carry her away. She'd curled herself in that stupid, cramped backseat and stared out the window at everything flying around them in the storm, listening to the

Bitch curse under her breath and Boon sing stupid made-up songs and hold conversations with Wolf, a pathetic monologue with responses only her dumb little brother could hear. He missed his booster seat, he'd whispered to Cassie, and she'd told him to shut up. So he'd ridden around beside her, sitting so low the seatbelt cut across his chin. She'd smacked his hand away each time he'd reached for her. At least he hadn't begged Sara to roll down the windows a few inches. At least there was that.

She'd climbed in and out of that piece of crap car into the pouring rain, so the Bitch could pick out a motel, each one crappier than the one before. Cassie had showered in that revolting tub, careful not to touch any surface she didn't have to, dried herself on those scratchy towels that reeked of fabric softener. Now her entire body reeked. So she did know exactly *how* she'd ended up here. What she couldn't explain was *why*.

Rain tapped against the motel window. The air conditioner rattled and hummed, frigid air whooshing into the room in stale bursts. She burrowed deeper, shivering. She grew warmer, then suddenly hot. As soon as she kicked off the covers, her skin prickled with goosebumps, and she had to yank the stupid sheets back up again.

Lexi had texted that morning. *Party!* Which meant Lexi's stepdad was hosting. Lexi's stepdad was kind of creepy, the way he laughed at everything everyone said, but he never charged for the beer. Not like Mikey P's sister, who made everyone pay before she went into the liquor store. When Lexi's text arrived, Cassie had gone to the window. Things were really blowing around out there. The rain was really coming down, too, striking the Paradise, and flooding the alley far below. Did she really want to walk in that? But she hated the way she'd left things the day before, her dad yelling at everyone, telling Cassie to cover up for Christ's sake. She glanced to Boon, on the couch and sucking his revolting thumb. He'd be fine, she'd decided, but the minute she went to the front door, he was there, pulling at her and wanting to know where she was going. She tried to shake him off, but he snatched at her sleeve, her shirt. *You can't leave,* he sobbed. *Don't leave.*

Something inside of her broke. *You're turning out just like your mother.*

All right, all right. Calm down, she told her brother. She'd stay until their dad got home — another *why* she couldn't explain. How was she going to sneak off to a party once their dad came home? He'd left a note stuck to the fridge. *Stay put,* he'd written. *Be back soon.*

A big, fat lie. Hours had passed. Was he home now? She hoped so. She hoped he was all alone, and freaking out about where they were. The Bitch sure seemed to think so.

Sara was a motionless lump in the bed. Cassie couldn't tell if she was asleep. Maybe she was in a coma. Cassie almost hoped she was.

"Sara?" Cassie whispered, and when there was no answer, she slid out of bed. Sara lay with her back to Cassie, her hair fanned across the pillow. Cassie was pretty sure that if she gave Sara's shoulder the slightest touch, Sara would be awake like a shot. Cassie reached for her jeans on the floor and pulled them on, quietly.

They'd all been responsible the night before for bringing in their own things, even Boon lugging his crappy backpack bulging with Lego and action figures. Cassie had stowed her own backpack under her bed and slid her purse under her pillow. The Bitch had left her bag on the chair by the desk.

Cassie padded across the oily-feeling carpet to the large canvas bag with the sturdy green handles, and tipped it toward her. The contents shifted, revealing the pale

312

block of a packet of tissues, a wooden-handled hairbrush, an interesting item that looked like a pen, but when Cassie held it up, squinting in the darkness, she found it was in fact a screwdriver. A canister of red pepper spray, a heavy black flashlight that looked like it meant business. A pocketknife with blades, corkscrew, nail file, and scissors. A roll of duct tape. Two protein bars. A silver laptop, which she opened, hoping against hope, only to find it was password-protected. Sara's wallet, thick with bills.

Cassie peeked across the darkened room. The Bitch lay utterly still. The closet door remained shut. Once Boon had moved into the closet for the night, he stayed there.

She carried the wallet to the lone window and hooked open one side of the heavy drapes just wide enough to let in a sliver of pee-colored light from the overhead bulb outside their door. Four hundred and twelve dollars. More money than Cassie had ever seen in her life. There was a credit card, a Visa card that Sara had signed on the back. Cassie's mom had a lot of credit cards. She was always filling out forms and sending them in. Cassie's dad tried to catch the offers before they arrived. There was also a North Carolina driver's license.

Sara had been born around thirty years

ago. She was five foot seven and weighed 112 pounds. Her eyes were brown, her hair auburn. She didn't smile for her picture. She signed her name Sara Lennox, the two names joined together in one flowing wave.

Cassie returned the wallet, pulled out a small bag of cosmetics, a neatly folded bundle of clothes: another pair of jeans, a couple blouses, underwear.

Two books lay beneath the clothes: *The Secret Garden* and *A Little Princess.* The pages were soft with age. They had drawings of girls in old-fashioned dresses. Cassie soundlessly turned pages, wondering why the Bitch was carrying around two beat-up old kids' books. She stopped at a bit of newspaper wedged into the spine. She pulled it out and unfolded it. A black-and-white close-up of a man's face. His dark hair was parted on the side and waved back. His eyes were smart and serious, his mouth curved in an almost smile. He wore a collared shirt, just the knot of his tie visible. He didn't stare straight at the camera, but slightly away, like he was holding on to a secret. He looked like Sara. Cassie turned the piece of paper over, found an ad for a vacuum cleaner.

In the bag's inside pocket, she found a ring of keys. A car key, a house key just like

Cassie's, a weird square one, a small brass one, and two tiny ones. She fingered the last two, toy-sized. She'd spent enough time trailing after her dad at the Seaside. She knew what a suitcase key looked like. But Sara didn't have any suitcases with her.

Frowning, Cassie carefully put everything back. She straightened the drape. The room fell back into darkness. The room was still. She was the only one awake. She tiptoed to the door and slowly dragged the chain across the metal plate, wincing each time it rattled. Chains were useless, her dad told her. Any thief could cut them in half and be in the room in a heartbeat. Solid metal bars were best. She turned the doorknob and stepped out into cold, foggy drizzle. The overhead light shone yellow on the front bumper of the blue car. Everything beyond it was lost in the rain. But out there were the mountains.

Her mom had taken her and Boon to the mountains once — maybe these same ones. The road had swooped and spiraled, climbing closer and closer to the clouds. Cassie sat in the front seat with Boon on her lap and ate saltwater taffy and told knock-knock jokes. She'd been young enough to think they'd actually get where they were going. But then Boon got carsick and the car broke down and Cassie's dad had to be called. He hugged Cassie and Boon hard, right there on the side of the road, then pulled their mom aside by her elbow. Cassie had heard what he'd said. *What the hell's the matter with you, Dee?*

Her mom didn't listen. She never listened. It didn't matter what anyone else said. Her mom had all sorts of plans. She wanted to take them to see Mickey Mouse, Luray Caverns. Once, she dropped them off at Grandma Helen's and drove away before Grandma Helen even opened the door. She put them on a bus with nothing but a crinkly paper bag filled with cinnamon buns. She piled them in the backseat of some bald stranger who turned around and very seriously told them Jesus loved them.

Cassie learned to sleep flat on her back so she'd have two ears open to hear her mom creeping around the apartment late at night. She always hurried straight home after school. Sometimes, she borrowed the school secretary's phone to call her mom at the dry cleaner where she worked, just to hear her impatient voice on the other end. And then came the time when Cassie wanted her to leave once and for good.

She shivered, teetering on the edge of the cold, wet concrete. Where was Danny right now? He was an idiot, but at least she knew where she stood with him. Would she ever see him again? Did she care? The strong pull of wanting Danny lessened, slithered away like a rope.

She peered up into the tumbling, dark clouds. Rain drizzled onto her head, pattered against her cheeks. Pastor Gleeson talked a lot about heaven, and how your only purpose on earth was to do good so that you made sure you ended up there, cradled in God's Mighty Hand. Cassie tried to picture it: people piled up like popcorn, slipping through His fingers, clinging to His wrist. Was that where her mom was now, looking down at Cassie looking up?

Maybe there was a heaven. Because Cassie knew for sure there was a hell.

CHAPTER 31
HANK

These days, Hank found himself waking long before dawn. It didn't matter how late he went to bed the night before, whether he'd had one nightcap or two. Some mornings, he lay there, staring at the shadowy ceiling. Some mornings, he got up. Used to be rainy days like this one would keep him sleeping through the alarm. It would be Barb's gentle hand on his shoulder, shaking him awake, that would finally tease him up through the warm layers of sleep. Now that she was gone, there was no reason for him to be awake. No reason at all. Still, he couldn't sleep. The rumble of thunder outside didn't help.

The diner was nearly empty, just a few people sitting here and there. Lou had the radio on back in the kitchen, Waylon Jennings. Hank shook the rain from his umbrella, grabbed the paper from the stand, headed over to his usual spot. Forty-four

318

years he'd been coming here, forty-four years of sliding across the padded black vinyl cushion, leaning an elbow on the wooden table, and looking out the front window. He knew the menu by heart, knew to the day when the strawberry pie would be replaced by blueberry, could look around the room at the faces and instantly tell who'd argued with whom, who'd gotten bad news or good, who was worried about making the bank payment. Still his town, though he was no longer in charge of it.

Ellie set a heavy white mug in front of him, tipped the glass coffeepot over the rim. "Really coming down out there, isn't it?" Her face was flushed, her shirtsleeves rolled up over her elbows. She fanned herself with a paper menu.

Hank peeled open a container of creamer and pulled the mug toward him. The coffee here wasn't good, but it was hot and plentiful.

"The usual?" Ellie smiled and adjusted the waistband of her apron. She was beginning to show. They were hoping for a boy this time. Three girls already.

He grunted, flapped open the paper.

After a moment, she moved off.

Yesterday's hurricane was still punishing the Outer Banks. There'd been four confirmed fatalities so far, thirty-seven missing. The cold light of dawn had revealed entire coastal towns washed away, million-dollar homes snapped like Tinkertoys. Families torn apart. They were calling it a superstorm, gusting all the way inland to this small town set among the foothills. Hank couldn't recall the last time they'd felt the effects of a storm so far away. They warned this was the new weather pattern, thanks to global warming. They said people should get used to it.

There was a Labor Day sale at the florist's. How did that make any sense? Barb would know. Barb would curl up beside him and rest her head on his shoulder and her hand on his bicep, making his heart beat faster. *Oh, Hank,* she'd sigh. High school sweethearts, that's what they'd been. Hank had taken her small, warm hand in his and placed his other hand on her slim waist, both of them fourteen and unsure. He'd tugged her toward him and she'd stumbled, just a little. She'd flushed pink and looked around. No one was looking. No one saw. Her hand relaxed in his, and they started again. This time, she allowed herself to be led, and after a song or two, she'd let him rest his cheek against her soft, slippery hair beginning to come out of its curl. The next song, he tightened his hand at her waist and she raised her eyes to his. He'd never known eyes could be as blue as hers. They'd taken all those first steps together. They had never wavered.

Ellie brought over his eggs and bacon. He frowned at his plate. "I didn't ask for toast."

"Eat up, Hank. You're getting too skinny." She patted his shoulder and headed back to the kitchen.

The ceiling fan whirred and clattered overhead. He ate, paper opened to the obituaries. When he was newly married, this was the section he'd sacrifice for washing windows. Then came the years when he avoided this section entirely. Now, he scrutinized each photograph. Goodbyes were overrated. You never knew when you needed to make them count. By the time you figured it out, the person on the other side was too far gone to hear them.

The knitters arrived, chattering about the wet morning and the storm, claiming their usual table in the corner. The decibel level soared. Hank edged aside his plate, patted his pocket for a ballpoint pen. He refolded the paper to the crossword puzzle and stopped at the headline running across the back page.

"More coffee?" Ellie stood beside him.

He pressed the paper flat. It had happened just a few hundred miles away, shoved off the front page by the hurricane and buried in this inside section.

"Hank?"

He tore the page along the seam, creased it carefully into a square, tossed some bills on the table. He pushed himself up and went home.

It was a small mention. A toddler snatched from a shopping cart outside Charleston while his mother had her back turned loading groceries into her car. What had she been doing, memorizing sell-by dates? There was a blurry photograph of the child, obviously an accidental shot taken from a distance of something or someone else, the boy having wandered into view, turning his face toward the camera at the last moment. His soft, unformed features made him indistinguishable from a million other nineteen-month-olds: high forehead, plump cheeks, blue eyes. Shave his hair, change his clothes, and he could walk right past without stirring a single wisp of suspicion. Forgettable. Too soon, he would be — pushed aside by the nine-year-old who wandered away from her family's campsite, or the twelve-year-old who should know better but still climbed into a stranger's car. The six-month-old infant last seen peacefully sleeping in her crib. The fifteen-year-old runaway.

Hank fired up his desktop. It was already going on fourteen hours since the child's disappearance. The most critical hours. The hours when memories were most reliable. When lies were still taking shape and vulnerable to a stiff jab or shaking.

Amazing what someone could find online. Made him wonder how they ever managed, back in the day. Of course, things were simpler then. The lines between cause and effect were clearer and more direct. None of this jogging here and there and taking bizarre turns. He typed the boy's name into the search field. The boy was last seen wearing a canary-yellow shirt and red shorts. Barefoot. Thirty-seven inches tall, twenty-nine pounds. Canary yellow. He wondered who provided the description, and whether or not the investigating officer did due diligence. Couple years back, there had been a mom in California who described her kid wrong just to throw off sightings. No one thought to correct her, not the kindergarten teacher who'd had the boy in class that day, not the school bus driver, or any of the residents living along the child's short walk home. Who was going to question a grieving mother? No one, it seemed, until it was too late.

He checked into the most promising chat rooms, to see if anyone was saying anything interesting. There wasn't much, a mutter about a cult kidnapping that no one had picked up on. People were always quick to suspect religious fanatics, but he couldn't find any information about a cult active in the area. He posted an entry. His printer hummed to life. He removed the sheet of paper and studied the blurred lost face. This was the best that mother could do? It said everything. It pointed the finger directly at her.

Barb took hundreds of photographs of their son at every stage. Hank had albums stacked in the basement bulging with photographs. She insisted on taking George's picture on the first day of every school year. But neither of them had seen it coming. They'd never felt it so much as puff chillingly against their skin.

What am I going to do? Barb had stood by the window after, eyes as bleak as the moon she was staring at. The ground was barren, embracing winter. *What am I going to do?* He had no answers for her. He himself had stopped asking why. The other questions were toxic enough.

He carried the photograph he'd printed out to the wall and found a place for it among the others. Barb used to hate the sight of them, begged him to keep the door closed so she wouldn't walk past and see their faces.

Eliza, 10
Henry, 7
Ruth Ann, 12
Michael, 9
Olivia, 6

Now, Christopher, nineteen months.

CHAPTER 32
SARA

Something pressed against her hip. Sara grunted, shifted position, flung out an arm, struck something soft and sturdy. A screech. Her eyes flew open. Boon kneeled beside her, plastic blocks scattered around him on the covers. He stuck out his lower lip and rubbed his shoulder. "You hit me."

"Sorry." Sara raised herself up onto an elbow. The room was shadowed, the thick curtains still drawn. The air conditioner muttered. The TV was on, muted images flickering.

"I told him to get down." Cassie was at the mirror nailed to the closet door, carefully applying lipstick, that ugly black shade she seemed so crazy about.

"How long have you guys been awake?" Sara was groggy, needed to pee. She fumbled for the plastic clock radio on the nightstand, turned its face toward her. Eight-fourteen. Way too early. She sat up, swung her legs over the side of the bed. The room swayed around her, settled into place. She'd slept harder than she'd intended, unmoving and dreamless. An unforgivable mistake. She was hiding from the FBI. She mustn't underestimate them. Not for one second.

Cassie leaned closer to the blurred glass. "A million years."

"You were talking." Boon jumped Wolf up and down along the mound of covers.

Sara glanced at him, alarmed. "I was? What was I saying?"

"Lots of things. You were loud."

"Sorry," Sara said, again. As far as she knew, she'd never talked in her sleep before. She might have revealed a name, a place. It was the small things, the Feds had warned, as if they were the first to think of it. But she'd learned it first from her father, watching the ways he did things and absorbing them through her skin like osmosis. Don't hang your coat so the label can be read. Keep ID and keys separate. Answer a question with a question. Most important, don't have a tell. That had been the hardest lesson to learn. It had been one of the guys she dated who'd pointed it out. *You always hold yourself so still when you're thinking.* He thought it was adorable. After that, she made sure to relax the muscles in her face.

She blinked, and breathed, and smiled. But inside, she was taut as a drum, humming with tension.

The kids didn't seem the least bit interested. Sara would drop the subject and maybe they'd forget whatever she had mumbled in her sleep. Cassie turned up the TV. Sara's head throbbed. Had she remembered to pack ibuprofen? "Call your dad, Cassie."

"Yeah."

"*Now*, please." Sara got up, used the bathroom, and washed her face. She put on the same clothes she'd worn the day before, brushed her teeth, combed her hair. When she came out, the two kids hadn't moved. They were in the same rumpled clothes, too. Chances were good they hadn't brushed their teeth. Cassie was still in front of the mirror, running her fingers through her hair, preening. "Any luck?"

"Nope."

"Where's the remote? I need to change the channel."

"Who knows?"

Sara looked around. "Well, you must have had it."

"I didn't turn on the TV. Boon did."

"See if you can peel yourself away from admiring yourself and help me look."

"Why? Are you blind?"

"Cassie," Sara said, warning.

"Here," Boon said, hurriedly. "I was sitting on it."

"See?" Cassie smirked.

Sara held up the remote, turned to the Weather Channel. A reporter wobbled in the downpour, holding up a microphone: *. . . still battering the coast and showing no signs of abating.* The reporter reached up to grab the hood of her raincoat as the storm gusted. In the water behind her, boats tipped and teetered.

"Where is that?" Cassie wanted to know.

"Richmond."

"What about the Outer Banks?"

"They'll get there in a minute. Just wait." Sara ignored the girl's impatient huff as the video changed to a map with that same huge, swirling white mass hovering over the Carolina coast. Dotted lines had been added, tracking various possible trajectories along the Eastern Seaboard. A weatherman paced, zestfully described how the hurricane had moved back briefly over open water, gaining strength before veering treacherously inland again. The storm seemed alive, breathing, filled with purpose and intent.

Now a new video, of churning gray sky filled with black-tinged clouds. The water below it chopped. "Here we go," Sara said, sitting on the bed. Boon rose up on his knees beside her to watch.

Seen from the sky, the Outer Banks was a feeble dribble of sand surrounded on both sides by water. The drone swooped lower. People waved for help from windows. Buildings lay in pieces, like mangled toys. The highway had buckled into undulating ribbons of asphalt, spattered with ponds of water and huge drifts of sand. Street signs tilted at demented angles. Uprooted trees sprawled across cars, roofs, roads.

Cassie edged closer. "Is that our bridge?"

"No. I think it's the Bonner." The middle of the bridge was underwater. Emergency vehicles lined the entrance, lights flashing. Sara had driven across that span mere hours before.

"I don't see the Paradise."

"I don't, either. But that doesn't necessarily mean anything." Sara read the words scrolling across the bottom of the screen. "They're saying the cell towers are still down. That's why you haven't been able to reach your father."

Now what?

Either she loaded up the kids and dumped them at some podunk police station out in the middle of nowhere, or she stayed put and hoped cell service was restored quickly. Both choices sucked. The cell towers could be out for hours, days. Possibly weeks. But holding on to the kids was also risky. Sara had noticed how people talked to kids. People asked questions, and Boon at least, answered them.

But if she dumped the kids now, she'd have to find another place to stay. Who knew how far she'd have to go before she found another gullible motel owner? She wouldn't have the excuse of two children with her. Keeping them with her could work in her favor. The Feds wouldn't be looking for her in the company of a small boy and a preteen girl. Pretty great cover. *Think light on your feet,* her father would say. *Be prepared to swivel, and swivel again.* She was swiveling, all right. The problem was figuring out whether she was facing the right direction.

Cassie had gone back to the mirror and was fooling with her hair, scowling. Boon had climbed down from Sara's bed and, with Wolf's help, was tugging the blanket off the mattress to the floor. What the hell was she doing here? Didn't she have enough to contend with?

She had no one to blame but herself. Somewhere, she knew, her father was shaking his head with disgust. *Told you.*

Turned out this little dumpy motel offered breakfast. Five small tables clustered beneath a TV on the wall, a counter holding plastic decanters of cereals and a large platter of pastries. Yogurts and fruit sat in bowls of ice. The place was empty, other than some old guy behind the front desk, pointing a remote at the TV. Steel-gray hair hanging over a square forehead, ruddy cheeks, washed-out blue eyes. Probably Joyce's husband. They appeared to be the same age.

The kids beelined toward the food. Sara headed for the coffee urn. She filled a Styrofoam cup and sat at a table where she could see the TV but not have to hear it. The old guy had tuned it to a weather station and kept the volume low. Boon ran toward her with a paper plate heaped with cellophane-wrapped pastries. His faded purple T-shirt was wrinkled. The pockets of his oversize shorts jingled as he moved. He grinned at Sara. "Want one?"

"No, thank you."

Cassie sat down with a cup of yogurt. "Don't touch me," she warned Boon as he leaned toward her.

"Don't. Touch. Me," he mocked.

"Shut up." Cassie peeled the foil from the yogurt cup.

"Shut. Up."

The old guy behind the desk had set down the remote. Though he stood a few yards away, he didn't seem to be paying them any attention. Maybe he was hard of hearing. "That's all you're having?" Sara asked Cassie.

"You're one to talk."

"Don't whine to me later about how hungry you are."

"You didn't even give us dinner last night!"

Was that true? "You're right," Sara agreed. "I'll have to do a better job staying on top of your feeding schedule."

"Hilarious."

Boon was having difficulty opening the cellophane. Sara took the pastry from him and tore open a corner.

He took a big bite. Crumbs scattered across his shirt. "Are you getting rid of us today?" he said around a mouthful.

Sara hadn't used that expression with him — had she? "I'm not getting rid of you. I'm just trying to get you back to your dad." She glanced to the old guy, now tapping a computer keyboard. "You must miss him."

Boon shoved the rest of the pastry into his

mouth. His cheeks bulged. He licked his fingers, then shrugged.

"Well, I'm sure he misses you."

Cassie snorted.

Sara eyed her. "Call him again. Leave a message if he doesn't pick up, let him know you're okay. He'll get it when service resumes."

Cassie banged down her spoon with a theatrical flourish and yanked her bag to her. It was a cross-body style that was currently popular. Expensive, though. Shoplifted? Cassie put her phone to her ear and waited. She sighed. "It's not ringing."

"Keep trying."

"Can I eat first, or do you want me to sit here listening forever to a stupid dead phone?"

"You're a clever girl. I bet you can do both." Sara stood.

Boon clutched at her. "Where are you going?"

His fingers were small and warm, and — to her horror — sticky. She tugged her hand free. "Just getting more coffee."

At the coffee station, she plucked a napkin from the dispenser and wiped icing from her fingers. She glanced into the lobby and was startled to see the old guy behind the front desk staring at her over the top of his computer screen. He nodded, and she nodded back. No big deal, she told himself. The place was empty. What else was he going to look at? As far as he knew, she was just a mom with two whiny brats. She returned to the table and sat down. Still, she felt his gaze on her. "Anything?" she asked Cassie, who sat there holding the phone against her ear and dramatically ignoring her breakfast.

"No. I told you. *Now* can I hang up?"

"Of course. Thank you for trying," she said, sweetly.

Cassie narrowed her eyes at Sara, dropped the phone into her bag, and reached for her spoon. "What are we going to do today?"

"After breakfast, we'll go back to the room." Boon had a blob of bright red jelly on his chin. Sara handed him a napkin, pointed to his face.

"And do what?"

"Watch TV. Read a book."

"I don't have a book. Can we go to the movies?"

"Movies cost money."

"So? You've got money." Cassie scraped her spoon noisily around the inside of the plastic cup.

Sara gave the girl a sharp look. "I've got work to do."

"So that's it? We're just going to sit in the

room all day and do nothing?"

"Yep."

"It'll be okay," Boon assured his sister. "You can watch cartoons with Wolf and me."

Cassie rolled her eyes. "I'd rather kill myself."

Boon held out another pastry for Sara to unwrap. "I know."

"You know what?" Sara ripped apart the cellophane, handed the pastry to him.

"How we can go to the movies." He broke the Danish in pieces. Apple, this time. "Wolf's tooth is loose. When it falls out, the Tooth Fairy will come. And she'll bring money for the movie."

Cassie snorted. "There's no such thing as the Tooth Fairy. And Wolf doesn't have teeth."

"Yes, there is. And he *does*!"

"Nope. It's just moms and dads, and sometimes not even them."

"You don't know *everything*!"

"No such thing as Santa, either."

"You're a *big fat liar*!"

"Go ahead, dumb-ass. You'll see."

Sara couldn't remember a time of Santa and the Tooth Fairy. She remembered once losing a tooth while drinking milk. She'd set the tooth aside on the sofa cushion beside her and finished her meal around the taste of blood, before getting up and tossing the tooth in the trash. Her father had been home, she thought, but he hadn't been sitting beside her. Where had he been? On the phone? Probably. He did almost all his planning over the phone. He kept a small notebook in his pocket, with names and numbers penciled on the pages, crossed off and updated. Sara kept her own contact list uploaded to the cloud. What would her father make of that? she wondered. How would it have affected his cons? She had never betrayed him, no matter how the cops hammered at her. They gave her all sorts of reasons for why she should speak up. Didn't she want to do the right thing? Make amends to the people her father had stolen from? None of it had swayed her. Her father's one guiding principle drilled into her very core: you had to watch out for your own self. You could never count on someone else to have your best interests at heart. Why would you? Over and over, he'd been proven right. Her mother had left her. Men had ended things. Friendships had faded. Her dad had died. She had herself. It made her resilient.

"Finish your breakfast," she said. She drank her coffee. She'd get through this meal. Then she'd get through the day. This must be what it was like for parents.

"Cassie has a boyfriend," Boon informed her.

Cassie whirled in her seat to face him. "Shut up! I do not!"

"Yes you do. He has orange hair. Not like yours," he told Sara. "More like crayon."

Cassie shoved him. "Shut up. He does not." Her cheeks were flaming.

Boon grabbed the table to keep from toppling. "He's skinny like a straw. He always wants Cassie to come over. Sometimes she does. They drink *beers.*"

"I hate you so fucking much."

"Be quiet," Sara hissed. She glanced to the old guy, who had returned his attention to his computer screen.

Boon picked up another pastry, thickly smeared with chocolate frosting and covered with bright sprinkles. The thought of all that sugar made Sara's stomach roil. Should she be stopping him? Would it make him sick? One of Sara's foster moms had served fast food every single night. Another mom wouldn't allow meat in the house. A third refused to cook entirely. For six months, Sara had eaten granola bars and canned fruit cocktail. "Are you allowed to eat so much crap?"

Alarmed, Boon looked down at the pile of

cellophane wrappers in front of him. He glanced back up at her, his eyes filled with tears. "Are you mad?" His voice wobbled.

"No. Jesus. Of course not." Poor kid. His parents had really screwed him up. Of course Sara blamed the mom, but where had Whit been? He'd played a role, too. If his wife had issues, and it certainly seemed like she did, then it was his job to have protected his kids from her. Sounded like he'd sided with her instead. Sara had caught a glimpse of him the other night, dragging his kids across the courtyard toward the storm surge. She had come out to carry down her trash and spotted the threesome, the spaces between the three figures narrowing and widening as Whit gripped Boon's hand and Cassie shone a flashlight around at the flying debris, the narrow beam jerking and swaying.

Sara nudged Boon's plate closer. "Go ahead. Eat as much as you want." It wasn't as if he was really eating the pastries. He seemed more interested in playing with them, tearing them into chunks and sucking his fingers, sharing bites with his stuffed dog. He was making a mess.

It was a small lobby. The TV muttered. The rain beating against the windows made the space feel close. Cramped and humid.

That old guy at the front desk was staring at his computer screen, but his hands were motionless on the keyboard and his head was tilted slightly toward them. Well, the best way to deal with curiosity was to meet it head-on. When Cassie pushed away her plate and demanded to go back to the room, Sara handed her the key. "I'll be there in a minute," she told the girl, who snatched up her mother's silver raincoat from the chair and wadded it in her arms, defying Sara to snatch it back.

CHAPTER 33
HANK

"Got some drop-ins last night." Joyce twined a filmy scarf around her neck, clicked her pocketbook closed. She had a doctor's appointment, and she was in a hurry to leave, given the unpredictable weather. Her face was crisscrossed with fine wrinkles, her eyes sunk deep. Her scalp shone yellow-pink through her silver curls. Hank saw past them through the years to the girl with strawberry blond hair glowing as she bent to retrieve the newspaper from her driveway, her merry eyes as she held up her glass for a refill. Well, who was time kind to? He wasn't the same man staring back at himself from the mirror. "Nice family. I put them around back."

Why can't one of your girls do it? he'd asked when she asked him to spell her the first time, years ago. Joyce had three of them. They'd given her enough trouble growing up: summonses to the principal's office, whooping cough, late-night exits amid giggly, breathless whispering. A car would be waiting at the bottom of the driveway, and off they'd go. Barb had told him that it had taken all she had not to burst out laughing the time Joyce confided with confusion that her eldest daughter had an alarming case of poison ivy in a particularly sensitive area. *She must have scratched herself, poor thing,* Barb managed to choke out before hurrying home to tell Hank. Now those girls were married and starting families of their own. Surely one of them could make time to help their mother. Joyce had just shot him a look. *The girls are busy.*

Meaning he wasn't.

He'd warned Joyce he didn't think it was wise for her to keep the Step On Inn going, now that Chester was gone. A woman alone, in her seventies at that. But she claimed she needed the money, as little as what trickled in since the Holiday Inn Express opened nearby. She could manage, she insisted. She wasn't going to spend her twilight years sitting around, watching weeds take over the flower garden. Another barbed jab at him.

"Family, huh?"

"That's what I said."

"Why here? This place isn't exactly on the beaten path." Joyce didn't advertise. She relied on word of mouth and repeat customers. There were fewer of them every year.

"Why not here?" She adjusted a fat, glittery earring. She wouldn't look him in the eye. "Wear your name tag, will you, Hank?" Another improvement one of her girls insisted upon. The Step On Inn. Ridiculous name for a motel. But Joyce had picked it long before Hank and Barb and George moved to town.

Her new guests showed up for breakfast.

Hank was behind the front desk, pointing the remote at the TV hanging on the wall in the breakfast area and trying to find a station that wasn't showing hurricane coverage. There had to be an update about that missing toddler. It couldn't be all about the weather. But channel after channel showed the same images of wind and rain. If he wanted to see weather like that, he could look out the damn window.

The lobby door jingled. A woman and two kids hurried in, rain jackets wrapped around them. The kids quickly shucked their jackets, dripping water onto the linoleum. Boy, about six. Dark hair that fell over his eyes. Purple shirt, tan shorts. Sneakers with no socks, both laces loose and flapping.

The girl's age was harder to estimate. Twelve, maybe. Thirteen? Long, thin hair, eyes ringed with God-ugly liner. Was that black lipstick on her lips? Flannel shirt that hung on her scrawny frame, jeans laddered with holes. Purple flip-flops. She wore a silver ring on one of her toes, a purse strapped across her chest.

The woman was slender, little taller than average, shoulder-length reddish hair. Thirty-something. Under the silvery raincoat, tailored white blouse, jeans. Black flats. Neither of the kids looked like her. She poured coffee, fitted a lid onto the Styrofoam cup. She had an economy of motion. No hesitation in her choices.

The boy whirled from the buffet and caught Hank staring. The boy grinned, lifted his hand in a wave. A dazzling smile, a dimple flashing high on one cheek.

Hank's shocked heart clenched with recognition. He lowered the remote. It couldn't be, of course not, but he found himself taking shallow breaths, almost panting.

The girl stalked over to the table to contemplate her choices. The boy had gone back to heaping his plate. The girl said something to him. He said something back. A flurry of elbow jabs.

Their mother took no notice. She was seated at one of the tables, with her back to the wall. She lifted her cup to her lips, took a sip. The boy ran to her, holding his paper plate with both hands. The woman pulled back a chair for him to sit. Hank wondered where the father was.

Hank would come home from work and call out, walk through the quiet rooms to the back door, where he'd find George digging at something in the yard or chasing a butterfly with a net, and Barb standing there on the deck, just watching. Hank would go to her and put his arm around her waist. She'd lean her head against his shoulder. Such simple happiness.

Hank shook himself. He pretended to be busy on the computer. Still, he couldn't keep from glancing over. The girl sat opposite her mother, dumping her purse on the floor between her feet. She'd flung her wet rain jacket on an empty chair, piled on top of the boy's. She slouched in the chair. The woman said something. The girl shrugged, picked at the lid of her yogurt cup. The expression on the woman's face tightened. The tension between them crackled.

The boy pressed a cellophane wrapper flat, studying it. Then he surreptitiously pushed it into his shorts pocket. Another shard of memory toppling into place: George had been a collector, too. Barb was always finding marbles and bits of string and rubber balls in his pockets. She was always shaking out his jackets and jeans and shorts. A few months after, Hank had found her in the laundry room, her hands on the machine and her head bent. She blamed herself. *I should never have let him walk home alone,* she said, weeping. *What was I doing that was so important? Nothing. I was doing nothing.* Hank had stood in the laundry room doorway and seen that she was holding a balled-up sock in her hand, and he had quietly backed away.

The girl pressed a cellphone to her ear. Then she shrugged again, dropped the phone back into her purse. The mother looked annoyed. She made no move toward either of them, not leaning forward to brush the boy's hair out of his eyes, not patting her daughter's forearm to tell her to stop slouching. Barb was always touching George, pulling him into her arms and resting her chin on top of his head, even as he giggled and squirmed to get away.

What were these three doing here? This place wasn't exactly on the beaten path.

The mother got up to refill her cup. She caught Hank staring. She hiked an eyebrow. Not confrontational, just letting him know. Hank returned his attention to the solitaire game on the computer screen, tapped a few keys, let the queen of spades gently float into place. He waited, then looked back over. The mother had returned to the table with her coffee. She seemed perfectly relaxed, but her roving eyes betrayed her. Hank felt another click of recognition. He straightened. The woman's mind was working, taking everything in. She scanned the room, noting what the other guests had left behind — the puckered napkins, crumbs. A pushed-back chair. She was counting exits — two, with a third down the hallway. She glanced to the rain-smeared window, saw the empty parking lot.

This was a woman practiced at surveillance.

The boy was bouncing a shapeless stuffed animal on the table. His sister rolled her eyes and said something. He leaned against her, his shoulder bumping hers. She shoved him away, but he resettled resolutely against her. This time, she didn't object. Her blond, flyaway hair against his deep chestnut cap. Hank saw George's narrow head, the pink tips of his ears. He had Hank's forehead, Barb always said, her hands. Together, they had marveled at their son's features as he lay wrapped in the hospital blanket, his eyes squeezed puffily shut, his impossibly tiny fingers endlessly flexing. He was uniquely his own person, and theirs.

Too soon, the two children were gone, collecting their rain jackets and shrugging them on, running to the lobby door. The mother watched them but didn't call out a warning to be careful on the wet floor. Then she turned her placid gaze to Hank.

He wasn't surprised when she got up and came over. She'd already telegraphed her intent with that composed gaze of hers. He smiled, more a baring of his teeth. "Morning." His voice was gruff. He cleared his throat. "Can I help you, Mrs. . . . ?"

"I hope so," she said, neatly evading the question. She was something, all right. She smiled. "I'm wondering if you have a recommendation for someplace I could take the kids for lunch?"

So they were staying. He wondered what for. He got the sense she was making chit-chat. He could always tell when someone was working to put him at ease. People did it all the time, even the innocent ones. "Well, there's the diner. Pretty much everyone in town eats there. It's not far, couple blocks. You'd have passed it on your way into town. There's a pizza place, too, but that's just delivery. Small town. Probably not what you're used to."

348

She nodded, with a flicker of a smile. Her eyes were steady, drilling into his. "A diner sounds great. Thank you."

She was good at sidestepping. Well, so was he. "Joyce might have a menu somewhere. Hold on." He yanked open a drawer, rummaged through the jumble of papers.

"Oh, that's all right —"

"No, no. It's around here somewhere. Unless you're in a hurry?"

"Not at all. Take your time. Though it's really not necessary."

"Don't mind at all." He tugged open another drawer. Pencils rattled. He bent to reach the next drawer. "So how did you find us?"

She didn't answer. He glanced up at her. She was turned away, staring at the TV in the breakfast area. He straightened, looked to see what it was that had caught her attention so completely. Another reporter standing in the rain. Behind him, the flashing lights of emergency vehicles. The hurricane had claimed a victim, Hank thought, fumbling for the remote and pressing the volume button.

. . . missing mom from the Outer Banks was found dead this morning, her body located by police in a septic tank in the backyard of the home you see behind me, which belongs to

349

Diane Nelson's in-laws. Her husband, Whit Nelson, has been arrested for her murder. Diane Nelson went missing back in May, and police believed at first that she had abandoned her family.

Hank snorted. "Police knew from the start. Just took them this long to put the pieces together."

The woman glanced at him. Her face had gone white. "What makes you say that?"

He shrugged. "I was sheriff for thirty years." He thumbed off the TV. He was tired of seeing weather, hearing other people's bad news. "Here you go," he said, and handed her the menu.

She thanked him. As she walked across the lobby, Hank thought: She was shaken by the news story. Well, who wouldn't be? People did terrible things to each other.

CHAPTER 34
SARA

If Sara had gone online first thing that morning, instead of tunneling ahead for coffee, she might have seen the news about Whit Nelson safely in her room. Instead, she'd learned about it in a freaking motel lobby in front of a man who turned out to be law enforcement himself. Sara knew — she just knew — she'd let her shocked reaction show. How could she have not? The kids' mother hadn't abandoned them. She was dead, murdered by their father. Now what? For the first time in a long while, maybe for the first time ever, Sara felt lost. Forget swiveling. She had no game plan. She couldn't even figure out a first step to formulate a plan.

She stole a glance at Boon, propped up against the bed pillows, eyes glued to a cartoon. He was sucking his thumb, his eyes half closed. Manic cartoon music rolled up and down. Cassie was in the bathroom, the

351

door closed, water running. A reprieve.

When Sara had overheard the reporter mention the Outer Banks while the old guy was bent behind the front desk, digging through drawers, she had automatically glanced to the TV. A man stood beneath an umbrella, speaking earnestly into his microphone outside a small house. The words BREAKING NEWS snaked across the bottom of the screen. The reporter was talking about Whit Nelson. Oh no, had been Sara's first thought. Whit had been injured in the hurricane. She had found herself turning toward the TV, collecting words that assembled into a different, utterly unexpected story. Had she gasped? She might have. Hank had said something, and she'd glanced back to see him standing there holding out that tattered menu, his gaze on the TV set behind her. What had she said to him in response? She had no recollection. Her only thought had been to get away from him as quickly as possible. A retired sheriff. No wonder he'd been watching her and the kids so closely. He wasn't some old guy with nothing better to do. He was a cop. All cops were like that, scanning the world with suspicion as though they owned it.

She had taken the menu, clutching it against her like armor as she strode back to the room. It had taken everything she had not to run.

She stepped into the room and saw the bizarrely normal scene of Boon mesmerized by the TV on the dresser while his sister hogged the bathroom. He didn't even glance over as she fished her laptop out of her bag. There had been no mention of Whit Nelson's kids, but Sara knew the police were searching for them. And until she figured out what to do with them, she wanted them right here, where she could see them. The police wouldn't suspect she'd had anything to do with what had happened to their mother. They couldn't. There was nothing — absolutely nothing — to link her to Whit Nelson.

Other than the fact that she had his kids.

Sara angled the laptop away from Boon, though there was no way he could see what was displayed there: a photograph of his dad, some official photograph taken off a website. Whit stood there in his cheap navy suit, looking charming and handsome, smiling like he was everybody's best friend, instead of a murderer. How had he done it? Had he shot her, knifed her, beaten her unconscious until she finally stopped breathing? Had he wrapped his hands around his wife's throat, choked the life out of her? It was hideous, too horrible to imagine. And yet Sara found herself casting up one grotesque mental image after another.

She had known plenty of thieves and liars, people who manipulated other people to get what they wanted. She herself had worked for a man who preyed on women, and she knew he damn well deserved whatever punishment the court finally doled out. But she had never in her life stood chatting at the railing with a man who had cold-bloodedly killed his wife and the mother of his two kids. God, what kind of monster would hide his wife's body in a septic tank? She prided herself on being a reader of people, watching their body language, searching for their telltale tics, listening for what they weren't saying. Nothing in Whit Nelson had sent up a red flag.

But Whit's father had apparently sent up a red flag among his neighbors. One of them had noticed unusual activity in the backyard, gone over to investigate. Whatever he'd found had been enough for him to call the police. Sara didn't want to think about what the neighbor had seen. It had been months since Diane's disappearance. Where had the murder happened? Right on the other side of the wall while Sara was watching TV, brushing her teeth, drinking her wine? Sleeping? The thought made her shudder. The police had never come knocking, demanding to know whether Sara had heard anything and what she'd observed of the family next door. Only the kids' social worker had done that. The old guy at the desk had been wrong. The cops hadn't suspected Whit of his wife's death. It had taken a snoopy neighbor to expose the truth.

She hit refresh. Nothing yet about Whit's kids. What the hell were the cops waiting for? More likely it was the media, more interested in covering the devastation of the hurricane than in the salacious details of a domestic tragedy. Or maybe, just maybe, no one knew Boon and Cassie weren't right where Whit had left them; or maybe the police were too busy dealing with flooding and power outages to check on two kids presumed to be okay at home. But she couldn't count on that.

Had anyone seen her usher the kids through the driving rain and into her car? Hers hadn't been the only vehicle in the lot. She shuddered again. Diane's garish silver raincoat — Boon had insisted she put it on. How could she have been so stupid? Had security cameras been working anywhere along the route she'd driven from the

Paradise to the bridge? What about the firefighter who'd shone his flashlight into her car? Had she mentioned the kids' names to Joyce last night as she was checking in? Had Hank overhead a name that morning at breakfast? At any point along the way, had she done or said anything the least bit memorable? Had the kids? She didn't *know*. Worse, she had no way of finding out.

She'd actually talked herself into thinking that having Boon and Cassie with her provided the perfect camouflage. She'd told herself a little story to appease the anxiety she had about acting impulsively and returning for Boon and Cassie. She'd lowered her guard. Her dad had warned her over and over. *When things seem to be going well, that's when you know something's wrong.*

She needed to get rid of the kids. Now. Before the nosy guy at the desk knocked on the door with some half-baked pretense so he could take another good look at them. It wasn't like this place was swarming with strangers. She and the kids stood out. She needed to drop them off somewhere — no, better yet, leave them in the room, pretend she had an errand to run. Eventually, one of them would get bored or curious enough to go looking for Sara. By then, Sara would be long gone. Before the old guy got it into his head to wander over and check her license plate.

She clapped her laptop shut. She plucked a tissue from the box on the nightstand, began rubbing light switches, doorknobs, anything she might have touched. Fallen strands of hair were okay. Her DNA wasn't in the system. At least, not that she knew of. Now that she was in motion, she couldn't move fast enough. She glanced at Boon, thumb in his mouth, enthralled by a cartoon in which squirrels appeared to be riding motorcycles.

What was she doing? She had to keep him away from that thing. What if he turned to the news? She snatched up the remote. A squirrel squawked, then silenced.

Boon looked up at her, startled. His nose was running. She averted her eyes.

"Just for now," she told him firmly, before he could protest, wiping the remote and dropping it on the other bed. She'd have to take her chances on what he might see on TV after she left. Thank God the news had broken when it had. Otherwise, Sara would have transferred the kids back into a killer's custody. Now at least they'd be okay. They'd have a chance. "Listen. I have to go out and get something."

He scratched his rib cage. "Okay," he said,

sounding uncertain.

She rapped on the bathroom door. She'd shoo Cassie out, wipe the room down, then she'd leave. She was already packed. Another lesson learned from her father long ago. She knocked louder. "Cassie, open up," she called through the door and the sound of the shower. "Cassie?"

"She's not in there," Boon said.

Sara turned to look at him. "What?"

He shrank back against the pillows, pressing Wolf against his chest. His cheeks flamed red. "Don't be mad, Sara."

The doorknob turned easily in her grasp. Steam boiled out of the room. Sara tore back the shower curtain. The stall was empty, just the water splashing down. Of course it was. It was a trick Sara had used, too.

CHAPTER 35
HANK

Joyce's Pontiac eased past the front window and crunched to a stop. Seeing it, Hank told the dispatcher, "Just make sure Tom gets the message." Someone had to be paying attention to that missing toddler in Charleston. It couldn't all be about the hurricane and, now, the man who'd killed his poor wife and dumped her corpse in a septic tank. He banged down the receiver and hurried across the lobby just as Joyce's headlights flared off. He let himself out into the wet, umbrella in hand, met her as she was climbing painfully out of the driver's seat. The rain always made her arthritis flare up. He held the opened umbrella over her head, and she glanced up at him in surprise.

He waited for her to gain her balance, then reached around her and closed the car door. They proceeded up the walk, arm in arm, skirting puddles. "What exactly do you know about that family?"

"What family?" She stepped into the lobby, glanced around. "I see you put away the breakfast things. You're a sweetheart, Hank." She undid her rain bonnet, held it dripping away from her body.

"You know what family. The only family staying here."

She shuffled around the counter, set down her pocketbook, fluffed her curls with her fingertips. "No *How did things go at the doctor's, Joyce?*" she said. "No *Did you have any trouble parking?*"

She was trying to change the subject. "You're here, aren't you? I assume they went fine."

She moved things around, the pad of Post-it notes, the basket of pens. THE STEP ON INN printed on each one, an effort by one of her girls to punch up business. "Your compassion is astounding, Hank. Did the plumber show? I called about that leak in 107."

"No record of their registration. No charge slip."

She pressed her lips together. "You checked?"

"There's something off about that woman. She's hiding something." Everyone lied. Thirty-three years of being a cop distilled to that single acid drop of truth. Even when

361

there was nothing to lie about, people lied. All the time, in every way.

"Oh for pity's sake, Hank! She seemed perfectly nice to me. Does this mean the plumber was a no-show?" She pulled out the keyboard and tapped a few keys, frowning. "That's the second time in a row. I'm calling his uncle. He owes me a favor."

"What is it, Joyce? What aren't you saying?"

She studied the screen, reached for the receiver. "It's all right, Hank. Trust me."

He'd learned to trust no one. "What did you do, Joyce?" He put a hand on her forearm, the bones fragile beneath his touch.

She glanced at him, color high in her cheeks. "It was late. The children were exhausted. They'd come a long way."

"Joyce."

She inhaled, lifted her chin. "She's paying cash. All right?"

"Why?"

"There's a husband."

A husband who could track his wife's credit card charges. He knew that woman would be watching doorways, counting escapes, mistrustful. "Don't tell me you've put yourself in the middle of a domestic dispute."

"Oh, Hank."

"Oh, Hank, nothing." He had to fight to keep his voice level. "What were you thinking? You have any idea how dangerous this is? Things can get out of hand. People could get hurt —"

"But she has children."

"— *especially* when there are kids involved. Jesus, Joyce."

"Sometimes couples just need a break." She withdrew her hand from his grasp.

"Did you check her identification?" A loaded question.

She kept her gaze firmly on his. "Of course I did."

He believed her, for what it was worth. "And?"

"Hank, what is this?"

"How do you know the husband's not going to show up?"

She considered him with pale blue eyes, then sighed. "Oh, Hank. Not everyone's a criminal."

"You have some nerve," he said.

"Hank —"

Maybe she thought thirty-seven years was long enough to forgive and forget. But Joyce had been the one to rent that room to that monster thirty-seven years before. She had been the one to let the darkness into their lives.

CHAPTER 36
CASSIE

Cassie sloshed along, huddled in her mom's silver raincoat, which the Bitch had dumped on the chair beside her like it was garbage. All yesterday, Cassie had endured the sight of Sara pulling it on, pulling it off. Acting like it belonged to her. Which it clearly didn't. It was way too short. The cuffs didn't even reach her wrists. Sara had looked ridiculous. On her way out of the breakfast nook, Cassie had seen her chance and seized it — literally. Sara hadn't noticed. She'd been too busy staring down that old guy behind the front desk.

He'd been watching them all, too. Probably bored. Or a perv, though Cassie didn't get that vibe from him. Her third-grade gym teacher had been a perv. Cassie had fallen once playing dodgeball, and had the breath knocked right out of her. The gym teacher had hurried over to make sure she was okay, helping her up and patting her down to make sure she was breathing. She knew in that instant the way he was touching her was wrong. It was bright daylight and all the other kids were standing around watching, but she knew.

They couldn't go to the movies, Sara had said. They couldn't do anything but sit in the stupid room all day watching that lame TV that got only twelve channels. Sara had work to do, she'd said. What a lie. Sara was a *cleaning* lady. Cassie had seen her coming and going at the Paradise wearing that ugly uniform, the logo swirled across the front pocket above a pair of crossed brooms. Unless Sara was going to start mopping floors and dusting, what sort of work could she be talking about?

Cassie stopped at an intersection, looked around. She thought they'd driven this way the night before, but she wasn't certain. Everything looked the same — houses this way and houses that way, green lawns and green trees, the road wet and shiny, a layer of mist creeping along the ground. Should she turn left? Right? She was wet, too. And cold. If someone stopped and offered her a ride, she would climb into the car, no questions asked. If she got raped and murdered, well — would anyone really care? Serve Sara right if she got murdered. But maybe Boon would care.

I'm going for a walk, she had told him, and he'd just nodded, crawled up onto the bed, and picked up the TV remote. He wasn't worried about Cassie leaving because he knew Sara was around. Boon liked Sara, but then again, Boon liked everyone. He had no filter.

A car drove past. Cassie jumped out of the way, too late. A wave of water sprayed over the curb. She was wearing flip-flops. Water squeezed around her toes with their blue-painted nails.

A short woman hurried by, holding a red umbrella. Cassie felt hollowed out by hunger, as if she could press her belly and reach all the way through to her spine. She didn't know why. She skipped breakfast a lot. Sometimes, she'd get to school and discover she had no money in her lunch account. On those days, she'd go all the way to dinner-time without eating. It had never been a big deal, so why did it feel like a big deal now? She stepped down into the street, following the woman with the red umbrella.

A restaurant glowed in the gloom. A family sat inside against the plate-glass window, a father, mother, and three blond kids squeezed into a booth. A baby sat in a high chair facing them, slapping the table with his chubby little palms and laughing. The mom reached over and dabbed at his round chin with a paper napkin. He grabbed at her fingers and tried to stuff them in his mouth.

Boon missed their mom, Cassie knew. When their social worker asked him how he was doing, he always cried. It made Cassie's throat squeeze tight. She had to swallow to keep herself from throwing up.

Sara would be pissed when she figured out Cassie was gone. But what could she do about it? Nothing. Sara would just have to sit there in that crappy motel room and wait. Which would serve the Bitch right.

No wonder your mother left you. If I was your mother, I'd have done the same thing.

Bitch.

Rain dripped through the branches, tapped on the hood of the silver raincoat. Cassie dragged the sides around her, as if it would help make her warm and dry. Water slid down her cheeks and with it, the faint vanilla smell of the lotion her mom liked to use. Oh, Mom, she thought. She ordered herself not to cry.

Kids had been leaving the same picture in Cassie's school locker, nudged through the metal slots, and then hanging around, waiting for her to find it. Cassie could never

367

predict when she'd open her locker and see it lying there. Not the same picture, obviously, Cassie kept throwing them away — but the same image, cut out of the newspaper. She imagined a room filled with newspapers stacked high, each one showing the same awful headlines and the same horrible picture of her mom on her way into the courthouse, her hand raised to block her face as she hurried up the steps. *It was a mistake,* her dad was quoted as saying. *My wife just made a mistake.*

He said it to the reporters, and later, he said it to Cassie — the two of them, in the hot yellow spill of the apartment light the night her mom died. Her father's eyes steady and dark on hers, but she saw the fear there. The panic.

It was just a mistake, honey.

A mistake was when you did something by accident.

CHAPTER 37
HANK

Rain still fell steadily, gushed off the eaves. Hank fixed his cap onto his head against the wet, rounded the corner, and saw the small, dark-haired boy crouched reverentially in front of the vending machine beneath the stairs. The kid had his hand in the metal tray and was leaning close to peer up inside. The boy was all alone, here in this hidden spot lit by a single overhead bulb. Hank frowned. "What are you doing?"

The boy wheeled. He held that stuffed gray thing in his other hand, by the leg. Barefoot, in his shorts and T-shirt, he had to be freezing. "Sometimes people leave stuff in there. Sometimes they leave money, too. But not today."

The boy's nose was running. Hank fished his handkerchief from his pocket and handed it to the kid, who took a dutiful swipe before giving it back. Hank folded the handkerchief and pushed it into his pocket.

"Does your mother know you're out here?"

"Maybe."

Where was the red-haired woman? If she was worried about her husband finding her and her children, why would she leave her child to his own devices like this? Didn't she realize how dangerous it was? It wasn't just her husband she had to be worried about. "You shouldn't be out here alone."

"I'm not alone. I got Wolf." The boy held out his stuffed dog.

He was a handsome boy. His eyes were a disconcerting deep blue, lashes thick and dark as a girl's. Hank remembered George at this age, the same intent expression, the dimple in his right cheek when he grinned. "You hungry?"

"A little."

"I'll get you something. What would you like?"

The boy's expression brightened. "Anything?"

"Sure."

The boy pushed himself up and stood in front of the machine, contemplating his choices, toy tucked beneath one arm. Then he stepped back and peered up at packages hanging above his head. He jumped to tap the glass. "That."

"A chocolate bar?"

370

"Yes. Please."

Someone had taught the kid manners. Hank fished change out of his pocket, held out his palm, showed the boy the coins. "Do you know what a quarter looks like?"

The boy reached out a small finger.

"That's right. You need five of them."

The boy hesitated, peeked shyly up at him.

"Go ahead," Hank said.

The boy took a quarter.

"That's one," Hank said. "Keep going."

The boy selected four more quarters, cradled them in his hand.

"Now, three dimes. Do you know what a dime looks like?"

"It's the smallest of all. It's my favorite."

"Okay. Well, you need three of them." *Can I have a nickel?* George would plead. *May I,* Barb would correct, but Hank would already be reaching for his change. "Good. Now slide them into the slot. One at a time. That's it. Now you need to tell the machine what you want."

"It can hear me?"

The boy looked amazed. Hank almost smiled. "No. You need to punch in the number. See that? What does that say?"

"B. And seven."

"That's right. Look over here. Can you find a B?"

"Right there."

"Exactly. Push that button. Now a seven."

The metal coil holding the chocolate bar slowly rotated. The boy watched intently. The moment the candy thudded into the tray, he crouched to retrieve it. He grinned up at Hank, that dimple flashing. "Thank you, mister."

The boy peeled the wrapper, poked the corner of the chocolate bar against his stuffed dog's mouth, then stopped. He held up the chocolate. "Want some?"

"I'm good. Let's get you back to your room. Do you remember which one it is?"

"I put my shoe in the door to keep it open."

"That was pretty enterprising of you."

The boy nodded, amiably. Had his George been this trusting? Had he looked up at the stranger with the same innocent eyes and agreed to follow him? "Do you know what a stranger is?"

"Someone you don't know."

"That's right." Hank didn't want to frighten this boy. Had he ever sat down and warned his own boy? Would it have done any good? Could it have changed things? "And you shouldn't ever go off with a stranger, even a friendly one who buys you a chocolate bar."

"Like you."

"Exactly. You can't trust people you don't know."

The boy thought about that. "Some you can."

"Well, that's true. Firefighters, police officers. But you can't tell from looking at someone whether they're a bad person."

"Wolf helps me. He tells me who's good. He knows you are."

The boy had been lucky this time. They stopped outside the door held ajar by a blue sneaker lying on its side. The DO NOT DISTURB sign dangled from the doorknob. Hank pushed open the door, nudged aside the small shoe. The TV played to the empty room. "You know, son. Sometimes even Wolf can be wrong. About who's good or bad, I mean. You have to promise. You can't go off with a stranger again. Not all of them would bring you back." Harsh, but the boy had to hear the ugly truth.

The boy merely nodded. " 'Kay."

Hank held out his hand, and the kid slipped his small hand in Hank's without hesitation. They shook on it. The boy started across the threshold, then he halted and turned. "Everyone comes back, though. Right?"

Those blue eyes so steady on his. Hank

felt panic blossom. He cleared his throat. "What do you mean?"

"My mom went away."

Yes, leaving her boy alone so he could wander out looking for food. "She'll be back."

The boy looked relieved. "No one's talking about it. Cassie just tells me to shut up."

Cassie must be the sister. "You lock the door behind you," he told the boy, standing there with his toy under his arm and holding his chocolate bar. His cheeks were bright red. "I'm going to wait and make sure you do it. You hear me? You don't let anybody in."

Hank didn't see the cruiser parked in the driveway, didn't see Tom Compton sitting back on the porch until Hank was halfway up the puddled steps and couldn't turn around without looking a damn fool.

"Hank."

Tom was in uniform, so this was an official visit. Hank picked up the other rocking chair to shake off the wet, then sat. He wasn't about to invite Tom inside. Rain pattered on the roof, dripped off the eaves. "What do you want?"

Tom removed his cap, tapped it against his knee. He'd always been a polite kid, even when he pulled up behind Hank on the dark road and told him his drinking and driving days were over. The day before Tom announced he was running for sheriff, he came by to break the news to Hank first, sat there with his big, meaty hands hanging down and his head canted to one side as Hank tried not to let on that his hangover was blinding him. A door slamming shut, that's what it had been. Hank understood he'd never be sheriff again. "For you to stop calling the station."

That again. "Your people don't pay any attention."

"My people have better things to do."

What could be more important than finding missing children? "They locate that boy yet? The one in Charleston?"

"A, Charleston is in West Virginia. B, what makes you think you know better than anybody else?"

"A, we're all brothers under the badge, and B, because I do."

"Bullshit, Hank. On both counts."

"So they haven't found the child?"

Tom looked away. He liked to let things play out. He wasn't hungry enough to push past what lay right in front of him. But things had a way of snowballing. Hank had seen it happen time and time again. Tom was too young to know that. Still, he'd turned out to be a pretty good sheriff. People liked him. They trusted him. He was developing a paunch, though. He'd always been one for the extra serving. "Not yet."

"They need to look at the boy's mother. My guess is she's hopped up on something." The telltale disorder in the photographed background behind the boy's hesitant face, his unfocused eyes. He'd been on the scrawny side, carelessly fed. "Opioids, most likely."

"You been following kids around town again. I thought we talked about that."

He patrolled the streets. That was what he did. Keeping an eye out. People saw things all the time. They made note of cars that didn't belong in their neighborhood. They noticed strangers. But, by and large, they rarely spoke up. They dismissed it, or waited for someone else to say something. They passed the buck. If someone had made a call thirty-seven years ago, George would have been found.

Tom frowned. "Look, Hank. I've gotten complaints. You're making folks uncomfortable. You know how sympathetic I am. I get it. I do. But some of those days aren't quite the way you remember them."

"That right, Tom? Tell me what the hell

you know about it." Tom had been a boy in short pants. A *boy*.

Tom rolled his hat between his hands. The plastic covering crinkled. "How many times did you call in last week?"

Hank fought back from the haze of emotion, refocused himself. Which had it been then? Right. "That little girl in Arkansas, the one playing in her yard. Just like that other one, couple years back." There were too many coincidences to ignore. The child's age, the time of day, the accessibility to a train yard. "There might have been a third child, hard to say." The grandmother had been uncertain how long the girl had been outside playing before she noticed her gone.

"Thirty-nine, Hank. Thirty-nine."

Hank knew his messages didn't get passed along. But ego didn't matter when a child's life was at stake. Tom was sworn to protect people. He took his duties seriously. He should be told about the red-haired woman renting a room from Joyce, on the run from her husband and leaving her small boy to wander a strange place on his own. Hank hitched himself forward in his chair. Tom leaned forward, too, canting his head to catch Hank's response in his good ear. Born that way, just like his dad had been. But hearing loss hadn't slowed this boy down any. He ran uncontested in the last election. He was married to a nice girl and they had two kids. "You need to move Mitchell off phone duty, stick him somewhere where he doesn't interact with the public."

Tom pushed himself up. "That's it, Hank. I'm telling Dispatch to stop putting you through. Get yourself a hobby. A life. Stop wasting mine."

Hank saw the boy he remembered, the towheaded kid with the gap-toothed grin, who could sit silent for hours in a rowboat waiting for a fish to tug the line. He saw the ten-year-old army crawling through the brush, his blue eyes startling against his mud-streaked cheeks, and the awkward fourteen-year-old with the crooked bow tie. The seventeen-year-old pushing himself up from the wrestling mat, arms raised in victory. He saw all the boys George had never been.

Barb had pleaded with Hank to move. There were too many reminders, she said, weeping. But Hank refused. There was always the chance George could come back. It didn't matter how much time had passed. Hank left lights on at night, shining like beacons. He painted the house the same brown. Everything fell to hell around him,

but Hank fixed this one place on earth for
his boy to come home to.

CHAPTER 38
CASSIE

Cassie was pretty sure the kids she found
standing outside the convenience store were
the same ones she'd spotted the night before
when they drove into town. It didn't matter.
There were four of them — two girls, two
boys — all dressed in dark colors, slouching
in the sheltering doorway of a building
down the block from the store, and sharing
a cigarette. Cassie had walked right up to
them and one of the boys had nodded at
her. She'd nodded back.

They weren't that much older than she
was, she decided. Maybe fourteen? It was
hard to tell beneath the droop of their
hoods. She huddled in her raincoat, keeping
her distance beneath the wide overhang.
They didn't say anything to her, but she
didn't mind. The street gleamed. Cars
pulled in and out of the parking lot between
them and the store, tires sucking the wet
pavement. People got out of the cars and

hurried through the downpour into the store. A little while later, they came back out, hurried to their cars, and drove away.

One of the girls started complaining about a party they'd been to. It had been lame. She couldn't wait to get out of this crap town. The other three agreed. There was nothing to do around here. Too bad fat, old Mrs. F was working today. She always came out from behind the cash register and followed them around. Just because she'd caught them before. One of the guys tossed the cigarette into a puddle. "But not you." He was asking Cassie.

Cassie had shoplifted plenty of times. "Sure."

She pushed herself away from the wall. Another car jolted into the parking lot, headlights sweeping, and braked to a stop. The window rolled down. "I've been looking everywhere for you! Get in the car." It was the Bitch, leaning across the seat.

"No!"

"I'm not playing, Cassie. Get in."

"I don't want to. You can't make me."

Sara narrowed her eyes. Then she reached for the ignition key. The engine silenced. She got out and marched over. Sara wasn't wearing a coat. She was drenched in seconds, but her gaze was locked on Cassie.

"What the hell do you think you're doing? You don't even know these kids."

They were all watching. Cassie lifted her chin. Sara looked like a freak, standing there letting the rain pour down on her. She sneered. "What's your problem?"

"You. You're my problem. Get in the car."

"No."

"Fine. Stay here. I don't care. But I need your phone."

Everything was on her phone. It was hers, and hers alone. "No way!"

"Where is it? Your pocket? Your purse?"

Sara grabbed her arm. Cassie tried to twist free. "Get away, you psycho!" She slapped at Sara, but Sara jammed her hand into Cassie's raincoat pockets, reached for Cassie's purse. "Help me!" Cassie yelled to the kids, just standing around staring.

The guy who'd handed her the cigarette shook his head. "Sorry, dude." He peeled himself away from the doorway. The others followed. The four of them turned the corner and disappeared.

Sara dug out Cassie's phone. She held it up high.

A white-hot rage churned up inside Cassie. No one ever listened to her. Her mom, her dad. Sara. She curved her fingers into claws. She lunged.

Sara's white, shocked face, falling away.

Cassie pressed her hands to her mouth. She couldn't breathe. "No no no no no no no no." She couldn't do this. She couldn't do this. She wouldn't. No way. No.

Sara looked dazed. "I'm fine. Jesus. Calm down." She got to her feet carefully.

Cassie wrapped her arms around herself. She swayed, hiccuping and gasping for air. She couldn't stop sobbing. She couldn't slow her thundering heart.

"Hey. It's okay." Sara put her hand on Cassie's sleeve.

Cassie jerked free, horrified. "Don't touch me!"

"All right, all right." Sara glanced to the store on the corner, its windows bright with light. "Look," she said, in a lower voice. "I was hoping to tell you in a better way. But the reason I want your phone isn't because I'm an asshole but because your dad's been arrested. It was on the news this morning."

This was a bad dream. This wasn't happening. "No. You're lying. You're nothing but a liar."

"The police are going to be looking for you. They can track you through your GPS. They're probably on their way right now. I want you to get that phone right now. It's under the dumpster."

Cassie felt dizzy. All her thoughts tumbling around. She couldn't make sense of any of them. The police were going to come for her. "But I already turned it off . . ."

"When?" Sara's hair was plastered to her head. Her shirt was sopping, showing the narrow straps of her bra. Her jeans were muddy.

"Yesterday." It had come to her suddenly, maybe the second or third time Sara told her to call her dad. They were halfway across the bridge and Cassie had been reaching for her cellphone to do exactly that when she stopped herself. She didn't want to talk to her dad. She found herself pressing the power button and watching the screen go black. Just for a little while, she'd promised herself.

"It doesn't matter." Sara looked impatient. "Someone finds your phone, they'll turn it back on. You've got five minutes, Cassie, then I'm out of here." She limped to her car, opened the door, and climbed in.

Icy rain tapped Cassie's bare head, her shoulders, slid down the back of her neck. The sky was dark. The air smelled of lightning.

She walked over to the dumpster. She got on her hands and knees, and peered underneath. She lay on her side, stretched out an arm. Her fingertips nudged smooth plastic. She wriggled forward, closed her fingers around her phone. She pushed herself up, swiped her gritty palms on her shorts, and sloshed across the parking lot to where Sara's car sat. She opened the door and climbed in. Every inch of her was water-logged. She showed Sara the black screen. "Happy now?"

Sara held out her hand. "May I?"

She didn't believe her. Cassie gave her the phone. Sara examined it, dropped it into her bag.

Cassie watched in disbelief. "You can't have that. It's mine."

"I'll get you a new phone."

Cassie didn't want a new phone. She wanted her old phone. She wanted to pick up her life exactly where she'd left it. But that life was gone, wasn't it? Her dad was in jail. What would happen to her and Boon now? She crossed her arms tightly, stared out the window at the gray world, but she couldn't stop shivering.

"You know," Sara said, after a moment. "My dad got arrested, too. It sucks, but it's not the end of the world. You'll be fine."

No, the end of the world had already happened. This was just what it looked like, after. A man walked past carrying a huge black umbrella. He stopped in front of the convenience store, snapped his umbrella shut, and went inside.

"Cassie? You haven't asked what your dad was arrested for."

Sara thought she was so smart. She thought she had it all figured out. But Cassie wasn't going to tell her a thing about what happened that night. Only Cassie and her father knew. And Cassie would never, ever tell. Especially to someone like Sara.

Sara sighed, then turned the key in the ignition. Nothing happened. The car wouldn't start.

Chapter 39
Sara

Sara and Cassie waited in the car for the town's only mechanic to show up. Rain drummed the roof. Cassie sat slumped in the silver raincoat. She was quiet now, lost in her thoughts. What the hell had just happened? The girl had been completely hysterical. Sara had slowly climbed to her feet and been stricken with the awful thought *This has happened before to Cassie.*

Cassie glanced over Sara's shoulder. "He's here," she said, and Sara turned to see the tow truck pull up beside them.

Sara climbed back out into the downpour to talk to the guy. She was cold and wet. She'd twisted her knee and scraped both her palms. He raised the hood and took a look at the engine, then reached in and fiddled with a few things. "Here you go," he said. "Looks like you need a new alternator."

Sara had heard of alternators, though she

didn't know what they did. "That's not a major repair, is it?"

"Nope. I can take care of it first thing Monday, soon as the part arrives." He lowered the hood, let it clang shut. Raindrops pelted his shoulders, dribbled off the brim of his baseball cap.

"I can't wait until Monday. I have to be on the road."

"Well, I could charge your battery for you, but there's no telling how long it'll hold. Could be hours, could be minutes. Use your radio, turn on your headlights, it'll all drain the battery. You'll end up right where you are now."

Sara could keep the radio off, drive as long as possible without turning on her headlights, but she needed working wipers. She didn't want the car to break down on the side of the road. A trooper might pull over to offer assistance. He'd run her plate, see that the FBI was looking for her. She started to push her cold hands into her jeans pockets, stopped at the stinging pain.

The mechanic glanced at her, then at Cassie sitting in the front passenger seat and watching them both through the windshield. "Maybe I could call around, see if someone in the next town over has it in stock."

"Now?" she asked, hopefully.

"I'd have to send someone to get it."

Sara understood. "I'll cover the expense."

When he offered to drop her and Cassie off at the Step On Inn so they wouldn't have to walk in the rain, Sara had to accept. It was the normal thing to do. She didn't want to stand out any more in the man's mind than she already did. Besides, she needed to rest her knee, which was throbbing. She couldn't afford to make it worse, not now.

Sara had no idea what was going on in Cassie's head. The girl didn't want the police to find her; she didn't ask why Sara didn't, either. Sara couldn't make sense of any of it.

Boon greeted them as though they'd been gone weeks instead of hours. He hugged Sara, then he threw his arms around Cassie, who elbowed him away. "I have to take a shower," she announced crossly and took possession of the bathroom before Sara could claim it. The shower jetted on.

The TV was playing. Sara had turned it off before she left. If Boon had seen the news about his parents, she guessed he was old enough to have understood something if not everything, but he showed no sign of it. Did she really want to spend all afternoon stuck in this motel room with two kids and nothing to entertain them? The mechanic needed four hours, minimum, he'd said — and that was only if things went smoothly. He'd try to have her car back by midnight at the latest. Eight hours. She heaved a sigh. "Sorry," she told Boon and switched off the TV.

He stared at the blank screen, then at her. Wolf drooped from one hand. "But why?"

"You've watched enough TV."

"It's okay."

"Don't argue."

His shoulders slumped. Then he crouched and upended his backpack. Plastic action figures and blocks rolled out. "Okay, but Cassie's gonna be mad."

But Cassie didn't get mad. She exited the bathroom, pink-cheeked and subdued. She perched on the bed and painted her finger-nails shiny black. She was starving, she said. Sara realized she was, too. Sara found the diner menu Hank had given her that morning. Cassie wanted chicken nuggets and a milkshake. Boon insisted he wasn't hungry.

"You have to eat something," Sara told him. "You didn't have any lunch. How about a cheeseburger?" It was what he'd ordered the day before.

He hunched a shoulder. He pushed Wolf around on the vehicle he'd constructed.

Sara took that for a yes. She called in the order, and when there was a polite knock an hour later, she opened the door to rain and a woman — mid-thirties and pregnant — holding out a paper sack. Sara stood so the woman couldn't peer into the room and spot the children. She paid her, adding a nonmemorable tip, closed the door, then locked it.

She spread everything out on the small table and told the kids to eat. Boon crawled over reluctantly and climbed into the chair Sara pulled out for him. He propped Wolf on the table and frowned at the burger nestled in its Styrofoam compartment. "Do I have to eat that?"

The burger looked fine to Sara. It had come heaped with steak fries, and a dill pickle wrapped in waxed paper. "Just try a bite."

"Okay." But he didn't reach for it.

Maybe he was homesick, Sara thought. Maybe he'd overloaded on cartoons, or was coming down from that morning's pastry sugar high. Cassie was tearing open ketchup packets with her teeth and squirting ketchup across her nuggets. She, at least, was eating. Sara carried her container of chili over to her bed and sat down with her laptop. She tapped and scrolled and spooned chili into her mouth while the kids ate, or in Boon's case, jumped Wolf around the small table. There had been no updates. Maybe everyone thought the kids were still at the Paradise, where Whit had left them. The police would check, as soon as they could. And then all hell would break loose. "Cassie," she said. "Did you talk to anyone today while you were out?"

"Like who?"

"Like anyone. Did you tell anyone your name, where you live?"

Cassie set down her milkshake. "Oh. Right. I stood in the middle of the street and shouted."

"Those kids I saw you with. What about them?" The girl had to understand how serious this was.

"No! I didn't tell anyone *anything*! Why don't you *ever* believe me?"

"Because you've lied to me before." *Because you're a liar.*

"Whatever. I don't care."

Sara closed her laptop. Her knee had stopped throbbing and her palms felt fine. She stood to look out the window. The parking lot was glazed with rain. What about the mechanic — Sara hadn't called Cassie by name in front of him, had she? She didn't think so, but she couldn't be sure.

"Can I turn on the TV?" Cassie was already reaching for the remote.

"No."

"Are you kidding me?"

"Do I sound like I'm kidding?"

Cassie glared at her with incredulity, then stomped over to the bed. "You are such a bitch." She opened her backpack and pulled out her silver makeup bag. Boon lay curled on the floor, murmuring to Wolf.

Forty minutes later, Sara saw the wash of bright light sweep through the crack between the drapes and was at the door before the mechanic had turned off his engine. He apologized for taking so long but he'd had a tow. "Not a problem." Sara shivered in the wet air. She hoped the guy had done a decent repair job, but how could she know? Better to take things as they came. Swivel. She'd tell the kids she was going out for a drink, and that she'd be back soon. "How much do I owe you?"

He cited a figure, then splashed through the rain to the back of his truck to release the chains attached to Sara's car. It was more than she'd expected. She wouldn't have much left, but she really only needed gas money. She thumbed through the bills in her wallet, frowned, counted them again. She calculated what she'd spent on dinner just now, the motel room the night before. The guy had come back around and was standing there patiently waiting. Sara tugged the bills free and handed them over. He gave her the keys and wished her a good evening.

Sara stepped back into the room. Boon kneeled on the floor, surrounded by action figures. His dinner sat untouched. Cassie was brushing her hair. She glanced up and saw Sara's expression. "What?" she challenged.

"Give me my money."

"What money?"

"You're not fooling anyone. Give it to me."

"I don't know what you're talking about. And I don't appreciate being called a thief."

"Don't be mad, Sara." Boon tugged on her shirt. "Please don't be mad."

"Stop it." She smacked his hand away. He looked up with horror, as though she'd actually hurt him. She turned her attention back to the girl, standing there with her arms defiantly crossed. She was so convincing, the look of righteous indignation on her face, but Sara saw right through it. "I thought we had a deal, Cassie. We help each other out. We don't steal from each other." Forty dollars was nothing in the larger scheme of things, but right now, forty dollars meant getting out of here. It meant freedom.

"I didn't steal from you!"

"Jesus, Cassie. You steal from everyone. The barista. That beach house you broke into. You don't even have the balls to admit the truth when you're caught."

"You've been *spying* on me? You some kind of pervert?"

"You can either give me my money, or I can take it."

Boon started to cry.

"Shut up, Boon!" Cassie yelled.

He ran to the closet and shut himself inside.

Sara wanted to shake the girl. What if Cassie had already spent the money? How the hell would Sara get to the bank then? She reached for Cassie's purse lying on the bed.

Cassie jumped into motion. "Stop!" she said, and grabbed her purse. She thrust the money at Sara. "Here, *Sara.* Like that's your real name."

Sara looked at her, stunned.

Cassie sneered. "You think you're so smart. *Sara* Crewe? Mary *Lennox*? Why do you have a fake name? Are you some kind of criminal? Why don't *you* want the police to know where you are?"

Sara felt something crack open within her. The girl had pawed through her things, held them up and inspected them. Had she fingered the keys dangling from her key ring? What about the photograph of Sara's father — the one thing from her past she couldn't bear to part with — carefully snipped from the newspaper when Sara was about this girl's age? Had she laughed at the headline citing his crimes? Sara was surprised to find she was trembling. Sara pictured herself slapping the girl, the pleasure she'd take in wiping that self-satisfied smirk off her face. Instead, she sucked in a deep breath, snatched the bills, and folded them into her pocket. She picked up her bag. The car was fixed. The kids could find their own way. She wasn't responsible for them anymore. She was leaving.

She swung open the closet door and saw Boon curled up on the floor inside. "Boon," she said, impatiently. "You need to move. I have to get my shoes." He was lying right on top of them, his knees tucked to his chest. Wolf's head poked out from the crook of his arm.

He didn't move.

"Boon," she said, sharply. "Now!"

Boon looked up. His mouth crumpled. "I don't feel good," he whimpered.

CHAPTER 40
HANK

The tow truck beeped to a stop behind Joyce's place, pulling along a small dark sedan. Hank stood by his dining room window, glass in hand, and watched through the line of poplars separating his property from Joyce's as Steve climbed out of the truck and ran to knock on the motel room door. After a moment, it opened and a woman stepped out into the yellow circle of light. She stood there talking with Steve. From this angle, Hank could see a glimpse of her profile, her arms crossed in front of her chest. She nodded, and Steve turned to walk back out into the rain.

Everyone comes back, though. Right? that boy had wanted to know.

Steve's headlights lit up the unruly bushes in Hank's yard. It used to be Barb's garden and it had been something in its day, a profusion of roses, hydrangeas, dogwoods she managed to coax into blooming, jonquils in the spring and fire-red lilies in the summer. Morning glories and lilies of the valley, so sweet they'd make a person's head spin. Now, the rock garden was thick with weeds. Vines had pulled down the lattice. The roses hadn't bloomed all summer. The yard lay tumbled and overgrown, not a splash of color among the muddy leaves. Barb would weep if she saw it. It hadn't taken long for the earth to snatch back what was hers. Hank had stood by this window and let it.

It had been the garden that won Barb over. She hadn't been sure about moving in next to a motel. She'd eyed the place as they drove up and parked in the driveway. *It's so close,* she'd murmured. *Family-run,* Hank had pointed out, wanting her to agree. The location was convenient. The price was good, the sellers motivated — as if they'd known what tragedy was to befall the new occupants of the place. Barb said nothing as the realtor showed them around, the living room with the fireplace that needed just a little work, the root cellar. Then the realtor swung open the kitchen door to show them the yard, and Barb clutched Hank's sleeve. *Oh,* she exulted, and he knew she had come around.

Joyce and Chester had turned out to be

decent, hardworking people. Good neighbors. Barb had marveled that it really wasn't a problem at all living next door to a motel. All the guests coming and going provided a source of gossip, a source of entertainment. In those days, none of them gave a second thought to any of the people renting rooms at Joyce and Chester's place. Until the stranger vanished into that long-ago autumn night, along with Hank and Barb's ten-year-old son. The whole town changed after.

Hank took another sip of whiskey. Rain blurred the panes. Lightning forked, too close. The tow truck drove around the corner. Headlights flashed across the windowpanes, blinding him momentarily. He blinked, craned to see through the trees. The woman had gone back inside. Her car sat parked in front of her door.

Hank turned from the window and went into the study. Barb's word. His mother would have called it the front room. The thick, patterned drapes reached to the floor. Barb had wanted something heavy to keep out the winter freeze. Later, it kept out the prying eyes of their neighbors and the press.

His old leather chair creaked beneath him. He reached over to switch on the lamp, then ran his fingertip across the framed photograph on the desk to dust it. Barb had insisted on having the portrait taken. Hank had grumbled at the expense, at the sentimentality, but now he thanked the good Lord she had prevailed.

He turned on his desktop computer, checked his email. There was an alert waiting. He tapped the link, and the story bloomed across the screen. The news had just broken. The toddler had been found in a stream not far from his mother's house. She'd made up the story of his being snatched from the shopping cart to hide the truth — the boy had wandered outside while she was passed out on the floor of her house. Opioids, just as Hank suspected. Same blurry photo of the boy staring out. Was it the only one taken in his brief life? Hank spun in his chair and studied the wall of photographs, found Christopher's, added just the day before. Nineteen months. The boy never had a chance.

George had wanted to be a pilot. That was all he ever talked about, from the moment he looked up into the sky and saw the contrails puffing like popcorn from behind a plane. *Wazzat, Daddy?* He'd cupped his hands to his eyes. *Wazzat?* Hank picked up a model plane from his desk, turned it in his hands. George and he had built this one together. The paint was a little sloppy on the wing, the decal crooked. *What war is this from?* George had wanted to know. *Were you a soldier, Dad?* Then, *I want to join the Army.* He was going to see all seven wonders of the world. He was going to travel across the ocean in both directions. George had made Hank see the world through his eyes. Every day with him was a miracle of discovery.

Hank drained his glass, pushed himself up. Had to be getting on to dinnertime.

As he washed his hands at the kitchen sink, he watched the small TV on the counter. He was hoping for an update about the dead toddler — maybe a press conference, a chance to hear the investigating officers speak about the case — but the coverage was still focused on the hurricane, now churning along the Virginia coast. The Outer Banks was drying out, but the devastation the storm had left behind was massive. Might be a while before the TV caught up with the online story. The two mediums didn't always synchronize. He'd learned to monitor both, especially when there was an active case.

A commercial played as he dried his hands. An actor Barb had admired hawking life insurance. *Let's go to the movies tonight, sweetheart.*

Hank would give anything to hear her voice now.

There wasn't much in the refrigerator. When had he last shopped? Behind him, the news was on.

. . . a small Outer Banks town hallmarked by tragedy. Diane Nelson, forty-two, first hit the headlines when she left her son alone in a car on a hot summer day while she went to work. The boy survived and was returned home, but Diane herself went missing a few weeks later. Her body has just been discovered buried in her in-laws' backyard. In a final, tragic twist, both her children, Cassandra, twelve, and Whit Junior, six, are now also missing. Were they swept out to sea during the hurricane —

The child left sleeping in the backseat. Hank remembered seeing something about that. He was surprised to hear they'd returned the boy to his parents. He pulled out a package of ground beef, peeled back the plastic wrap, sniffed, and grimaced. He turned to toss it in the trash, glanced at the screen.

A narrow-faced blond girl. A dark-haired boy. The image changed before he could be certain.

CHAPTER 41
SARA

Boon lay flat on his back. His eyes were open, staring up at the hangers dangling over his head.

"How don't you feel good?" Sara asked.

He drew his gaze to hers, blinked. His eyes seemed to glitter. "I think . . ." His voice fell away.

Instinctively, Sara crouched and put her hand to his forehead. He felt warm. But he always felt warm to her, every time he slid his hand into hers, or leaned against her. Were his cheeks flushed? "Do you feel hot?"

He dipped his chin.

"Do you feel *too* hot?"

He shook his head.

"Does anything hurt?"

Peering up at her, he put his hand to his throat.

She didn't know anything about sick kids. But weren't kids always sneezing, wiping their runny noses? They were hotbeds of germs, weren't they? "Are you thirsty? Do you want some water?"

"He wants *medicine.*" Cassie twisted a stringy lock of hair so tightly around her finger Sara wanted to yank her hand away. "Obviously."

"Like what?"

"Like, how do *I* know?"

Sara glared at her, picked up the motel phone, called the front desk. It rang a dozen times before Joyce answered. She sounded sympathetic, told Sara she could help herself to whatever she had in her medicine cabinet. Sara thanked her and hung up. "I'll be right back," she told Cassie. She threw one more glance at Boon, who still lay staring up at the empty hangers, and let herself out into the rainy night.

Joyce stood waiting in the lobby, bundled in a pink quilted bathrobe. She unlatched the glass door and held it open for Sara. "I made you a box," she said, indicating the plastic bin on the front desk. "I just tossed everything I had in there. Help yourself."

"Thank you so much." Inside the box was a jumble of cold medications, pills and tubes, and a thermometer.

"Try not to worry, honey. Kids always get sick in the middle of the night, fevers especially. They give you a real scare, and then. Poof. It's nothing." She patted Sara on the shoulder, smiling.

Sara hoped the woman was right. She couldn't take Boon to the doctor. That was the last thing she could do. She elbowed her way back out into the chilly downpour. "He threw up," Cassie announced, even before Sara had pushed open the door. "I got him to the toilet. *Thank God.*"

Boon slumped on the bathroom floor, cheek pressed against the rough floor tiles. The toilet lid was propped open.

"Let's get you into bed, okay?" Sara set down Joyce's box and stooped to slide her hands beneath his armpits. He was surprisingly heavy.

He wrapped his legs around her waist and howled, "Wolf!"

Sara stumbled a step. "Cassie, grab that thing, will you?"

"Ew. No way."

"Cassie!"

"Fine." Cassie crouched, gingerly rolled Wolf over with a fingertip, then pinched him up by the ear, dangling. "But you *owe* me."

"Have we been keeping score?" Sara shot back, tartly.

Boon slung his arms around Sara's neck, put his forehead against her shoulder. Now even his breath felt hot. "I wanna sit," he whimpered.

Maybe that was wise, given that he'd just vomited. Sara ladled him into the chair by the desk. "Want me to get you some ginger ale?"

He just shook his head, refusing to look at her.

"You'll be okay," she reassured him. After all, he'd been fine just hours before. He was a sensitive kid. Everything set him off. He rested his forehead on his folded arms, Wolf in his lap. "Does your throat still hurt?"

He started to cry.

She pulled a box of cough drops from Joyce's box, scanned the directions. Boon was six, over the age of concern. He might like the sweet honey flavoring. She tipped the box over and squinted at the tiny lettering stamped into the cardboard. The drops had expired seven years before. Would he know not to swallow them? She tossed the box aside. "What about your head? Do you have a headache?"

"Uh-huh." Tears slicked his cheeks. He hiccuped.

She sorted through the bottles. Why didn't people throw old medicines away? Maybe he hadn't been fine earlier. Maybe this — whatever it was — had been brewing for a while. He'd sat for hours in the backseat yesterday, completely drenched. He hadn't complained. She hadn't thought twice about it. She hadn't even thought once about it. She held up the aspirin.

"Stop." Cassie was standing right behind Sara. "You can't give him that."

"I can't?" Sara looked at the bottle, shook it. What did the girl see that she didn't?

"Little kids can't have aspirin."

Sara brought out a container of ibuprofen and one of acetaminophen. "What about these?"

"Are they kid-strength?"

She studied the labeling on both, shook her head. "Can I just give him less?"

"That's not how it works. Don't you know *anything*?"

Cassie was convincing. She would know more than Sara did about this.

Boon moaned. "My tummy hurts . . ."

All that crap she'd let him eat. "It's okay, honey. You'll be better soon."

Did he need a doctor? There had to be an ER nearby. Joyce could give her directions. Sara would load Boon into the backseat and set Cassie in the passenger seat beside her. But how would she explain her relationship to the children, provide insurance information? The hospital personnel would insist on seeing Sara's ID. They'd plug her new social security number into the computer. It would instantly send up a red flag. The Feds would know where she was. Agents would swarm the hospital. They'd set up roadblocks, search surveillance footage. They'd catch her, and the bargain they'd made would be off. She'd go to prison.

"Everything hurts," he whimpered, miserably.

It occurred to her to check his temperature.

101.2, the thermometer read. Was there a dangerous level for children? How would she know? She sat on her bed, opened her laptop. Quickly, she scrolled through medical websites, selected one run by a pediatrician. The banner showed a colorful cartoon of a smiling teddy bear wearing a stethoscope. The pages she clicked through, though, weren't as cheerful. Who knew kids could get so many illnesses? Some of them began benignly — a stiff neck, a bruise — then turned deadly, almost without warning. How the hell did kids survive? Because they had a parent taking care of them. Not someone like Sara. She'd never babysat as a teenager, never even once felt the slightest urge to admire someone's baby.

"Has he had his shots?" she asked Cassie.

The girl shrugged.

"Shots?" Boon lifted his head.

"It's okay," Sara assured him, longing to shake his sister. "No shots. What about ticks? Did a tick bite you?" Hadn't he talked about ticks once? "Or a snake? Did a snake bite you?"

"He'd know if a snake bit him." Cassie was gnawing her thumbnail. "He's a big baby, but he's not stupid." *Like you,* her tone implied.

Boon crawled out of the chair to sprawl on the carpet with Wolf wrapped in his arms. He was freezing, he whispered, begged for two blankets, not just one. All she could see of the toy was one threadbare ear poking out from beneath the blue paisley spread she'd stripped off the bed. She decided on the ibuprofen, brought over the bottle and a glass of water. "This will make you feel better," she tried, shaking the bottle playfully.

He yanked the covers over his head.

"It's medicine for big boys. Only big boys can take it."

"I'm hot like fire," he moaned.

Sara pulled the blankets off him. He lay flat on his back, arms and legs extended, looking impossibly small and unhappy. She dampened a washcloth and patted his cheeks and forehead. She rinsed the washcloth and worked the terry between his fingers and across his palms. She touched the cool, wet material to his wrists, then his chest. "Are you sure you won't try some medicine, sweetheart? It'll make you feel better."

He clamped his mouth shut.

"Are you hungry? Thirsty?"

"I have to go to the bathroom."

Sara asked him if he needed help, and he nodded, so meekly that for the first time, a bolt of true alarm flared in her. She helped him lower his shorts and lifted him by his underarms to set him on the toilet. His narrow ribs beneath her hands, his skin so unnaturally hot that she was afraid of holding him too tightly. And then it occurred to her that maybe his getting sick was perfect timing. She could call 911, slip out before the paramedics arrived. Cassie could stay with him. Boon would get real medical attention. She'd be miles away before anyone would think to look for her. It would be a win for everyone.

She helped him down, pulled up his shorts, and flushed the toilet.

"Sara . . ."

"What can I do for you, honey? What would make you feel better?"

"Can you make me a pillow fort?"

Kids got sick all the time, she reminded

herself. Joyce said so. The Web said so. "Sure," she told him. "I can try." She dragged the cushions off the chair and the pillows off the beds. She and Cassie constructed an elaborate structure on the floor, over which she draped a sheet. He sat with Wolf gripped by the tail and watched, eyes drooping. When she was done, they all crawled inside.

"How about one teeny-tiny pill now?" Sara coaxed, but he shook his head.

"Can you tell me a story?" His cheeks were ruby red. He looked like a child in a Disney cartoon, almost glowing with health.

Sara had never told anyone a story. Well, except for the lies she'd been telling her entire life. Wasn't telling a story like that? "There once was a little boy who lived in the forest. He had a warm, cozy house made of stones guarded by an army of acorns. At night, he would watch the stars twinkle and listen to the river singing." Boon lay on his side, thumb in his mouth, his eyes on her, Wolf protectively under his arm. "All the animals loved him and would talk to him. The birds taught him songs and the squirrels taught him how to climb trees. When other people came, the animals would run away. But they told the little boy every one of their secrets. They showed him where the best berries were, and how to make flour from nuts. He made jam and delicious pies. He grew big and strong."

"He was all by himself?" Boon spoke around his thumb.

"Yes, but it was okay. All the animals were his friends."

"That's a sad story."

"Is it?"

"Yes."

Didn't every child want to grow up big and strong, completely independent? She had. Maybe independence in this case translated to just desperately lonely. He was on his own now, too, even though he didn't know it. He and Cassie both. "Oh, well, I'm not done. One day, a little girl showed up. She knocked on the door of his cozy little house and asked if the little boy wanted to play. He liked this little girl because she had long, long hair and eyes the color of honey."

Cassie snorted.

Sara ignored her. "The little girl knew all the ways in and out of the vast forest. She had a very special carpet that they could sit on and take trips."

"Like Aladdin." Boon's hair was damp at his temples; were his eyes glassy?

Okay, she'd stolen that one. "Exactly. Just like Aladdin. Together, they flew all around the world. They had lots and lots of exciting adventures, and they were the very, very best of friends."

"Oh, my God" came Cassie's protest.

"That was a good story." Boon's eyelids drooped.

When Sara took his temperature again, it had climbed to 102.9. He refused to eat or drink. He started to shiver. Sara piled the blankets back over him. His small body barely made a shape beneath them. What if he died? No — the websites said kids ran fevers all the time. Joyce had said it, too.

Cassie sat motionless, her eyes never leaving her brother. That sight, more than anything, scared Sara. She turned on the air conditioner, opened the vents. When Boon coughed, Sara spun toward him. "Are you looking for Wolf, honey? Here he is. Wolf would never leave you." Sara tucked the toy beneath his chin.

He stopped flailing, coughed softly, wetly. "There's a mark on the wall."

"There is?" There was nothing there.

"Can you put the picture over it? To hide it?"

"Sure. Is that better?"

But his eyes had closed. Was he delirious?

"Is he going to be okay?" Cassie whispered. No eyeliner, her lipstick worn away, her blond lashes pale, freckles dashed across her nose and cheeks. She looked so young, suddenly. Nothing like the surly, spiky teen she usually was.

"He's a little under the weather. But he'll be all right." How many times tonight had she made that same thin promise? "Has your brother gotten sick like this before? What did your mom do?"

Did, not *does.* As soon as the words were out, Sara wished she could snatch them back. She didn't want to be the one to have to tell them their mom was truly gone, that she'd never again take care of them when they were ill. Someone better equipped to handle kids had to deliver that news, not her. How had she gotten herself into this disaster? Why couldn't she have just left the kids behind at the Paradise? They'd have been fine. She'd always been fine.

"Mom hated it when Boon got sick," Cassie said.

"I'm sure she did."

"Not like that." Cassie tore at her thumbnail, eyes on her brother. "She got mad."

"She must have been worried." That pretty blond woman on the balcony, arguing with her husband.

"No. She was *pissed."* Cassie's thumb was bleeding. She rubbed it against her jeans.

414

"She had to go to work. She told Boon to suck it up, but he cried. So she gave him medicine to make him sleepy and told him to lie down in the backseat. And she went to work anyway."

"I thought it was an accident." That's what the papers had said.

"That's what she told everyone. But she *lied.*"

Cassie sounded spiteful. But she also sounded certain. Sara believed her. The police would have questioned her before deciding whether to arrest her mother. Certainly the social worker would have before deciding to return the kids to their mother's care. But Cassie had successfully convinced everyone that everything was fine at home. Sara eyed the girl, kneeling beside her brother, her head bent and her blond, flyaway hair falling forward and hiding her face. Cassie couldn't know her father had murdered her mother. Could she?

"You know," Sara said. "You haven't asked why your dad was arrested."

Cassie had been patting Boon's sleeve. Now her hand stilled.

Sara's heart sank. So Cassie knew the terrible thing her father had done. How? Was it possible she'd witnessed the murder? What a mess. What a horrible mess. No wonder the kid was filled with rage. And what about Boon? How much did he know? "I'm sorry," Sara said, helpless.

"Why? It's not *your* problem."

"No," Sara agreed. It wasn't. She knew what it was like to be surrounded by adults claiming they understood when they clearly couldn't. How could Sara know what Cassie was feeling, or going through? She couldn't. She wouldn't lie and say otherwise. "But I am sorry about what happened."

Cassie's head shot up. Her eyes blazed. "Like you know *anything?*"

"Okay," Sara said, wanting to be agreeable. Cassie was beginning to work herself into one of her tantrums. Sara had her hands full dealing with Boon.

"Don't say that! Don't say it's okay. You don't know *shit!*"

Sara cast around for something positive to say. "At least you have Boon —" Which was more than Sara had had.

"I *don't* have Boon! They're going to put me in jail. I'll never see him again."

"No one's going to put you in jail." Sara was confused. "Why on earth would you think that?"

"Just forget it. It's none of your business."

"Was it your dad who told you that?" Was

that how he'd gotten Cassie to stay silent about what he'd done? Sara tried not to think about the times she'd lied to protect her father. But he'd never killed anyone.

"He said he'd fix it! He told me to be quiet and he'd take care of everything. But he lied!" Cassie shrieked. Her face white. Her chest heaving. She clenched and un-clenched her fists. She was losing it, just as she had that afternoon. *This has happened before to Cassie,* Sara had thought earlier. "Cassie," she said, slowly. "Did you do something bad?"

"She said my dad didn't want me!"

"Your mom?"

"She said if it wasn't for her, I'd never have been born!"

Sara was in over her head. What should she say? How could she comfort this kid? "That's a mean thing to say. I would have been angry if my mom told me that —"

"Stop! You don't know anything! I didn't mean to push her!"

The truth. Sara felt dizzy with it. The girl wouldn't look at her. Sara spoke hesitantly, feeling her way. "Your dad . . . he didn't hurt her?"

"My dad *loved* her!"

Whit Nelson also loved his daughter. He loved her so much that he was in jail right now, telling the police he was the only one to blame for his wife's death. "Sweetheart, it was just an accident. I promise. Nothing's going to happen to you."

Cassie was sobbing, her shoulders heaving. Sara tried to take her in her arms, but the girl scrabbled at her, flailed and kicked. "Make this go away!" she wept. *"You have to make this go away!"*

"I can't, Cassie. I wish I could. But I can't."

"Shut up! Shut up! I hate you!"

"Look. You're old enough to deal with this. It's horrible, I know. But you have to find a way to move on. You don't have a choice. You just don't."

No one could help Cassie. Not Sara. Not Social Services. Not Whit Nelson, who had promised his daughter otherwise. Sara's father had told her lots of things, too. She had clung to his advice and wisdom, let them mold and guide her, even as they began to reveal themselves as lies. She was who she was because of him, and she was where she was now, too, for the very same reason. Her father could have easily walked away after her mother abandoned them both. But he hadn't. Sara had thought it meant he loved her.

CHAPTER 42
HANK

Barb had been the first to say it. *You have to stop, Hank.* She had been the only one who could say anything, but still he had not listened. He had tried to explain, but she had brushed off his hollow promises, stepping back and shaking her head, her face rinsed with tears. *This obsession of yours is killing me,* she'd wept. *You can't bring him back.* Then, there had been the lies that drove her out of the house and into her sister's place a hundred miles away. She wouldn't answer his phone calls. Her sister told Hank to stop calling. The divorce papers arrived in the mailbox. Then one winter day she had shown up on the doorstep, her large pink suitcase on the sidewalk behind her. He had stood there astonished at the sight of her. She had put her finger across his mouth. *Do what you have to,* she'd told him. *But don't you say a damn word to me about it, ever.*

What would she say now, seeing this?

Those two children staying at Joyce's place, Hank had even spoken to the boy. Whit Junior, who went by the name Boon. Cassandra, known as Cassie. Their father had foolishly left them home alone as the hurricane bore down, and after the storm, the police had finally been able to check the apartment and found it empty. A neighbor reported seeing them leave in the company of a woman in a silver raincoat driving a small, dark-colored sedan. An Amber Alert had been issued.

He adjusted his reading glasses and, scowling, leaned closer to the computer screen. School portraits. The kids' faces fixed in wide smiles. One dark-haired, one fair. He couldn't be sure about the girl. The photograph appeared to be of a younger child, with a fuller face. But the boy. He had that dimpled grin. George's grin. Hank didn't recall hearing their names over breakfast that morning. He hadn't asked the boy later that afternoon. None of that mattered, though. He'd noticed the pretty red-haired woman in that shiny silver raincoat. The one on the run from an abusive husband, who had gone quite still upon hearing the news about Whit Nelson's arrest.

What was she doing in the middle of all this?

She looked nothing like the children's mother. Hank studied Diane Nelson's mugshot. Her blond hair gleamed around her face. Still, she looked miserable, her mouth a downturned, stubborn curve. *Look up,* Hank imagined the charging officer directing her, just as he had himself hundreds of times. *Just look into the camera.* And now she was a homicide victim and her husband charged with killing her. His parents had been charged as accessories to the crime. How was the red-haired woman involved? Was she the husband's lover? Had they conspired to murder the kids' mother?

There were other photographs, too. Nelson was a good-looking fellow with hair dark and thick as his son's, combed back from that same square forehead. One taken on his wedding day, standing beside his golden-haired bride, her arm possessively through his. They'd made an attractive couple. No mention of another woman. No photographs of her at all.

The news stations were embracing the story. One of them had found the kids' social worker, an earnest, dark-haired woman named Robin McIntyre, who leaned into the microphone. "Please tell your viewers —" Her voice broke, and she looked away for a moment, composing herself. "Someone has to know where Boon and Cassie are."

Mistakes got made in every investigation. It was inevitable. Adrenaline, fear, pushing away the facts that didn't fit. It was especially true when kids were involved. But Hank wasn't about to make any mistakes now.

He fetched his windbreaker and cap from the hall closet, took the Maglite from the kitchen drawer, and let himself out the back door. Rain slanted down, tapping leaves and pavement. The temperature had dropped another ten degrees. Chilly for an August evening. He flipped up his collar and waded out into the deluge. Lights gleamed here and there, a blurred string of them outside the motel doors. Every window was dark but one.

The blue Kia was parked right up to the curb. He flicked on the Maglite, shone it through the driver's-side window. No jumble of items in the console, nothing dangling from the rearview mirror. The rear windows were tinted, but if he stood by the side mirror, he could see between the front seats and into the backseat, a gray stretch of material scattered with debris: a wad of crumpled paper napkins, a red-and-white-striped straw, bent at the tip. He circled the vehicle, raindrops hitting his shoulders, slanting off the brim of his cap. North Carolina plate. The metal was mud-spattered. He wiped rain from his face, held the beam of his light steady. He studied the number, committed it to memory, clicked off the light.

Tom would run down the plates, bring the red-haired woman in and ask a few questions, contact the cops in North Carolina and let them know he had the kids they were looking for. Tom might think Hank was an idiot, call him paranoid, but he followed procedure. Hank turned and hurried through the rain around the corner of the building to the lobby, shining bright in the gloom.

The teenage girl behind the front desk scarcely glanced up as Hank entered, didn't put down her pink phone. "Hey."

One of Joyce's grandkids. He could never remember which one. They all looked alike, small blondes like their mothers. As if the fathers had no say in the genes handed down. This one had her nose pierced, both ears multiply pierced, tiny silver bars and chains and glittering stones. Joyce despaired of what her grandkids did to themselves. Piercings, tattoos. Shaved heads. *They're such beautiful children. Why would they mutilate themselves?* "Your gran around?" he asked.

"She's in her apartment. Want me to get her?"

"Don't bother. I just wanted to follow up on something."

"Whatever." She sounded bored. But as he came around and reached for the keyboard, she leaned back to watch over his shoulder.

He resisted the urge to elbow her away. "Slow night?" he asked, to get her talking.

She came alive, as he'd known she would. "The slowest. I don't even get good reception here. I have to stand outside to get any signal, but I can't tonight, not with the rain. I don't know how Gran stands it."

Nothing on the motel computer. Joyce had been cannier than usual. No registration at all. That red-haired woman must've really struck a chord. Joyce might bend the rules, but she'd never cheat the IRS. So there had to be a record of that rental somewhere, where Joyce could access it but not an angry husband. Whom Hank now knew was probably fictitious. The red-haired woman, whoever she was, had played Joyce like a pro. She'd played Hank, too, coming up to the front desk that morning and making small talk. He began opening drawers. "That plumber ever show?"

"What plumber?"

He found a battered ledger among the take-out menus and crumpled receipts. Pages of Joyce's angular handwriting, jotted down every which way. *Set ant traps. Check dates of antique fair. Offer special HNYMN rate?* Ah, Joyce. The eternal optimist. Who would ever honeymoon here? He stopped at a lone entry scrawled in the margin and reached for the pad of Post-it notes. "Joyce mentioned there was a leak in one of the rooms."

"Oh. Right. I don't think so. I heard Gran talking on the phone to someone when I got here."

"She get it sorted out?"

"Don't think so."

"Tell her to let me know if she wants me to take a look."

"Sure."

He closed the ledger, slid it back into the drawer. With any luck, that was what the girl would remember. She'd tell Joyce that he stopped by. She'd say he asked about the plumber.

The girl spun herself around on the stool, holding on to the counter and pushing. Her hair was long and fine, cut high and blunt across the forehead into bangs. She smelled of some fruity shampoo. Her fingernails sparkled with glittery polish. He tucked the Post-it into his pocket. "You left the lobby door unlocked. I walked right in."

"It's okay. I got my phone." She held it up as proof, the pink case glittering with silver rhinestones.

He leveled a look at her. She sighed, climbed slowly down from her stool. "Fine," she muttered. She knew about George. They all did. Her mother would have told her as soon as she was old enough.

"Hank?"

They both turned at Joyce's voice. She shuffled into the lobby, belting her fuzzy robe, gray curls matted. "What's going on?" She looked from Hank to the girl, who obligingly answered.

"Uncle Hank wanted to follow up on something."

"This time of night?" Joyce shot a look at Hank.

"It's nothing," Hank lied. "Just a loose end."

"Mellie," she told her granddaughter. "You go on home now."

426

"You sure?" But the girl brightened.

"I'm sure, honey. I can't sleep anyways."

"Okay. Thanks, Gran. Bye, Uncle Hank!" Mellie twisted the latch and slipped through the door into the rain.

"I'd better head out, too," Hank attempted, but Joyce put her hand on his arm.

"Oh no you don't. You tell me what you're up to, Hank Peterman."

Accusing *him,* when she was the one who needed to be held accountable. "That woman you took in? She's not who you think she is."

"Don't tell me you've been snooping around that poor young woman and her children. You leave them alone."

"You have no idea what's going on."

"And you do? You have no right! You're not sheriff anymore!"

"You've learned nothing, Joyce. Not a damn thing. You're just as gullible and blind as you've always been."

"Blame me all you like. Lord knows I've blamed myself for what happened. But what about you, Hank?" She stepped close, the frill of her nightgown cupping her chin, her eyes blazing. "Where were *you* when George got taken?"

"You know better than to listen to gossip."

"Barb waited for you to admit the truth. She died never hearing the words."

"Shut your mouth. You don't know what you're talking about."

"I'm your friend, too, Hank. And I'm telling you. You need to stop lying to yourself."

It had been only a couple beers. Enough to give the world a soft focus. It hadn't slowed Hank down. The instant the call came through about George, he was off that barstool and into his black-and-white. No one could say any different.

CHAPTER 43
SARA

The hours dragged by. Two in the morning. Snoring softly, Boon slept on the floor beneath the draped bedspread. Cassie refused to leave his side. She made no response when Sara told her Boon looked better, that it was good he was getting some rest, that his temperature had gone down slightly. She ignored Sara's suggestion that she try to get some sleep, too. She paid no attention as Sara used a washcloth to wipe down the bottles and boxes in Joyce's medicine box. They hadn't spoken since Cassie's outburst.

Sara rose to tackle the bathroom, glanced over at Boon. He was lying so still, flat on his back, arms stretched out. Was his chest even rising? She dropped to her knees beside him. "Boon? Honey?"

"What is it?" Cassie pressed closer. "What's going on?"

"Hold on." Sara held her palm to his

chest, closed her eyes with relief when she felt the slight rise. When was the last time she'd checked his temperature?

He made no protest as she slid the tip of the thermometer beneath his tongue. His hair was stiff with sweat and matted against his forehead, his cheeks bright splashes of crimson as though someone had slapped him.

The thermometer beeped and she removed it.

104.6.

"Is it okay?" Cassie crouched beside her, her shoulder bumping Sara's.

"His fever's pretty high." She had no idea how to interpret a sudden spike in fever. It had been going down. She looked at the motionless boy. Watch for lethargy, the website had warned. "Boon, honey. Wake up. Tell me how you're doing."

His head lolled as she gently shook his shoulder. His eyelids didn't even flutter.

This was on her. This was all on her. She'd consulted websites instead of listening to her instincts. She'd taken risks with a child's life and he was paying the price. She'd always thought she was smarter than anyone else, and now a boy's life was at stake. "Come on. Grab my bag. We have to take him to a hospital."

Cassie scrambled to her feet.

Sara hoisted the boy into her arms. His head rolled against her collarbone. She fitted her feet into her shoes, reached for the doorknob and opened it. The rain thundered down. Water roared along the gutters. The sky was impenetrable, no stars piercing the downpour.

"Find my keys. Do you know how to unlock the car?"

"Yes." Cassie held up the keys and pressed the button. The headlights blinked.

"I'm going to put him in the back with you so he can lie down."

Cassie scooted in. Sara laid the boy across the seat, so his head rested in his sister's lap. She looked up at Sara with terrified eyes.

"It's okay," Sara told her. All these empty promises. How could she possibly know whether he was going to be okay? Those websites had warned of things like meningitis, appendicitis. Rotavirus. The ugly words reeled in her brain.

Sopping, she slid behind the wheel, pulled her phone from her bag, and located the hospital. It was only three miles away. What if the mechanic had done a lousy repair job? But the car started up instantly. Weak with relief, she flipped on the wipers and put the

431

car in reverse.

"I don't feel good," Boon wailed from the backseat as they reached the highway.

Surely it was a good sign that he was alert and talking. "I know you don't, sweetheart. I'm taking you to the doctor."

"No shots!"

"No shots," Sara lied. Let the medical staff tell him otherwise.

CHAPTER 44
HANK

Sara Lennox.

No middle initial. No address. Joyce hadn't taken down any helpful details that could refine Hank's search. Even so, a woman matching Sara's description didn't appear to live anywhere in the state of North Carolina. A person didn't have to do much to pop up in an online search. Attend a high school reunion. Have a Facebook page. But the red-haired woman was a total cipher. What was her connection to Whit Nelson? Were they lovers? Had they hatched a getaway plan after the murder that included her snatching his kids and running? The children seemed willing, but of course they were too young to know otherwise. She would have filled their heads with lies. He could be wrong, of course. She might be some kind of do-gooder. It was possible she was trying to protect the children from their murderous father. But it wasn't for Hank to decide what was in the children's best interests. It wasn't up to Sara Lennox, whoever she was. It was up to the courts.

He picked up the phone hanging on the wall, dialed the number he knew by heart. The call went straight to voicemail. Hank frowned. It was well after midnight, but Tom should have picked up anyway. Unless he'd known it was Hank calling. Damn caller ID.

Hank would have to try the station, tell whoever answered to contact Tom ASAP. Hank would have to summon his rusty persuasive skills. Tell the officer working the late shift to look and see for himself — Boon and Cassie Nelson would be on the missing kids database. Their mother was a homicide victim. All the fellow had to do was drive on over to Joyce's, check it out for himself. He'd be a hero, Hank would tell him.

Hank dialed the station, got a busy signal. Had he misdialed? He tried again. He stood by the kitchen window, looking through the rain at the line of poplars. He'd poured himself another glass. The back of the motel and parking lot were scarcely visible. Was that movement? He scowled, stepped closer to the glass. The dim yellow bulb shining over the motel door allowed him a glimpse of Sara carrying the limp form of a child, another child trailing close behind. What the hell? Had Sara drugged that little boy, injured him in some way? The headlights flared on. Sara's pale face behind the windshield, carved with shadows, dappled with rain.

The busy signal bleated in Hank's ear. He banged the receiver down, scooped up his cellphone from the table. He ran to the front door and out into the wet night. Behind the wheel, he stabbed the buttons for 911. Rain dripped from his hair. He swerved down the driveway. He fought to keep the car on the slick pavement. That long-ago night reared up.

Maybe it had been more than a couple beers.

CHAPTER 45
SARA

The hospital sign emerged glaring in the dark. Sara took the turn, followed the winding road, and braked in front of the emergency entrance. "Stay here. I'll be right back."

She ran to the broad entrance, where two wheelchairs sat together beneath the overhang as if in conversation. Grabbing the handles of one, she steered it to her car. She opened the back door and reached in for Boon. "Come on, Cassie," she urged, and the girl crawled out after her brother to stand on the sidewalk beside Sara.

"Cassie, take Boon inside, out of the rain. Tell the nurse he needs to see a doctor right away. Tell him you might need to be checked out, too, if whatever he has is contagious. Tell them he's running a high fever, that he vomited a few hours ago."

"Why can't you?"

"I have to park the car. I can't just leave it here."

Cassie hesitated.

"We're getting drenched. I'll only be a minute or two. I promise."

Cassie glanced behind her to the bright entrance, then back to Sara. Rain splashed around them, puddled the pavement.

"Go on, sweetheart," Sara coaxed.

Cassie shook her head. Then, to Sara's surprise, she grasped the handles of the wheelchair.

So much trust in that simple action. Sara felt moved to say, "Cassie, hold on. You need to tell someone what happened. You need to. It's the only way you'll be able to move on. Okay? I know what it's like to live a lie. You don't want that."

Cassie had stopped. She stared up at Sara with confusion. Sara could see the questions tumbling behind the girl's eyes. She'd said more than she should have. Sara gripped the car keys tightly in her hand. "What are you waiting for?" she snapped. "Take your brother inside. Hurry."

CHAPTER 46
CASSIE

The nurse sitting behind the front desk glanced up, then stood. "Hey," she said, coming around to Cassie. "Look how wet you two are! What's going on?" She bent, placed the flats of her hands on her thighs. She was wearing pea-green scrubs. Her black hair was braided tightly back in tiny rows. She had a photograph of her smiling face swinging from a lanyard. She'd gained a lot of weight since that photo was taken, Cassie thought. "Hey, sweetie."

"My brother's sick."

"I see. Are you alone, sweetheart?"

"No. Sara's coming." Sara had said this. She had looked Cassie in the eye and said so.

"Who's Sara? Is she your mom, sweetheart?"

Cassie had no words for who Sara was. But the nurse wasn't paying attention to Cassie anymore. Boon's eyes had rolled back up in his head and his legs were kicking. After that, things happened quickly. The nurse scooped Boon up and ran, elbowing through a pair of swinging doors. Heart pounding, Cassie stood waiting for someone to come back and tell her what was going on. She was trying with all her might not to cry. Why did things always have to happen to Boon? Why not her? She was the bad one. Boon never hurt anyone in his life. He only tried to make people happy. The outside glass doors whooshed open behind her. It wasn't Sara but that horrible old man from the motel. "What's going on?" He touched her shoulder. He was soaked, rain dripping off the brim of his cap, running down his sleeve and splashing onto her leg. She smacked at her jeans. He didn't seem to notice. "Are you okay?" he said. "Where's your brother? Where's that woman?"

"Sara's coming," Cassie insisted. "Sara promised."

He gave her a weird look. He pushed his lips in and out, thinking. He carefully removed his windbreaker and cap, set them on a chair. "Okay," he said. "Let's wait for her." He slid his phone into his pants pocket and sat. Cassie looked at him, then at the blank glass doors. She felt completely alone. After a moment, she sat down beside him.

Cassie hadn't been allowed to visit Boon the last time he was in the hospital. But this time, she got a seat right beside his bed. He had an IV and medicine to bring down his fever. The nurse brought them both cups of Sprite and crackers. Breakfast was going to be in a couple hours, she told them. Today was pancake day. After breakfast, someone was coming to talk to them. Cassie knew that meant a social worker. Two policemen had tried to talk to Cassie, hammering at her with questions. Cassie had refused to say anything. The doctor had finally called a halt to it, coming in and insisting she needed to examine Cassie. She had taken Cassie into another room, looked in her eyes and mouth, pressed a stethoscope against Cassie's ribs, trying to find the heart Cassie knew wasn't there.

The nurse turned on the TV hanging from the ceiling and found an old movie playing. She showed Boon the button to press if he needed her. She'd be outside, sitting at that desk where she could see him. "You two good for right now?"

Cassie just looked at her. Like they had a choice.

440

"Yes, thank you," Boon whispered.

That was the way Boon talked to adults. They thought his politeness was cute. Cassie hated it. She knew that he only did that because he'd learned it was the best way to keep their mom from losing her temper.

The nurse smiled at him and swished out. The second she was gone, Cassie climbed onto the narrow bed. Boon wiggled over to make room. She'd seen this movie before. She'd watched it with her mom sitting close beside her, her mom's arm slung over her shoulders. Her mom had memorized the lines. She repeated them along with the actress. Cassie had pretended to watch the screen, but she was really gathering her courage to talk to her mom. *What if I never have a boyfriend?* Or, *What if I flunk out of school? What if I'm a big loser?* What she really wanted to say was *Are you and Dad getting a divorce?* But her mom just cuddled Cassie closer. She never took her eyes off the screen. Now, Boon pressed against her, restless and a little stinky. His soft hair tickling her chin. He'd been sucking his thumb again. She could smell his spit. He didn't always suck his thumb. He didn't always sleep in the closet, or wet the bed. What was going to happen to him now that he didn't have a mom or a dad?

Cassie didn't remember pushing her mom. But she remembered her mom falling back, the sound her head made against the table corner. The blood after.

"Sara left," Boon mumbled, around his thumb. He sighed, pressed in closer to her.

Yes, she had. Cassie was furious with herself for believing in Sara, for believing in anything. "Everyone leaves," Cassie told him.

CHAPTER 47
SARA

She watched the speedometer. Five miles over the speed limit, not too high and not too low. The sweet spot that made her invisible to cops and other motorists.

The rain had finally eased, spitting occasionally at the windshield. She'd have to stop and pick up a box of hair dye, drive to the next rest stop and apply it. A dark color. She'd hack off the waves, wear big-framed sunglasses and a hat. She'd change her walk, maybe use the southern drawl she'd gotten used to. It would be enough to get her to Columbus. She'd already taken a Sharpie to her license plate, changed the *O* to a *Q*, the *F* to an *E*. It wouldn't hold up under close scrutiny, but she didn't intend to be pulled over.

The car. What was she going to do about the car?

The needle moved higher. Sara eased her foot off the accelerator.

The Feds knew her associates. They'd be watching. Maybe not forever, but for a while. She couldn't take the chance of tapping any of them for help. It would be risky going with people she didn't know, but what choice did she have?

The two kids would be okay. The doctors would take care of Boon. He'd be fine. The hospital would notify the authorities. Cassie would tell the cops everything she knew. What Sara looked like, that she lived next door to them at the Paradise, that she'd driven them away from the hurricane. Cassie might remember the make and model of the Kia. With any luck, she wouldn't mention the mechanic, who certainly would remember. The cops would be curious — someone would talk to Joyce at the Step On Inn — but they'd be more focused on figuring out what to do with Boon and Cassie. Nothing had happened to the kids. All she'd done was rescue them from the storm. There would be no need to waste manpower looking for a Good Samaritan.

Still, she hoped she'd managed to wipe away all her fingerprints from the room.

Fifty miles east of Columbus, she'd stop at the post office where she'd rented a box some years before. An envelope would be waiting inside containing the identification she'd mailed herself. It wasn't the best quality — nowhere near the caliber of the one the FBI had provided her, but it only had to fool the bank officer. Then she'd head into the city to the bank and access her safe-deposit box. She didn't have much cash stowed away — certainly not enough to start over completely — but it was better than nothing. She'd thought of it as her retirement plan. She never thought she'd be withdrawing the money so early.

It had been a cumbersome system, necessitating that she regularly make the trip from Minnesota to Ohio to maintain both the post office box and the safe-deposit box. At times she'd wondered if it was worth it. She was so small-time. Did she really have to hide her money this way? But now, as she drove along the road skirting the foothills, watching in her rearview mirror for any car that might be following, she was glad she'd paid attention as her father conducted business. He'd taught her well. She'd become just as skilled a liar. Look how she'd fooled the Feds. The secret, he'd explained, to lying successfully was to stick to the truth as much as possible. Lies by themselves gave way under scrutiny. But if you hooked them to truth, they bore up. Convince yourself that what you're saying is true, then you can convince someone else.

Whit Nelson had shown his daughter how to lie. He told her it was to protect her, but Sara was struck by the sudden thought that maybe he'd been protecting himself, too.

Was she forgetting anything?

The car was a problem.

After she got her money, she'd hit the road, figure it out as she went along — sleep in the Kia, wash in public restrooms. Find an average-sized town without traffic cameras where she could waitress or bartend. Stay off the grid until she got new ID. Working with the cops had taught her a few things. Living with her father had taught her more.

She'd never hot-wired a car. How hard could it be? You could google anything these days. She glanced at the anonymous roads bisecting the gray ribbon of highway that curved away deep into farmland. All that isolation, no witnesses to observe her jimmying open the driver's door. Unless some angry farmer showed up with a shotgun or pack of dogs. Damn it. She needed a city.

She'd clean out the car and leave it in a rough neighborhood, then replace it. She wished her dad were sitting beside her, leaning back against the seat, telling her how to avoid satellites and drones. He'd make it sound easy.

She'd figure it out. She was her father's daughter, after all. She never forgot that.

Forty minutes later, the fuel gauge arrow hovering around E, she pulled off the highway. The gas station was busy and well lit.

A plump woman stood pumping gas across from Sara, her eyes narrowed on the display as the damp wind whipped her coat around her; an older man climbed out of his sedan, flicked his cigarette into a puddle. Another man sat behind the wheel of a red pickup, his head tilted back. None of them glanced over. She kept her face averted as she got out of the car. She couldn't see a security camera, but that didn't mean there wasn't one.

A cold wind gusted around her as she strode to the attendant's booth. She'd just crossed into West Virginia. The Appalachians rose all around her. The teenager set down his magazine to open the window and take the twenty Sara extended. "Need a receipt?" He didn't even look at her.

"No, thanks." Sara walked back to the Kia, unscrewed the gas cap. She fit the nozzle into the tank and pressed the lever.

There was a sandwich shop attached to the station. The food would be tasteless, but she had an endless day ahead of her. She should pick something up, a caffeinated drink, too. She couldn't remember when she'd eaten last.

Sara tapped the last drop out of the nozzle and slid it back onto the pump. She yanked a paper towel from the dispenser and wiped her hands. She felt chilled and deeply tired. The hurricane, the past two nights in the motel, all had happened to a different woman.

She locked the car and walked over to the sandwich shop, hooking the canvas bag over her shoulder. The sharp corners of the two children's books inside poked her waist. She reached in to adjust them, felt something. She stopped, drew her arm out of one of the thick canvas straps to let the bag sag open. She rummaged inside, turning over her clothes, pushing aside her laptop. There — the point of a gray ear, a shining blue eye. Her hand closed around it, drew it up. Wolf.

Shortly after she'd arrived at the Paradise, Boon had been leaving her things. She didn't know why. First had been the cicada shell, hunched and gleaming. A matchbook, a Lego car made of red and white blocks. It didn't take long to figure out who was placing gifts on her windowsill. She'd almost caught him one day, her hand on the door-knob on her way to work when she heard the rustling noise outside her window and froze. When she stepped outside, she'd found a sparkling red sequin. It began to be a game between them. She'd leave the object for a day or two, enjoying its mystery, then she'd bring it inside and set it in on her nightstand. The next day, she'd discover something new on the sill. A pinecone, a pink button — the world's treasures as seen by a small boy. After a long and miserable day pretending to be someone she wasn't, she felt herself smile.

Sara had never seen Wolf without Boon, but here he was.

No one had ever given her anything so valuable. Not a friend, not a lover. Not one of the people who'd fostered her. Not her father, who Sara always understood had been incapable of such gestures, incapable of love. He knew loyalty, though. He'd gone to prison rather than tell the police anything about his accomplices. He had left his young daughter to fend for herself. Sara had grown up knowing and understanding loyalty in all its guises. But — like her father — she had lied to herself. She knew nothing about love.

Cars drove past, tires spitting rain. People

walked around Sara on their way into the sandwich shop, laughing, bickering. The bleat of a car horn. She stood motionless, holding Wolf. *Go,* her father would have urged her. *Get the hell out of there. What the hell are you waiting for?*

He wouldn't have wanted her to fall into the same trap he had. The cops who had arrested him had tried to rattle her. Her father was a thief, they told her. He stole people's life savings. He stole your childhood. She hadn't listened, just as Cassie had refused to hear the truth from Sara about her own father. Kids made their own truths.

Well, maybe Sara's father hadn't been a loving one, but he had always been smart about the world. He had tried to teach her what he knew. His lessons had saved her, time and time again. Chief among them had been this: no one could save you but yourself. She was wasting time, standing here.

She walked decisively back to the Kia, unlocked it. Climbing in, she dropped Wolf on the seat beside her, turned the key in the ignition, and put her hands on the steering wheel. No point in looking back. All that mattered was looking ahead. She laughed bitterly, softly, feeling hot tears in her eyes.

The sun was rising, a glowing globe above the distant smudge of mountains, casting long shadows. It shone steadily in the corner of her windshield as she got back on the highway, following the signs heading east. Going back to the hospital, where two children were waiting.

EPILOGUE: BOON

"Have you heard from her?" Boon asked. He didn't look up. He concentrated on the fork — cheap metal, the tines all bent.

"No," Hank answered. Then he added, "I don't always, you know."

Yes, Boon knew. He dropped the fork with a clatter, rubbed his palms on his new khakis. His foster mom had wanted him to look nice for the campus tour. First thing Boon had done when he got here was yank off his tie.

"So how was it?" Hank asked.

"Pretty good. I got to sit in on a computer science class. That was cool." The bell over the door jingled, letting in a customer. Boon glanced over. No one he knew.

"So where does this one rank?"

Hank was hoping Boon would end up at App State, which was only an hour away. Hank said they'd be able to see each other more than they had these past ten years.

452

"First, maybe second. It depends on how much financial aid I get."

"Offer still stands."

"I know." Hank had told Boon he'd help pay for college. Boon knew he meant it, but he couldn't say yes. It was complicated. "It's okay. I'll figure it out. But thanks."

Hannah Rose came over to take their order. She grinned at Boon as she set down a glass of soda in front of him. "Hey, loser."

"Hey, toadfish." Hannah Rose was cool. Sometimes, they hung out together when Boon was visiting Hank.

"Mom made meatloaf today," Hannah Rose said. "It's pretty good but it's going fast."

Boon glanced to Hank. Did it mean anything that they were ordering now? That she wasn't coming? But Hank just nodded at Hannah Rose. "We'll take it," Hank said.

"Two orders of meatloaf, coming right up." Hannah Rose swayed off toward the kitchen. Boon watched her go, glanced back to find Hank trying to hide a grin. Boon blushed. Hank was always trying to set Boon and Hannah Rose up, but Boon already had a girlfriend.

"So how are your foster parents doing?" Hank set the menu aside and leaned back in the booth.

"Good. They would have come, I told them you said it was okay, but they wanted to stay on campus, check out the library." His foster mom had dropped him off at the corner. He knew she'd been dying to come in, but Boon hadn't wanted her to. He needed to keep this part of his life separate. He couldn't explain why. He glanced to the door again.

"Things good with your dad?"

Boon shrugged. "Okay, I guess." He'd gone to visit his dad a couple times in prison, even as Cassie refused, but he and Cassie had never been back to the Paradise. And as far as Cassie was concerned, that was fine. *There are things you don't under-stand, little brother,* she'd said, and he'd known she was right.

Look at all the things he'd never known, even while he was in the deep thick of them. *What do you remember?* Boon's therapist had asked. Not much from his early life, and nothing at all from the night his mom died. He didn't find out the details until his dad and grandfather were charged, and even then he didn't understand. It had been an accident. His dad was just trying to protect Cassie and keep them a family. Still.

Hannah Rose brought their food. Boon looked down at his plate, suddenly not the least bit hungry. She wasn't coming, he knew that now. She'd promised, but she didn't always keep her promises.

"How's your sister?" Hank asked.

"She's okay." Two years ago, Cassie had definitely *not* been okay. But now she wasn't dating that jerk anymore, and she seemed a lot happier. She seemed excited that Boon was going off to college.

Hank smiled, touched his arm. "She's still a pain in the tail, isn't she?"

Boon laughed. Only Hank knew how mad Cassie could make him. And how much he adored her. And she *was* the world's biggest pain sometimes.

The bell over the door jingled again. Boon glanced up. A woman stood there, a purse slung over her shoulder, red hair pulled back into a ponytail. She saw Boon at the same time, her face breaking into a smile. He knew he looked like an idiot grinning back and jumping up to hug her, but he didn't care. Sara was here.

A gray wolf big and brave enough to sit on a lap, with shiny blue eyes and a long pink tongue, one two three four paws, and a fluffy tail ready to wag hello.

ACKNOWLEDGMENTS

With true and deep gratitude to my editor, Kate Miciak, and to my extraordinary team at Penguin Random House: Gina Centrello, Kelly Chian, Toby Lousia Ernst, Jennifer Hershey, Kim Hovey, Alyssa Matesic, Cindy Murray, Allyson Pearl, and Kara Welsh.

Thanks to my agent, Dorian Karchmar, for keeping me focused on the right things, both story-wise and life-wise, and to my wonderful William Morris Endeavor team: Tracy Fisher, Alex Kane, and Hilary Zaitz Michael.

Gratitude to those who generously shared insights into their respective fields of expertise: William Buckley, Susan Friedman, Thomas Hutchinson, Allison Leotta, Jenny Milchman, Madelyn Milchman, Lisa Preston, Sande Roberts, Harley Schwartz, Colette Scult, and Alan Siqueiros, MD.

Thanks to my partner-in-crime, Chevy Stevens, for encouragement, insight, and general all-around awesomeness.

Thanks to my sister, Liese Schwarz, for great wisdom, laughter, and for always, always being there.

Thanks to my children, Jillian, Jonathon, and Jocelyn, for making my dreams come true, and to my husband, Tim, for making love at first sight real.

ABOUT THE AUTHOR

Carla Buckley was born in Washington, D.C. She has worked as an assistant press secretary for a U.S. senator, an analyst with the Smithsonian Institution, and a technical writer for a defense contractor. She lives in Chapel Hill, North Carolina, with her husband, an environmental scientist, and their three children. She is the internationally bestselling author of *The Liar's Child, The Good Goodbye, The Deepest Secret, Invisible,* and *The Things That Keep Us Here,* which was nominated for the Ohioana Book Award for fiction and a Thriller Award as best first novel.

carlabuckley.com

Twitter: @carlabuckley

Instagram: @carlasbuckley

Find Carla Buckley on Facebook